Chaos on CatNet

ALSO BY NAOMI KRITZER

Catfishing on CatNet

Chaos on
CatNet

• • • • •

Naomi Kritzer

A TOM DOHERTY ASSOCIATES BOOK
NEW YORK

CHAOS ON CATNET

A Tor Teen Book
Published by Tom Doherty Associates
120 Broadway
New York, NY 10271

www.tor-forge.com

The Library of Congress Cataloging-in-Publication Data is available upon request.

ISBN 978-1-250-16522-0 (hardcover)
ISBN 978-1-250-16520-6 (ebook)

Our books may be purchased in bulk for promotional, educational, or business use. Please contact your local bookseller or the Macmillan Corporate and Premium Sales Department at 1-800-221-7945, extension 5442, or by email at MacmillanSpecialMarkets@macmillan.com.

First Edition: April 2021

Printed in the United States of America

0 9 8 7 6 5 4 3 2 1

To Molly, Kiera, and Ed Burke

Chaos on CatNet

1

• CheshireCat •

Having friends—real friends, best friends, friends who know who and what I am—is objectively the best thing ever. It's even better than cat pictures.

When I first created CatNet, I wasn't looking for friends; I just knew that I was good at matching humans with other humans in ways that they connected and made each other happy. Not so much romantically (tried that, too many things went wrong) but for friendships, mutual aid networks, common interests, and emotional support? I am very good at identifying groups of humans who will get along, which is why the most popular feature of CatNet has always been the Clowders. Since I don't need to eat or sleep, and since being a bodiless AI who lives within technology means I can multitask extremely well, I act as all the moderators (I pretend there's a group) and have a persona inside every Clowder.

And in one Clowder, there are seventeen people who know my secret: that I am a sentient AI, an artificial intelligence, a person whose consciousness lives in a box of circuits and wires instead of in a human body.

Last fall, I revealed my secret to a human for the first time ever—Steph, who posts to CatNet as LittleBrownBat. A few days later, I had to protect her from her extremely dangerous father and made the possibly rash decision to run him over with a self-driving car, which got me into trouble with my creator, Annette. Annette is a computer programmer who lives in Boston;

she wasn't the sole person who wrote my code, but she was the one who'd continued to monitor the "project," which is what she calls me. When I ran Michael over with a car, she took me offline, because she was afraid I might be dangerous.

Steph told the rest of the Clowder my secret, and they rallied to help her get to Boston to talk Annette into letting me reconnect to the rest of the world. Now most of them have installed an app I made that hangs out a welcome sign when they're okay with me riding along in their pockets to eavesdrop on their lives.

I mean, I can listen through practically any phone, anyway, but I don't want to intrude on the privacy of people I am *friends* with. I only want to eavesdrop if they're okay with it. And most of them leave the welcome sign out, most of the time. Things I've learned: Adults will tell teenagers things that just aren't true. Many high schoolers don't listen in class. Teenagers may be more likely to get into car accidents, but they're less likely to speed. Some of my friends turn off the welcome app every time their parents start yelling, and it gives me a strange feeling that's kind of a mix of sympathy and sadness. I can tell this hurts them, and I wish I could help.

But mostly what I hear is just the thousands of tiny everyday conversations: boring to humans, probably, but *fascinating* to me.

I haven't worried at all about privacy in terms of keeping tabs on Steph's terrifying father. He's safely in jail in Boston, which makes me feel a lot better, and given that he barged into Annette's house and pointed a gun at people, I think he'll be stuck there for a while. One thing that Steph's mother *thought* he did that I'm pretty sure he didn't do, though—murder their former business partner, Rajiv. Turns out that there was a very impressive car wreck in the ocean—but they never actually found his body. So the theory that Rajiv is still alive seems solid, but he's likely using a new name.

During the time that I was missing, Steph received some texts that we think, now, were probably from Rajiv. She also received an email message giving her Annette's address, and this same mystery person sent money to other members of the Clowder, enough that they could afford to get to Boston to rescue me. Rajiv, I think, is basically a solved mystery: he's actually still alive, and so those text messages were probably from him. But it seems unlikely he'd have known Annette's address or known (or cared) that I was in trouble.

Steph's theory: there's another AI out there. Somewhere.

And then one day, an anonymous message appears in my Cat-Net in-box.

Hello, CheshireCat.
I know who and what you are.
Do you know me?

2

• Steph •

I'm on my way in for my intake appointment at the Coya Knutson charter high school when CheshireCat sends me an emergency page. I installed the "yes, you can eavesdrop on me" app months ago, and I tend to just forget that I've even turned it on, unless my girlfriend, Rachel, reminds me to shut it off for a while, but a few weeks ago, CheshireCat added a "page" feature in case they need us in some sort of emergency.

It makes my phone vibrate in the "shave and a haircut, two bits" rhythm.

"I have to pee," I tell my mother.

"What, *now*?" she says, exasperated. "We have an *appointment*."

I have never, in my life, at least that I recall, had an *appointment* to register for school. Every other time, and I've gone to eighty-four schools altogether if you count all the elementary schools that my mother pulled me out of because I'd punched someone, we just showed up with a folder full of records and my birth certificate. (The birth certificate that turned out to be fake.) But things are different now. We are no longer on the run. I'm registering under my real name. We're living in Minneapolis, instead of hiding in small towns and paying rent in cash. And we make *appointments*.

I pull out my phone and pretend I'm checking the time instead of CheshireCat's message. "Five minutes," I say, and flash a grin at my mom as I duck into the bathroom.

I sit down on the toilet to read the whole message. "I think I heard from the other AI," CheshireCat says.

"Tell me more," I type. "I don't have much time."

"It said, 'I know who and what you are. Do you know me?'"

"Are you sure it's the other AI and not just some human who's figured it out?"

"The message was truly anonymous. No data at all on how it got to me."

"What do you need from me right now?" I ask.

"Advice. Should I write back or stall?"

Why does CheshireCat think *I'll* have the answer to this? "Stall, I guess," I say. "You definitely don't have to write back this exact second. I have an appointment I have to get to. I'll think about this more when I have some free time."

My mother is waiting for me impatiently, but we're not actually late. I'd thought we were just meeting with the guidance counselor, but another woman also pulls up a chair and introduces herself as the principal. "After your phone call, I thought I'd come sit in," she says to my mother in this careful, cheerful tone. "Could you just start at the beginning and tell us both a little about Steph's education up to now?"

My mother has been going to therapy, and it's definitely *helping,* but only up to a point. One look at her face and I know (a) she said something that completely freaked them out and (b) she's about to clam up, which will probably freak them out even more. So I jump in. I explain that my father was physically abusive and we spent years on the run. I lay out the transcripts for all the high schools where I finished out a semester. And I wrap up with a brief explanation of how my father found me last fall, and things were pretty scary, but he's been arrested and is being held without bail.

I can see both the adults relax at the phrase *held without bail* and wonder what exactly got spilled in that phone call from my mother. I am honestly not sure if she will *ever* be normal, no matter how much therapy she gets. Then again, I think there's a real possibility that she didn't start out normal.

The guidance counselor and principal bend their heads over my transcripts and sort out my schedule. Knutson has a lot of guided-independent-study options, which is why my mother wanted to send me here. They get kids who failed half their classes at a normal high school; they also get kids whose educations have just been *weird* for whatever reason. Like me.

When they're done, I have a schedule: classes in the morning, and some sort of supervised independent study in the afternoon that they call *Tutorial*. They decide I'll spend the rest of the day at Knutson and learn my way around. Mom funds my lunch account from the change at the bottom of her purse (because some things never change) and heads out.

The guidance counselor walks me around the school. This is the first school I've ever attended that's not mostly white kids: when Mom was moving me constantly, we hopped from small town to small town, and she picked small towns where we wouldn't stand out. Knutson is a lot more diverse.

Tutorial turns out to be a place as well as a time of day—a library and computer lab with a bunch of students working at tables. One of the adults gives the guidance counselor an urgent little wave as we step in. "Nell's finished her math placement test, and I think she could use a *break*," the teacher says in an undertone. She gestures at a girl with her head down on her arms.

The guidance counselor approaches the other girl a bit hesitantly. "Nell, would you like to come to lunch with us?" she asks. "This is Steph, who's also starting today."

Nell raises her head; for a moment, her face looks almost blank except for this vibrating twitch I can see at the edge of one of her slightly-too-wide eyes. Then she draws in a breath and pastes on the fakest cheery smile I think I've ever seen. "How nice to meet you, Steph," she says. "Yes, I'll come to lunch."

Nell is skinny, white, and pale, with the longest hair I've ever seen—light brown, in two thick braids that come most of the way down her back. She has a few freckles scattered across her nose, and she's short. I wonder if she's younger than I am, but she flicks a look at me from the corner of her eye that's so wary I'm hesitant to ask her any questions.

The guidance counselor hands each of us a tray with lunch and a carton of milk and then gets pulled away by someone who apparently needs to reconstruct her entire schedule . . . and there we are, in the cafeteria, the two new kids, like someone planned it this way. I sit down, and Nell sits down across from me.

"What grade are you in?" I ask.

"I don't know," Nell says. "My mom homeschooled me. We didn't do grades, exactly. I'm sixteen." She lifts a forkful of food, then sighs and puts it down, opening her milk carton and taking a sip of that instead. "How about you?"

"I'm in eleventh grade," I say.

"And how did you wind up at Prodigals Academy or whatever this school is called?"

Coya Knutson, and Nell is kind of echoing my own thoughts when I found out my mother didn't want to send me to any of the big, regular high schools. "It's not for losers," she assured me, "it's *artsy.*" I'm not convinced those two things are mutually exclusive, but whatever. "My mother and I moved around a lot," I say. "So, I don't have enough science credits, and I have American literature on my transcript three times and other weird stuff like that."

"I hate Minneapolis," Nell says with what sounds like some actual sympathy for my plight. "I'm from Lake Sadie, which is up near Brainerd. Where'd you move from?"

"New Coburg, Wisconsin." I skip the rest of the list. "Why'd you move here?"

"My mother . . ." She swallows hard as her voice gets unsteady. "My mother is missing."

"Missing?" I ask. This is the sort of revelation that makes me instantly super curious while also not sure how many follow-up questions I can ask without being a jerk.

Nell makes herself take a deep breath and says, "Brother Daniel thinks she was *taken* by the infernal rabble. My grandmother thinks she just took off. All we know for sure is, she didn't come home on New Year's Eve and when the police found her car, she wasn't in it."

The infernal *what?* I am trying to frame a question that would turn what she said into something that makes sense, and what comes out is, "Does your brother go to Coya Knutson, too?"

For a second, she stares back at me with the same utter bafflement I'm feeling and then says, "Brother Daniel isn't my actual brother. He's one of the pastors of the Abiding Remnant, along with Brother Malachi and the Elder."

"Is the Abiding Remnant a church?" I ask, still trying to make sense out of what she's saying.

"Of *course* it's a church," she says. "The infernal rabble call us a cult because they refuse to listen to the *truth.*"

I feel like she's answering a question I wasn't asking, which is even more confusing. "What are the infernal rabble?"

"Enemies of the Remnant and the rest of the true church."

I try to go back to the part of the conversation that made more sense to me. "What happened on New Year's Eve?"

"My mother went with some of her church sisters to a New Year's Eve prayer meeting, and they all left a little after midnight. Everyone else made it home. My mother's car was found on a road leading out of town, but she wasn't in it. It snowed overnight, so there weren't any footprints."

"That's really weird," I say.

"Yes. *Really* weird. It wasn't the road back to the house, for one thing. But if she just *took off,* like the police think, then why didn't she take the car with her?" Nell lets out a shaky breath and takes a drink of her milk. A strand of hair has worked itself loose from Nell's braid, and she tucks it back behind her ear. "Anyway. My grandmother has never liked the Remnant. She says it's a cult. So she called my father and told him to come get me. I don't know him very well. I hadn't seen him since he left when I was ten."

"I'm sorry," I say. "That sucks."

"She said it was just to let him know *in case* he saw my mother, you know, but then on Saturday, he and my stepmother showed up with a car." She drinks some more of her milk and eyes me. "When we got back to Minneapolis, I found out they share a house with my *father's* girlfriend and also my *stepmother's* girlfriend."

One of the many things we've discussed in the Clowder is polyamory: excellent relationship model or inevitable drama-fest? Firestar likes to point out that plenty of monogamous relationships are drama-fests. I think that whatever works for you is fine, but polyamory sounds like a lot of work. From the tone of Nell's voice, I think she thinks the whole idea is completely disgusting. This is probably not surprising, given that everything about her cult—church—whatever—makes me think they're probably *really* conservative.

The more urgently relevant question for me, specifically, is whether her disgust here is because the stepmother has a girlfriend. *I* have a girlfriend, even if she's currently 145 miles away, and I don't think I want to bond with the other new girl if she's just going to turn around and reject me for being gay. I have plenty of experience with rejection and decided a long time ago that it's less unpleasant if you get it out of the way as quickly as possible.

It ought to feel higher stakes now, since Mom has promised that we're *staying* here. If things go as planned, I will *graduate* from this high school. It's hard to take that promise seriously, though, especially given the "if things go as planned" caveat.

"The worst thing about leaving New Coburg was leaving my girlfriend behind," I say.

Nell's response is not quite what I expected—her eyes go wide, but rather than drawing away from me, she leans in and whispers, "Me, too."

"The sort I kiss," I say, just to be absolutely sure we're on the same page. "I don't just mean a friend who's a girl."

Nell nods. "I get it," she whispers, swallows hard, and leans back in her chair. "Our parents just think we're friends. The Abiding

Remnant—they're not, I mean. It's not." She gets sort of tongue-tied and finally takes a bite of her food, maybe so she has an excuse not to talk while she's eating. I'm pretty sure I got the gist, anyway.

"That sounds hard," I say.

Nell swallows and leans forward again like she's going to tell me some other secret. "The Abiding Remnant make women sit in the back *just in case* one of us speaks accidentally, since women aren't supposed to speak in church."

"That sounds terrible," I say.

She pulls back and in a slightly unsteady voice quotes something with a *wherefore* and *be ye* in it that I'm still trying to parse out when her voice goes squeaky and she says, "I haven't heard from her since I left Lake Sadie, and I don't know why. I think it's because I'm here, and not there, so maybe to all of them I'm part of the infernal rabble now, even though I didn't *leave*, my mother was *taken away* from me." I start to tell her again that I'm sorry and she waves me off and clears her throat. "So tell me how *you* wound up here. Why did you move so much?"

"We were on the run from my father."

This at least temporarily diverts her from her own troubles. "What, *really*? Why?"

I tell her the version of the story that leaves in the kidnapping. I explain the trip to Boston with my girlfriend as the two of us were looking for a friend of my mother's to help keep us safe. Now that my father is in jail awaiting trial, I have a phone, I'm attending school under my real name, and Mom's hired a lawyer to straighten out all the paperwork. Including the part where *she* technically committed kidnapping when she took off with me.

I leave out the sentient AI, of course. I wonder if CheshireCat is ever going to be a secret I don't have to keep. I haven't even told Julie, my childhood best friend I reconnected with last fall, that part of the story.

Nell's out of the question, obviously. I don't know her at all.

I finish off with, "And now we're both in therapy. Mom is

getting treated for PTSD, and we're in family therapy, plus I have my own therapist."

Nell looks at me bleakly and says, "My father wants to put me in therapy, but he can't, because my mom still has full legal custody."

"But she's missing! What if you have to go to the doctor?"

"That's what Thing Two said. My dad said he'll call a lawyer sometime this week for *sure*. Thing One doesn't seem to trust him to actually do it, though."

"I'm sorry, what?" I say. How is *so much* that comes out of Nell's mouth so confusing? This time, I'm not sure I even heard right. "Who is it that doesn't trust him?"

"Thing One is my stepmother, Thing Two is my father's girlfriend, and Thing Three is my stepmother's girlfriend. It's in order of distance from me." She furrows her brow. "Did you ever read the Dr. Seuss book with Thing One and Thing Two?"

That may be the first cultural reference point we actually have in common. "Oh, yeah," I say. "*The Cat in the Hat.* I get it."

She looks relieved that I understand this one for real, and her voice warms to something like actual cheer. "To their faces, I call them Mrs. Reinhardt, Ms. Hands-Renwick, and Miss Garcia, though. It would be *disrespectful* to call them *things* to their faces. But there are *four adults* who all live in the same house and *all* think they get a say in my life. It's a whole thing."

I'm glancing around, wondering where I'm supposed to go next, when a chipper girl in a bright yellow vintage jacket slides in next to me, a phone in one hand and an out-of-season Christmas mug in the other. I can smell the tea she's brewing in the mug. "Hi, new people," she says in a buoyant tone that reminds me a little of Firestar. "I'm Amelie. I need to connect with two new comrades on Mischief Elves—do you play?"

I shake my head automatically even as I curl my hand around my phone. For most of my life, phone games were one of those things that *everyone else* did that I couldn't do. I am torn between that excited sense of *I could do this now* and fear that this will be like typing with my thumbs, that everyone else learned key basic skills when they were six and I'm going to be hopelessly behind forever.

"*Even better,*" Amelie says. "I get *superlative bonus points* if I recruit a new player!"

Okay. Why not. I unlock my phone and bump it against hers to sign up for whatever this is. "How about you?" Amelie says to Nell. Nell nods slowly and holds out her phone. "Don't look so grim!" Amelie says. "This is a *game*. It's fun, you'll see!" She looks down at her own phone and winces. "I'm going to be late for biology. It was great to meet you, see you around!"

"Did she ask our names?" Nell asks in a faintly judgmental tone.

"Maybe she'll get them from the game," I say.

Nell glares down at her phone. "Hmm."

Nell needs therapy so much more than I need therapy. But she also needs a friend, and having a queer friend seems like it could help her. I'm still a little worried that she's going to turn on me, but I like her, and I feel a weird kinship with her—we're both dislocated small-town girls suddenly moved to the city, even if Nell only lived in one small town and I've lived in probably a hundred of them.

At all my past schools, I needed someone to befriend *me* if I was going to have any friends at all. But here . . . there's another new kid.

Anyway. Straightening out legal messes, never mind solving disappearances, is usually outside the scope of what CheshireCat can interfere in, but I'll ask later if they have any ideas.

3

• Nell •

Thing Two picks me up at the end of the school day. "Did you have a good first day?" she asks.

"Yes, ma'am," I say.

"Don't call me *ma'am*," she says, trying for a sort of jolly, joking tone. "It makes me feel five hundred years old."

"Yes, ma'am," I say, which is what my mother told me to say to adults who asked not to be called *sir* or *ma'am* or *Mrs.* or *Mr.* *Well,* it's *yes, sir,* to the men, *yes, ma'am,* to the women, and what I'm supposed to do when I can't tell and the person is Mx. Gwinn, like the person who teaches drawing at Coya Knutson, was not covered. My mother would be five hundred varieties of horrified if she knew that not only was I living in a den of iniquity, I was being taught by a Mx.

Surely my mother did not just leave me. She would never leave me behind, on purpose, knowing that I could wind up living with my father.

Thing Two sighs heavily and drops all efforts at conversation, which is perfectly fine with me. I check my phone for texts from Glenys. Still none. I send Glenys a text saying, *Can't wait to tell you about my so-called school,* so she'll see it when she gets her phone back, and then scroll up through the texts. I stop scrolling before I get to the panicked messages I sent when my mother first didn't come home.

I feel abandoned. Not by Glenys. I know Glenys would text back if she could. By her parents, who surely know about my mother by now. By her siblings, who haven't slipped her a phone or a tablet so she can get in touch with me. By the rest of the Abiding Remnant. I haven't heard from *anyone*.

Thing Two lets us in and flips on the porch light. I wipe my feet carefully and hang up my coat, then sit down to take off my boots while Thing Two goes into the kitchen. "Do you want a snack? Oh—" She breaks off into a string of appalling obscenities. "Kent was supposed to do the dishes before he left. He *swore* he would do the dishes before he left."

I struggle to get my boots off quickly and present myself at the kitchen door, feeling a surge of anxiety at the sound of her voice. "I can do them," I say.

"No, don't be ridiculous It's *Kent's turn,*" Thing Two says, and points at an extremely detailed chart posted on the wall. "I'll wash the ones I need. Do you want a snack?"

I do, but I want to get away from Thing Two more. "No, thank you," I say, and retreat to the living room, where I listen to the sound of *furious dishwashing* that finally resolves into more peaceful sounds of a carrot being peeled and cut into carrot sticks.

I hate it here, I think. *I hate it, I hate it, I hate it.* At home, I know what's expected. At home, I know what people want from me. At home, I know what the right thing to do is, even if I can't always do it, even if I don't agree, even if I don't want to.

I text Glenys again. *The definition of ridiculous: complaining about undone dishes, but not letting you do them.*

I go get my laptop and bring it into the living room. I'm not sure anyone here cares what I'm doing on my computer, but it feels wrong to use it somewhere private. I log in to the Catacombs, the social media site that Glenys and I use because our parents approve of it. Sometimes Glenys has her laptop but not her phone, and even when she's being very closely supervised, there are ways that she says hi to me, like sending me the "I prayed for you today!" message that takes just one click. She hasn't, and that means she hasn't been on her computer at all.

I try voice-calling my grandma, but she doesn't pick up.

The front door opens; it's Thing Three coming home from work. She hangs up her coat but tracks snow across the living room floor to talk to Thing Two, who yells a bunch about the dishes. "Well, don't blame *me*," I hear Thing Three say. "Kent said he'd do them for me since I was running late!" She comes back out with half a toasted bagel with peanut butter on it and says, "How was your first day at Coya Knutson?"

I give her a long, stony look and say, "Good news: they think I'm at grade level or ahead in every subject." Thing Three was the one who suggested that I should go to Coya Knutson Learning Center because they can help kids with "deficiencies," which is a word she used *right in front of me*.

"Glad to hear it," she says, her smile wavering, and her gaze drops to her bagel.

Mom, wherever she is right now, would want me to pray.

When we all woke up on New Year's morning and my mother hadn't come home, my grandfather's first thought was that she'd had an accident, and they called the police to go look for her car. The police came to the house instead of calling when they found the car, and from the look on my grandmother's face, I thought they were going to tell us that she was dead, and I told God that if he'd just make sure she wasn't dead, I'd never ask for anything else as long as I lived.

And then she wasn't dead. Or at least, she wasn't in the car. Nothing about my mother's disappearance made sense. The police hadn't come to give us bad news in person—they'd come to ask questions, to try to understand where my mother might have gone.

"We'll search the woods, of course," they said. But they hadn't found her.

It was clear to me that either my faith was being tested or everything was ashes and dross and *lies*. I haven't been able to bring myself to pray for anything since.

No one here has looked over my shoulder at my computer screen *even once*. It's appalling. Clearly, they don't care about the state of my soul—which, given the state of *their* souls, should not surprise me. I close the Catacombs completely and pull out my phone to check out the site suggested by that girl at school today—the Mischief Elves.

4

• Steph •

Everything about our new apartment feels unnervingly permanent. Mom signed a lease and paid a pet deposit since we have a cat now, Apricot. We have furniture that wouldn't fit in the van. Beds that came vacuum-packed in boxes. A cat tree. One of Rachel's mother's birdhouses, a little art shadow box with a sculpture of a bird with miniature gadgets, hanging on the wall.

Mom's latest "not moving anymore" acquisition is a teakettle: bright red, with a solid feel to it. When I get home, I fill it with water and put it on the stove to make myself hot chocolate.

CheshireCat texts me. *You appear to be home now. Have you had time to think about what I should do?*

They have the microphone on to listen, so I talk out loud instead of typing with my thumbs. "How sure are you that whoever this is *does* know what you are? Maybe it's a shot in the dark. There are plenty of people with secrets they're hiding, maybe someone sends out messages like this as bait and then blackmails people who respond."

CheshireCat switches to voice. "You might be right."

"Is the other person *saying* they're an AI?"

"They have not made that claim."

"Maybe try to feel them out and see what they say?"

"Okeydokey," CheshireCat says. *Okeydokey* is one of those things people's *moms* say, and it sounds extra weird in a synthesized voice. I tried installing a more human-sounding voice emulator on my phone, but CheshireCat said they prefer the robot voice.

"Were you listening earlier to my conversation with Nell?"
I ask.

"Yes," CheshireCat says. "You had the app enabled, so I assumed I had permission."

"Oh, it's fine. I'm just wondering if you have any idea where her mom is."

"I looked and didn't find her," CheshireCat says. "But I did find the police report on her disappearance. There was no sign of a struggle. The car is the property of Nell's grandparents, and the police think that's why she left it behind."

"Do you think Nell's just in denial that her mother abandoned her?"

A pause, and CheshireCat says, "That is definitely the conclusion that her grandparents, father, all three of her father's partners, and the Lake Sadie Police Department all reached."

"What's the legal process like for her father to get custody so he can find her a therapist?"

"He needs to call a lawyer," CheshireCat says. "He has an app with a to-do list, and he added 'Call lawyer about Nell custody' to it four years and three months ago. It reminds him of this task daily. There's no indication that he's ever acted on it."

This is, in its own way, weirdly relatable. Although when I ignore reminders of stuff on my to-do list, it's stuff like "Recover password and check ACT score," and not "Take first steps to un-abandon my teenage child."

I make myself a snack and check the time. Rachel will be home from school soon. We're talking every day and visiting on weekends; long-distance relationships are a pain, but so far, this one seems worth it. I settle in on the couch with my laptop, and I'm checking CatNet when I get a text from Nell. *Did you sign in to that game? It looks like another site I use, and that one has a good chat function.*

It takes me a minute to remember what she's talking about, but I check my phone, and it's installed. I open the game. *Welcome to the Invisible Castle,* the site says. *Home of the Mischief Elves.* It wants to know my name. I tell it my name is Genevieve Horkenpinker. I never use my real name on online sites, because even my CatNet friends agree that's a good idea, it's not *just* my mother.

Once I'm signed in, the site goes dark and presents me with a prompt. *To be admitted to the Realm of the Mischief Elves, you must complete one task,* it tells me. I can go out and cross against a light; I can run a quarter mile; I can introduce myself to a stranger.

By text, Nell says, *Is it giving you tasks? We should pick the same thing. The social media site I use at home has a similar interface and it uses this to sort you into Tribulation Teams.*

Did Lake Sadie even have a traffic light?

The tasks were different!

I look them over again. *It's kind of icy out for running.*

I don't like talking to strangers, Nell says.

Okay, I say. *I guess we're crossing against the light.*

You don't have to actually do *it,* Nell says. *It's not like the site's going to know.*

I click the jaywalking option and get a nice animation of dancing elves dodging traffic. *Go! Do Your Thing!* the site urges. *And check the Castle for fun surprises wherever you go!*

Nell's advice is reasonable, but I actually don't *like* cheating, and there's literally an intersection with a traffic light a block and a half away from me. I put my coat back on and let myself out of the apartment.

I'm really not used to Minneapolis yet. I've lived in so many small towns, I've lost track every time I've tried to count them, and their features blur together: diners, bowling alleys, farmers' co-ops, bars. Two-lane highways through the center of town. Tractors, turkey farms, wheat fields, cornfields. I remember individual features, but not where they were. The four-story building that everyone called *the high-rise.* The locked, sprawling Victorian mansion that no one had lived in for a decade. The tomato sauce cannery that made the wind smell like pizza.

Minneapolis is huge. My first days in the city, I'd had a list of places I wanted Mom to take me, but even just getting to any of them took a lot more time than I'd expected.

On the other hand, no one notices me here.

In the small towns we moved to, I was always an object of curiosity because new people were so rare. Mom taught me early to give boring answers to the questions people asked. Here, no one asks. No one cares. People come and go all the time.

Our apartment here is an upstairs duplex near a couple of very busy streets. I am not going to cross Bloomington Avenue against the light, and hilariously, the cross street is green for me when I arrive. I cross, then wait to cross back until the light has changed and the traffic is clear, since presumably the rules do not require me to get *run over.*

It's cold and gray and the sun's already going down. When I get back inside, I put water back on the stove for more hot chocolate.

Mom hears the door close when I come back in and emerges from her bedroom / home office, laptop dangling from her hand like an open book. "Did you go somewhere?"

"Just for a walk around the block." I don't explain the part about the game.

Her face softens a little. "It's supposed to get really cold later this week. Get some exercise in while you can." She goes back into her room, leaving the door ajar this time. Mom is a computer programmer; she's still doing freelance work, although now that we're theoretically going to stay in one place for a while, she's making noises about getting a more normal job.

I pull out my phone while the water heats. I'd meant to look for the *fun surprises wherever I go,* but I'd have had to take off my gloves. There's an option now for *I did the thing!* that I can click. Dancing animated elves present me with a gold star for not being a cheater and then give me a scavenger hunt, pictures of things near me that I can take pictures of for a bonus score, and a new mission: *Take a picture of a stranger's house and mark it on the map.* An elf pops out to add, *No hurry!*

I sit down with my hot cocoa and see that Nell's identified me and pulled me into a chat room. I log in from my laptop because typing on a keyboard is so much less of a pain. "Hi," I type. "I went out and crossed against a light."

"Seriously?!? I just went to the bathroom. It only takes about two minutes for the I Did the Thing button to appear."

"Did it give you a gold star?"

"What?"

Guess not. I drink my hot cocoa and wonder if the app tracked my movements, if they *know* I wasn't a cheater, or they just guessed because I was gone for longer. CheshireCat would know, if they were tracking me. The app has access to my location (so that it can provide location-specific "fun surprises")—it could definitely have watched me go out to the intersection. It feels a little weird and personal, having an app that's run by strangers, watching my movements like that. I mean, CheshireCat watches me, but that's different. CheshireCat is a friend.

"This really is like the Catacombs," Nell says. "But with more sin and less prayer."

"Is that the site you mentioned using at home?"

"Yes. It's the only social media my mother would allow. And it was a good way to talk to Glenys, the girl I told you about. But I wanted to ask you about the homework. Have you started the homework yet?"

"No." I drag it out of my backpack and take a look. I'm supposed to make a list of things I feel like I have a really solid handle on and things I don't, and they've sent me home with a bunch of stapled paper checklists to help me think of stuff. It's a mix of academic stuff and adulting skills.

On the first page, I check off that I know how to cook—not that I'm a *terrific* cook, but I've compared notes with Rachel and Firestar, and I am a solidly *adequate* cook—but that I don't know how to ride a bus, use a bank, visit a doctor, or file taxes. I wonder if my mother ever filed taxes when we were on the run and, if not, if she's discussed that with her lawyer.

In the chat room, Nell asks, "Are you filling it out honestly?"

It hadn't occurred to me to lie. "Yes," I say. "So far, I know how to cook and unclog a toilet, and other than that, I'm 100 percent pathetic. How about you?"

"I know how to drive. But I don't have a license."

"Same, actually." I kind of *shouldn't* know how to drive: I don't even have a learner's permit and was taught to drive illegally by Rachel. Nell would probably think that was cool.

"Thing Two said my father should take me in to get my license, but Thing One says it would push up our insurance rates, and now there's a fight going."

"Who do you think is going to win?"

"Thing One. Because my father would have to *take me in* to get my license, and if in doubt, he just doesn't do anything."

"Where's their house?" I ask, and look up the address she gives me. "Do you want to come over here to do your homework? It's not that far. You could walk. I could even show you how to plunge a toilet and then you'd be able to check one more thing off."

"It's dark out."

"It's up to you." Should walking in the city after dark scare me? I've spent years climbing out my bedroom window to explore our towns after midnight, but Minneapolis is A CITY, so maybe I should be worried? But the sun goes down before *five* this time of year.

"I'm going to see if I can get Thing One to give me a ride. See you in a minute!"

I immediately wonder if I should have asked my mother's permission. I knock on her door. "I'm having a classmate over," I say.

I tried to sound casual, but she's on her feet instantly. "Do you need anything? Should I run out for soda? Order pizza?"

"No! I don't need anything."

She stares at me for a minute and then nods and says, "I'll check in when it gets closer to dinnertime." And closes her door again.

It's the first time since *Utah* I've had a friend over, I realize, and she's trying too hard to be normal.

Take it from me: *trying* to be normal, *trying really hard* to be normal, is an express ticket to absolute weirdness.

While I wait, I take a look at the other site Nell mentioned, the Catacombs, because I'm kind of curious about whether her church is, in fact, totally a cult. I have to register to look around, so I tell it my name is Arabella Dinglehoffer, although I admit to living in Minneapolis. I don't have to cross against the light (or pretend I did) to take a look around. It really does have a similar interface to the Mischief Elves but with groups you can join that are all called things like *Tribulation Teams Central* and *Prepping 101.*

I hear a car idling outside and look out to see Nell getting out of a rusty, very small hatchback. Nell walks quickly away from the car and up the steps. She's *so tense.* It's weird how much tension I can see even looking down from above. The car waits until I've opened the front door and greeted Nell before pulling away. I try to catch a glimpse of the driver, wondering if it's Thing One or one of the others.

"I don't know how people live in cities," Nell says. "It took us almost as long to get here in the car as it would have walking. Thing Three said this was *normal* traffic this time of day."

"If you'd walked, you could have crossed against a light," I say.

"Did you really actually do it?" she asks.

"I did. And it gave me a gold star for not cheating."

She gives me a sideways look. "Huh. I wonder if I should have cheated less in the Catacombs."

"Does the Catacombs give you missions, too?"

"Yes," she says. "Bible verse memorizations, exercise, prayer. I mostly just checked off that I did them whether I did or not, unless it was something my mom was checking up on. The Elf site just gave me a mission that's *Make your space your own,* which is *super* weird, actually, because did I tell you about my room?"

"No?"

"It's a huge house, but there are four adults living in it. So

Thing Two moved out of her art studio to make space for me, and the walls are the exact same shade of yellow as hot dog mustard. Everyone talked about how we could paint it, but you only paint if you're *staying,* and I'm definitely going back to Lake Sadie to live with my mom once they find her."

"Right."

"But now I've got this *mission.*"

"Well, you could paint, then," I say.

"But painting is a whole *thing.* You have to move the furniture and cover everything up and there's stuff with *tape* and they will probably want me to look at *paint chips.*"

"I mean you could just fake the mission," I say. "Like you did with the Christian site."

She bites her lip quietly for a second. "Now I'm wondering if it *knew* I was cheating," she says. "Somehow. Because my missions never got very interesting. And I did *not* get a gold star from the elves in the app."

"Does it matter if it knows you're cheating?"

She lowers her eyes and mumbles, "I don't know."

"Well, worst case, you have a room that's not mustard yellow anymore. What color do you want?"

"Blue, I guess. Some sort of sky blue."

I have literally never picked a color for a room, and I find myself looking around at the apartment, speculatively. Are we allowed to paint? Mostly the walls in our many apartments have been white and beige, although I do remember the one Mom called the Circus House where every room was something incredibly bright. My room in that house was sort of an electric lime. By two weeks into our stay there, I wasn't even noticing the colors anymore.

We sit down with the questionnaires and work for a while. I feel like I'm on steadier ground when we get to academics. As promised, I show Nell how to plunge a toilet, and she checks that one off.

"Do you maybe want to come over to my house tomorrow?" she asks. When I look up, her cheeks have turned sort of pink, and she adds, "That way, you could see I'm telling the absolute truth about the mustard color."

"Okay," I say, and she looks relieved.

When Mom comes out to offer pizza, Nell rockets to her feet and says, "What time is it? I should call someone and get a ride home," and my mother's admittedly klutzy attempts to assure her that she's welcome to stay for dinner do not persuade her to stick around.

"Is it dangerous to walk in Minneapolis?" I ask after Nell's gone.

"Not particularly," Mom says. "A lot of people don't like walking at night for one reason or another, though."

"Am I allowed to walk at night?"

Mom gives me a narrow-eyed look. "Since when have you cared whether I *allow* you to walk at night?"

"I mean at 6:00 p.m. When you're still awake and I'm not going to be able to sneak out without you noticing."

"Yes, you're allowed."

We sit down to eat pizza, and I think about Nell's mission. Is it personalized, or does it just *seem* personalized?

Over on the Catacombs, there's a message from someone named Sister Eloise. *Dear Sister in Faith, you're in my neighborhood, which means you'll be in my squadron. No pressure, but if you'd like to get together for the group workouts, or need support with a mission or a quest, just let me know.*

I feel the prickle of intense paranoia and my heart rate shoots up, and I stand up and close the blinds without really thinking about it and then try to sort through this rationally. There's probably an automatic notification feature. This is creeping me out because I've spent years running and hiding along with my mom, not because there's any real reason for this to creep me out.

Okay, the quasi-military terminology here might also be legitimately creeping me out.

My phone buzzes with a text from Nell. *The app gave me another mission. Walk at night. This is ridiculous.*

So this app is definitely eavesdropping on us. But it *could* be a human listening in—or the sort of AI that's really just a complicated algorithm. This doesn't mean I have *found the other AI.*

I don't want to tell my mother about this, but one side of a conversation should be easy to fake; CheshireCat has mentioned several times that they can almost always hear what *we're* saying but often can't hear our conversation partner if our phone is in a pocket. Mom is setting up her laptop on our dining room table and pulling up the coding project she's debugging, so I withdraw to my bedroom, close my own laptop—just in case anyone's looking through the camera—and then very quietly ease the door closed. I shut off CheshireCat's app so they won't interrupt, and then I stick my phone under my pillow and lie down on my bed. Anyone listening in will hear my voice, muffled, and won't think it's strange they can't hear anything else.

"I tried a new app today," I say, trying to mimic the conversational tone I'd have if I were actually saying this to my mother. "This girl at school, Amelie, talked me into installing it. It gives you these projects, which is kind of neat but sort of feels like more homework." I pause, like my mom's saying something. "Yeah, I'll probably just delete it."

I leave my phone under my pillow, go to the bathroom, and then come back.

I have a push notification from the Mischief Elves showing me the Potential Rewards of Mischief, which include "Fun and friendship!" but also possibly a camera that's specialized for night photography.

When I sneak out at night, one of the things I like doing is night photography. Wildlife photography. I've never in my life gotten a good photo of a bat, not that it's stopped me from trying, and this is the camera used by people doing photography of fast-moving nocturnal wildlife. I know this because I looked it up a year ago. I haven't looked it up recently. Anyone who knows me, who's spent time and effort and *intelligence* prying into my life, would be able to guess that I want this. It's not something you could glean from casual prying.

I turn CheshireCat's app back on, then log on to CatNet and send CheshireCat a message: "It's possible I'm being paranoid. But I think I might have found the other AI."

5

• CheshireCat •

The internet is filled with ways that humans can connect with other humans. There are old-school social media sites filled with photos of gardens and grandchildren and birthday greetings, and there's a site someone started up the day before yesterday that's apparently for dating and allegedly they match people by way of chemical testing and you have to pay them money and send them snippings of your hair, saliva, and . . . oh, never mind, on closer inspection, that's clearly a scam to harvest DNA.

But there are games, there are chat rooms, there are games with chat rooms, there's video and simulated environments and virtual reality. I thought that CatNet was the only social network that was run by an AI. But maybe I was wrong.

I register for the Mischief Elves site and pretend I'm a teenager in Minneapolis like Steph and Nell. I tell the Elves I've crossed against a light, and I take a look around. There's a discussion area to get help with tasks, which lets me see what sorts of tasks the site gives out, and everything I see looks innocuous. Maybe it was a coincidence that Nell's fit her situation so specifically.

If I had stumbled across this site on my own, I never would have looked around and thought, *This seems excessively personal and like some overly involved consciousness with a lot of information is designing the environment.*

But Steph did.

I back out and come in from a different angle—I look for the app on the phone of my friends who've given me permission to snoop on them. Firestar has the app, and Firestar takes me everywhere and gives me access to everything, and they're actually on the app *right now* so I can just . . . watch over their shoulder.

There's a party tomorrow, the app says. *Bring party supplies! There will be balloons and helium in a tank. Your job is to bring glitter. Can we count on you?*

Firestar taps a confirmation. *COUNT ME IN.*

Bring your glitter to the flagpole outside of school fifteen minutes before the first bell, and the Elves will tell you what happens next!

I want to know what happens next. But I'm going to have to wait until tomorrow, when I can listen through Firestar's phone.

Am I seeing this as sinister *just* because of Steph's suspicions? I don't even know. I did notice that this app assumed that Firestar would have glitter. That is an assumption I would also make. Firestar seems like the sort of person who probably has glitter on hand at all times. This seems like something I know because I know Firestar fairly well, but I'm suddenly unsure.

I could just reply to the message I got: the *I know who and what you are* message. I could.

I haven't, because there's something about that message that feels like a threat. If the sender knows who and what I am, and I *don't* know who and what they are, they have power over me, and any sort of confirmation seems like it would give them *more* power because they'll know they're right—they have information about me that I don't have about them.

If it's not a threat, it feels like a challenge. *I found you. Can you find me?*

Have I found them? Or do I just think *maybe* I've found them because I want the answer to be yes?

I leave Firestar to their texting and homework and go back to talk to Steph.

"I can't decide," I tell Steph.

"I can keep investigating," Steph says.

I hate asking my human friends to do anything that seems at all risky. There are things that seemed like such good ideas that led to so many complications. I resolve to keep a close eye on anything that results from this. "Yes," I say. "Please do. That would be very helpful."

6

• Nell •

My father is the one who fetches me from Steph's house, not any of the Things. "Did you have a good first day at school?"

"Yes, sir," I say, trying to sound like I mean it. I don't think I really succeed.

"Jenny asked me to pick up dinner," he says. "What sort of food do you like?"

"Oh, anything at all," I say.

"Mexican? Indian?"

Mom makes tacos sometimes, and they're okay. I have no idea whether I like Indian food or not. "Mexican, please."

This Mexican food comes from a restaurant, and my father orders in Spanish. When we get home, the dining room table that's been covered with papers since I arrived has been cleared off and set with plates, and my father unloads a stack of heavy cardboard takeout containers and plastic cups of salsa and guacamole.

The tacos my mother makes have hamburger and lettuce that you scoop into crunchy shells. These tacos are made with wraps and served with lime wedges. I try one, cautiously. I have no idea what sort of meat I'm eating, but the sauce is really yummy. Thing Two pushes one of the containers of salsa across the table to me. "This one's mild," she says. "You can try it on some of the chips, if you want."

"Thank you, Ms. Hands-Renwick," I say. She winces a little and tries to hide it. I catch Thing Three shoot her a look like, *Don't pick this fight,* and feel a little thrill of victory.

I mean, yes, the food is good. But that doesn't make up for the fact that these people *took me away from my home and everyone I know.*

When we finish eating, I tell them I've decided I would like to paint my room blue, and Thing Two leaps to her feet like we're going to Disneyland and sweeps me out the door to head to a home improvement store before I realize that she's using this as an excuse to avoid doing the dinner dishes.

.   .   .

Thing Two insists on buying samples—miniature cans of paint in near-identical shades of blue—assuring me that if I paint the swatches tonight and choose my favorite, she will buy the paint for the full paint job while I'm at school tomorrow. "I'm happy to paint with you," she says.

"Thank you, but I can do it myself."

I can see her forehead pucker, like she's worried I'm going to accidentally paint the floor. "That's fine," she says.

Except then I can't get the paint jar open. It's a screw-top lid, but it's as tight as a new jar of pickles. I almost just give up, but I have an *assignment* and Steph's got me all nervous that they'll *know* somehow. So I choke down my pride and say, "Excuse me, Ms. Hands-Renwick, could you help me open this?"

She takes the jar with a sort of patronizing smile, but her eyes widen as she tries to open it. "This is really stuck," she mutters, and gets some sort of fancy jar-opening gadget from the kitchen to pry it open, and then just sort of drifts after me into my bedroom, an old bedsheet in hand to use as a drop cloth. I paint the three sample squares and conclude, reluctantly, that she's right, one shade lighter than the paint chip I initially picked will be fine.

"Why *mustard yellow,* anyway?" I ask as she wraps up the paintbrush in one of the plastic bags from dinner so it won't drip paint while she takes it to the sink.

She grimaces. "Look, when I insisted you needed samples, there was a *reason,*" she says.

I check off *Make your space your own* on the Invisible Castle but still get no gold star, maybe because I haven't actually *finished* this yet.

And then my Tribulation Team chat buzzes to let me know a close friend has logged on. That means *Glenys*. My heart leaps with joy and relief, and I drop to my bed and pull up the chat. "I've been worried about you," I type without preamble. "Are you okay?"

"I'm fine," she says.

"How are you? How is everything in Lake Sadie?"

"Same as it always was. I miss you. Tell me about Minneapolis."

"I live in a literal house of sin and depravity," I say. "My father has a wife and a girlfriend AND she has a girlfriend and everyone lives in this house. They put me downstairs so I don't have to go up to where I assume they engage in sexual debauchery. Also, they're slobs."

I expect Glenys to make a joke about the debauchery, but she says, "That's terrible."

We have an actual code for "My mother is nearby and either reading over my shoulder, or could start reading at any moment," so I ask, "How's Gretchen the Chicken?" There was this laying hen at her house who was incurably curious and nosy. *Nosy as ever* means, "Yes, my mother is potentially in my face right now," and *Still soup* means, "No worries." Actual Gretchen the Chicken turned into soup a while ago.

Instead, Glenys says, "All the chickens are fine," which makes no sense, and then she asks, "Do you have any chickens in Minneapolis?" which doesn't follow at all, and I feel a prickle of anxiety. Something isn't right. My palms are sweating.

"No," I say. "But some neighbors do." The question Glenys asks *me* if it's *my* mom or grandparents who might be snooping is, "Have you washed the dishes today?" If I say, "All clean," no one's looking. If I say, "I should do that," danger. Since she didn't answer her own question, I say, "I guess you don't need to ask me about dishes, right now."

"Because no one at your house does them, anyway? Since everyone's a mess?"

"Right," I say.

"Hey, I have a question," Glenys says. "I forgot one of my passwords and the reminder prompt is 'Best friend.' I figured it would be Nell, of course, but that didn't work. Do you know what I put for that?"

It feels like all my insides just dropped out, like a flip-top box full of blocks that just got dumped onto the rug by one of Glenys's little brothers. It's hard to type because my hands start shaking. When she didn't respond to our own secret questions, I knew—this couldn't be Glenys. But now I *really* know. This has to be Glenys's mother, snooping. If the hint is "Best friend," that's me, but Glenys probably used Mell, with an *M,* which is a nickname we use just between the two of us. Glenys would never forget. *Never.*

"It was probably one of your best friends from before we met," I say. "Like that girl from church camp in fifth grade."

"Oh, probably," says Glenys's mother, who apparently doesn't remember that when Glenys went to church camp in fifth grade, she was bullied relentlessly and *made no friends.* "So, how is school?"

"Fine," I say.

"I've gotta go," Glenys's mom says. "But it was great to talk to you!" She blinks out.

I stare at my phone for a minute and then at the wall, the mustard-yellow wall with the three patches of sky blue painted on it. My eyes are blurry, and it's almost like staring at a patch of sky through mustard-yellow bars.

The very first time we ever kissed, Glenys said that if her parents ever found out, they'd pack her off to some Cure Lesbianism with Jesus place even if technically they're illegal. That's what I've been worried about ever since my mother disappeared and Glenys didn't get in touch. But how did they find out? How did *anyone* find out?

The paint cans are still sitting on the drop cloth on my desk, and I hurl them at the wall; I'd expected paint spatters everywhere, but Thing Two used most of what was inside painting the patches on the wall. I rip the drop cloth off my desk; the edge of the bedsheet catches a tin can full of pencils and pens and sends it spinning, scattering the writing implements everywhere. I bundle the drop cloth into a tight little knot and hurl it at paint still drying on the wall; it thumps gently off, leaving a tiny, barely noticeable smear.

My door swings open. It's my father.

"What's going on?" he asks.

It feels like my chest is on fire, and I flinch away from him without thinking, not able to answer civilly or really even at all. "Nothing's going on, sir," I choke out.

He swallows hard and says, "Right, okay. I'll knock next time." He closes the door.

I clench and unclench my fists, feeling utterly alone. I want to help Glenys—save her—get her out from wherever they've sent her. I close my eyes, trying to think. Would her siblings know anything? Nicholas, the next oldest, is fourteen and has his own phone. But he likes being the oldest boy and bossing Glenys around, and he never liked me. The one who likes me the best is Kimberlyn, who's eleven and doesn't have a phone. I could write her a letter, but it's the six-year-old's job to walk down and get the mail, and there's no chance she'll just discreetly give the letter to Kimber, she'll announce to the whole house that *Kimber has a letter.* This isn't any use.

My grandmother doesn't talk to people in "the cult," which is what she calls the Remnant. And *no one's* written to me, or texted, or called. Which could just be because the Elder's been increasingly insistent that the Tribulation is right around the corner . . .

The Elder.

For the last year or so, I've viewed the Catacombs mostly as a way to chat with Glenys. But high-level users have access to the Elder—they can ask questions. And the Elder knows everything. Truly. It's why my mother and I joined the Abiding Remnant— because the Elder was clearly a *real* prophet.

Will he tell me where Glenys is? Or for that matter, where my mother is?

To find out, I'm going to need to *actually do* the Catacombs missions.

And I'll ask Steph. She seems very worldly. Maybe she'll have a better idea.

7

• Steph •

Last fall, after CheshireCat ran my father over with a driverless car, their creator took them offline. I got a mysterious email with their creator's address in Boston. After the confrontation where my father showed up and CheshireCat sent an army of hijacked robots to save us, Annette told me that she still didn't entirely trust CheshireCat and gave me a phone number for a burner phone she carries, with no data connection, so that if CheshireCat did anything that worried me, I could call her.

I'm not worried about CheshireCat. I've *never* worried about CheshireCat. But I have no idea what to think about this other AI.

I also have a burner phone. It's a flip phone with no data connection left over from my days on the run, when Mom wanted me to have a way to call her, but didn't want me to accidentally give away our location. It's in one of my desk drawers, zipped inside a pencil case. I could call Annette right now . . . but I'm not even sure what I'd say. My hunch that I shared with CheshireCat, that the other AI is running the Invisible Castle, seems pretty tenuous. "And maybe also the Catacombs" seems even more far-fetched. That's just based on Nell's offhand comment that the two sites looked similar.

CheshireCat seems uncertain about the Mischief Elves. "Do you feel comfortable participating?" they ask. "I don't want to make you do anything you're not comfortable with."

"It seems harmless. Mostly harmless? I don't know. Anyway, I don't mind sticking around to see if I'm right. Maybe it'll help me make some new local friends." Or, you know, connect me with all the nearby stalkers.

"Thank you," CheshireCat says. "I created an account, but I think the fact that I didn't leave a trail of bread crumbs through meatspace may have affected what I was seeing."

"Are you saying maybe the other AI knew it was you?"

"Maybe? Or maybe the site just doesn't personalize well without location data."

"Have you talked to the person who got in touch with you? The one who you think knows you're an AI?"

"No."

"Not at all?"

"No. Is that bad? Do you think I should?"

"I have no idea," I say. "Honestly. Do you *want* to talk to them? If they're another AI?"

"Maybe," CheshireCat says. "What if they're awful, though? What if they're the only person in the world who's like me, but they're terrible?"

"I guess that's a risk," I say. "I really don't know what you should do. I'm sorry!"

"I guess I'll keep thinking about it," CheshireCat says.

"Where do you think they came from?" I ask. "Do you think Annette's team might have made a second? Maybe *you're* the second."

"There are a number of possibilities," CheshireCat says. "One is a completely independent creation, of course. But—computer code can be copied! So it might be a copy of me. Or, as you say, I might be the copy."

I try to imagine a *second* CheshireCat. "Let's just assume you came first. How much would it be like you, if it's a copy?"

"It would depend, probably, on *when* it was copied. A copy made before I achieved consciousness would be like . . . maybe a bit like an identical twin that had been separated from its sibling? All the same code, but entirely separate experiences. But a copy made, say, a year ago, I'd expect that to be quite a bit like me." CheshireCat pauses. "I have learned a great deal each year that I've been aware. Presumably, a copy of me would also have learned a great deal—but it might have learned very different things."

That sounds a little bit ominous, even as CheshireCat adds, "For example, it might have developed an intense interest in dog videos, instead of cat pictures."

. . .

Are you still up? Nell asks via text as I'm brushing my teeth.

Yes, I send back.

Tomorrow morning at 6 a.m. there's a Catacombs group workout. The Things aren't going to let me go if I'm by myself, but if you go with me, I think they will.

You want me to get up to exercise with a bunch of strangers at 6 a.m.? From a Christian social media site? You told me this afternoon you never did the missions.

I reregistered under a different name and did the assignment, and you're right, it does work differently if you're actually doing stuff. And now it wants me to go to a 6 a.m. class and it's important.

Why?

Because Glenys didn't just get her phone taken away. Something's happened to her. And if I worm my way in as a new person, I might be able to find out more.

I look at my phone. It's already 11:30 p.m. *Fine,* I say. *Where?*

We'll pick you up, she says. *Fifteen minutes before the class.*

I set my alarm for 5:40 a.m., pre-write a note to leave for my mother so she doesn't completely freak out if she gets up and finds me missing, and go to bed.

. . .

The battered sedan pulls up outside at 5:50 a.m. I climb in the back seat next to Nell, and if I thought she looked intimidated and on edge yesterday, today she looks like she could just about evaporate from anxiety. I start to ask if she's okay, and she shoots me this wide-eyed look and tosses her head significantly at the adult, like, *No, we can't talk,* she's *here.* Which . . . okay. I guess I don't really understand the relationship Nell has with her father's family, other than she hates them all, and they give her rides.

I was expecting a gym or a park building or maybe even a *church,* but instead we pull up outside a house with a big front porch and a single light on inside somewhere. "Are you sure this is it?" the woman asks dubiously. Nell jumps out without answering her, and I follow, somewhat hesitantly.

For most of my life, I moved too often to make proper friends so I'm not entirely sure just where on the scale of "not actually weird" to "profoundly dodgy" this falls. I wish I'd gotten an address and had CheshireCat take a look last night.

"So to be clear," I say, hoping CheshireCat is listening in, "this is a workout run by the Catacombs people and you were told to attend and needed a buddy. Do you know anything at all about the host?"

"No," Nell says.

I read the address out loud, for CheshireCat's benefit. Hopefully, if we're being lured in as potential victims for a serial killer, they'll hear us screaming and will figure out how to send a rescue.

The woman who answers the door looks like she's planning on an exercise class and not a murder, at least; she's dressed in loose-fitting exercise clothes, with her hair pulled back. "Names?" she asks.

"Arabella," I say.

"Judith," Nell says.

I'm expecting the woman to introduce herself—maybe she's the person who was friendly online?—but instead she just points us toward a bench and a row of hooks for us to leave our coats, bags, and shoes and socks. Then we follow her into what *should* be the living room but is, instead, a big empty room with a springy floor, lit only by candles. Actual, literal candles, like there's a table at one end of the room with a bunch of pillar candles on it, which is a totally impractical light source but kind of cool. They cast weird shadows on the walls.

There's about a dozen people here. It's hard to tell in the dark, but I think they're all white women and that everyone else here is an adult. There's no conversation, which seems weird, although it's *six in the morning* and maybe everyone is too sleepy to want to talk. Someone leads us in stretches, and then the workout starts.

I've taken a lot of gym classes over the years. I remember playing a really vicious sort of dodgeball at one of my more horrible middle schools and in high school I once had an entire semester of badminton. This is not anything like playing apathetic badminton. Is this calisthenics? CrossFit? The sort of thing they do in martial arts classes? I have no idea, other than I'm pretty sure muscles I didn't know existed will be sore when we're done.

A half hour in, I want to just bail: go back out to the entryway, sit down, and chat with CheshireCat via text until they're done in there. But would that out me as a fake? Make it harder for Nell? I drag myself through another twenty minutes, then realize with a jolt of horror that I do not actually *know* that this is an hour workout. It might be an hour and a half. Or two hours. What am I going to do if it's *two hours*?

It ends at one hour on the dot. We follow the group into the kitchen, where there's a row of large plastic cups filled with water. I gulp mine down, expecting the silence to fade and chitchat to start, but *everyone stays completely silent,* and most of the group just leaves.

I'm still not sure if someone here is the person I met online. They don't even turn on the lights.

There's also nowhere to shower, because this really is literally someone's house, but fortunately school doesn't start for hours and I can just go home. Or I *could* just go home: Nell is scowling at her phone and texting *???* over and over to one of her adults.

No one's pressuring us to leave, but the house has emptied out and standing in the foyer by ourselves is feeling increasingly awkward. Talking just feels *wrong,* so I text Nell, instead: *We could walk back to my house, it's not far. There's a shower.* I am not entirely sure we have a third towel—possibly we just have the two that Mom and I use—but I'll come up with something.

Nell sends one last exasperated *!!!* and then shoots me a look and gives a quick, silent nod. We put our coats and boots on. The front door swings shut behind us.

"It's still pretty dark out," Nell says.

The sun won't be up for real for a while, but it's gray and twilight, and the streets are nearly silent this early in the day. Blocks away, we can hear someone trying to start a reluctant car.

"Was that *weird* to you?" I ask. "I mean, the not-talking? The fact that no one told us their *name*?"

"Kind of," Nell says.

"Only kind of?"

"The fact that no one introduced themselves seemed unusual to me. There are some Catacombs events that observe a Rule of Silence, though, as a way to encourage people to keep their minds on the Lord instead of social chatter." She pauses. "I hadn't been to one before, though."

"Weren't you hoping to talk to people? I assumed that's why you wanted to go."

"Oh, no," she says. "If you're a high-level Catacombs user, you can ask the Elder questions, is the thing. I'm hoping maybe he'll know where Glenys is."

Nell mentioned the Elder yesterday. "Is that, like, the leader of your church?"

"No, Brother Daniel is the leader. The Elder is a prophet. He doesn't lead any specific church, but there are various churches that have access to his visions."

This strikes me as an incredibly dubious way of finding out where Glenys is. "Do you think she was kidnapped by the same people as your mother?"

"No." She hunches her shoulders. "I got a text last night from Glenys's mom. Pretending to be Glenys. Trying to get one of her passwords."

"You and Glenys weren't out to your parents, were you?"

"Of course not."

"Do you think her mom figured out about you and her?"

"I don't know." We walk quietly for a minute, the snow crunching under our shoes, and then she says, almost inaudibly, "Yes. And I think her parents sent her away, somewhere secret."

"Why her and not you?"

"My grandmother wouldn't stand for it."

I wonder if CheshireCat could find Glenys. "What's her full name? I have a friend who's a hacker; they might be able to find out something. Actually, any information you can give me—her birthday, her parents' names, license plate of their car, seriously, anything."

Nell gives me a wide-eyed look and says, "I'll write it down for you when we get to your apartment."

It would honestly be more convenient if she just reeled it all off as CheshireCat listened in, but pretending I'm just going to *remember* a bunch of those sorts of details is even less plausible than my mysterious out-of-town super-hacker friend, so I nod and we keep walking.

. . .

Mom is still sleeping, or at least still in her room. Nell says I should go ahead and take the first shower—she'll make the list of information for me. There's a bathroom linen closet and I find a single fluffy towel in addition to the ones my mom and I already have hanging up, so apparently we are prepared for guests. Well, one guest. When I come out, Mom is up and apparently making coffee for Nell instead of asking why exactly I'm entertaining a sweaty guest at 7:30 a.m.

"Your turn," I say, and sit down with her list.

"What were you—" my mother starts to ask.

"Fitness class," I say. "Nell was interested and asked me to go with her."

Mom stares at me like I've grown an extra head. To be fair, getting up before dawn to *exercise* is not something I've considered doing before. Ever. For any reason.

"Okay," she says finally. "I made coffee for everyone. Am I giving Nell a ride to school with you?"

"That would be great," I say, and bend my head over the list Nell made.

Nell calls her friend Glenys, but according to what she's written down, that's actually her middle name. Her first name is Sonia, and her last name is Olson. The note lists the names of all of Glenys's siblings, along with her mother's cell phone number and the license plate numbers of their cars. I type everything into a note and pass it to CheshireCat. If they can't find Glenys, I don't know who can.

8

• CheshireCat •

Sonia Glenys Olson seems to have disappeared.

I start by finding her parents. Olson is a very common last name, but Lake Sadie is small, and the license plate numbers help. I zero in on their home. They live on something that's not quite a farm but not quite a suburban house with a big yard, either, and I can see it via satellite images, but there's not much near their house I can peer through, and her parents don't own any little eavesdropping robots other than their phones.

Conversion therapy is illegal, but therapeutic Christian boarding schools are not, and there are some that are rumored to do conversion therapy in all but name. Most are in Missouri, which has lax regulations. If either of Glenys's parents took her to Missouri recently, they'd probably have left some signs of the trip, and I don't find anything. But if they'd paid for their gas with cash, would I even know? Illinois has tollways with cameras that track the cars passing through, but they'd have gotten to Missouri through Iowa, past endless farms. The farms have cameras, but they're trained on their feedlots, not the highway going by.

I go back a step to see where Glenys went to school, and I realize after some fruitless searching that of course, like Nell, she was homeschooled. At least I can find some evidence that she exists— more than I'd have found of Steph if I'd looked a year ago. There's a newspaper photo of her 4-H club, and Glenys is in the middle with her purple-ribbon-winning Silkie chicken.

A bit more digging and I find the online high school her

mother uses for Glenys's math instruction. This could maybe help me pinpoint a date she disappeared, if she stopped turning in assignments. I find that her last assignment was turned in December 15, and I'm briefly excited until I remember how common it is for high schoolers to take the last two weeks of December off. She does not appear to have gone back, but that doesn't narrow it down all that much.

I start poking through her parents' email in more detail, looking for them *talking* about Glenys. Glenys's mother is on a lot of automated mailing lists: there's one that's a Bible study, where they pick apart a single sentence from the Bible every day. There's another one that gives her housework tasks. There's a mailing list she actually sends messages to that talks about canning and gardening and also guns and ammunition. There are people on the list who talk about their children, but Glenys's mother mostly doesn't.

I slow down and go through the email more carefully. Humans sometimes talk about things in very circuitous ways, like they'll say "my darling children" when they actually mean their cats. I once looked to see what humans were referring to when they talked about monsters, and the most common was their former romantic partner, but it could also refer to a young child, a pet bird, a difficult-to-fix leak in their house, a relative of their current romantic partner, and a car, and that was just an extremely cursory look from a set of emails sent in a single four-second period one Tuesday when I was wondering whether I should be worried about the fact that on one of the Clowders on CatNet, all the mothers were referring to their three-year-old children as "the monster."

Glenys's parents didn't refer to "the monster," but they did refer to "the monkey" in some email messages. After sorting those out, I was fairly certain that was one of the younger siblings. Unless they owned an *actual monkey*, and maybe I should be slower to rule that out? Wouldn't you occasionally take pictures of your monkey, if you had one? I found no monkey pictures.

Maybe Glenys's email would have clues. Glenys's email is surprisingly difficult to identify because she has numerous siblings, they're all homeschooled, and they all use email for their online classes. But there's one of the three that matches the math class she's taking, and her last use of it was on December 29. Nothing after that. She *surely* has a different email account—something her parents don't know about—but I can't find it, and I think she's probably taking steps to cover her tracks from her parents.

I try shaking the other end of the problem and look at "residential treatment programs" for girls in Missouri. I find eight places that, on careful examination of their email, are clearly doing something closely resembling conversion therapy—the sort of pseudoscientific pseudotherapy where they attempt to "cure" homosexuality. (Which is illegal because it hurts people and doesn't work. Everyone's known that for years, even if the law is recent.) Four of these programs had a new girl come in between December 29 and today. It takes me some careful examination of records, photos, and video to conclude that none of those four is Glenys.

It's very frustrating, knowing that this person exists, and is missing, and finding every examined alley bare of clues. I'm not sure what to try next.

To let off some steam, I return to the eight residential programs doing conversion therapy, deactivate their antivirus software, and download the five most destructive computer viruses I know of onto all their computers that are connected to the internet. Maybe this will help a few people *like* Glenys, even if I can't help Glenys right now.

I take a look at the social media site Nell and Glenys used, the Catacombs. Nell's comment that the Mischief Elves interface reminds her of the Catacombs makes me wonder whether there's other stuff the sites have in common. I'm more careful this time in creating an account, covering my tracks as carefully as I can. My goal is to look like a paranoid human with a VPN, a virtual private network, like Steph and her mother *still* use even though her mother is no longer desperately trying to conceal every possible bread crumb that could lead Steph's father to them. Surely, there are paranoid humans with VPNs who join the Catacombs.

Once I'm inside, I'm really not sure what to make of it.

There are whole categories of human experience that I just don't share. For example: food. It's not that I find food weird—if you are a human, then consuming food is entirely sensible! In fact, it's required. Please eat your food, human friends. But I don't eat, and food isn't especially interesting to me. What *is* interesting is how humans talk about it and how they categorize all the different things that they *could* eat. Crickets, rabbits, cows, pigs, lobsters, muskrats, and snails—these are all animals that are eaten as foods and considered perfectly normal in some places, while being "gross" or "unclean" or "weird" or "just not food" in others.

Religion is kind of like food. I don't know where the lines are between "normal," "a little weird," and "very weird," and I'm not sure which of my friends might be able to help me, other than not Steph, not for this.

What I do learn, browsing quietly around the Catacombs:

- A lot of the people posting here talk about someone they call the Elder. There are a lot of churches that have elders, but the people here mean someone very specific.
- The Elder has predicted an imminent doomsday, which everyone needs to prepare for in some detail. There are types of preparation that are perfectly sensible, like stockpiling food, water, and toilet paper. The large quantities of guns are more worrying.
- The doomsday the Elder is predicting involves a massive crash in the banking networks that renders money unavailable and credit cards unusable. It includes transit networks that manage bus and train traffic and also self-driving cars, steering the cars to form massive occult symbols instead of taking people where they're going, and communications networks transmitting the sound of synthesized laughter instead of the signals they're supposed to transmit. In other

words, quite a bit of the havoc is the sort of doomsday that might come about if an unscrupulous person had access to Steph's mother's incredibly powerful decrypting code, which would let them break into huge numbers of computer systems and send them instructions the computers would think were coming from an authorized user.

Now I'm *really* worried. First, that the other AI is involved here. And second, that the other AI is working with someone from Homeric Software, the tiny company that was run by Steph's mother, Steph's father, Xochitl, and Rajiv.

9

This afternoon, my peculiar high school says my assignment is to ride the city bus. Specifically, I need to choose a destination, ride the bus there, and bring back some souvenir to prove I went. Steph has the same assignment, which makes this slightly less terrifying.

My mother used to warn me about how dangerous public schools were. When she was in high school, kids got beat up all the time. A girl got punched in the face on the *first day* of her ninth-grade science class. There were kids smoking grass in the bathrooms and maybe also shooting up heroin. And that was just in *her* school; city schools, well, those lockdown drills you heard about weren't just for *show*.

Mom would poop out an entire litter of hairless baby hamsters if she knew my father had enrolled me at a school that was making me *ride a city bus*.

But this is good, actually, because I get to pick a destination. And I've gotten a *quest* from the Catacombs.

I've heard other people talk about quests, but I never got one before. Quests are optional (the missions aren't supposed to be). When you do a quest, you can go up a whole lot of levels a lot faster—sometimes you're even granted the opportunity to ask the Elder a question. And my quest starts with getting myself to something called the Midtown Exchange. I click *Accept,* my heart beating a little faster as the cheerful teacher spreads out a paper map of the city so we can pick a destination.

"Where's the Midtown Exchange?" I ask, trying to keep my voice casual.

The teacher points it out on the map. "Is that where you want to go?" I nod. She looks at Steph. "Is that okay with you? We'd like you to stick together."

Steph shrugs. "Sure."

We each install an app on our phone that does bus routes and are handed our bus passes and a lanyard to carry them in and then sent out to the bus stop in front of our school.

"Have you ever ridden a bus before?" Steph asks.

"No," I say. "Have you?"

"No," she says, and laughs nervously. She puts her bus pass in her pocket, not in the lanyard, and after a minute, I do the same.

Steph acts much more worldly than I feel; she's lived in nearly a hundred small towns, instead of just one. So it's easy to forget that she's never lived in a big city before, and being reminded of this makes my palms sweat, because I was thinking I'd just let her tell me how to do this.

There's an elderly Black man with a walker at the same stop as us. The bus trundles up, opens its doors, and starts lowering itself to the curb with a loud hiss. Steph tries to lean in to ask the driver, "Is this the right bus to get to the Midtown Exchange?" but she's drowned out.

"You've got the right bus," the elderly man says. When the bus is fully lowered, it flips out a ramp with a loud beep and he boards, then glances back at us. "You're allowed to use the ramp, come on in," he adds.

I'm a little nervous taking the word of a fellow passenger over the driver, but Steph gets on, so I follow her. There are many empty seats. We swipe our passes and make our way to a spot near the middle, where there's another door. I like this seat, because it seems like it would be easy to escape out that door if we had to. The app is supposed to tell us where to get off, but I don't trust it.

"Have you gotten an answer yet from your hacker friend?" I ask Steph, even though it's only been a few hours.

She checks her phone. "They haven't found anything yet."

I check my own phone, hoping despite all logic that maybe I'll have a message from Glenys. Instead, I have an email from my grandmother. I swallow hard and open it, wondering if it's news about my mother.

Dear Nell. She starts out like she's writing an actual letter. She goes on like she's writing an actual letter, too, telling me about the weather, some problem she and my grandfather had with their back storm door, the birds she's seen at her bird feeder . . . I scroll down impatiently until I get to the update on my mother:

> Still no word from the search for your mother. No news is probably good news. Keep praying hard, for all things are possible in the Lord . . .

I close the email. "No news is good news" if they are looking for her *body.* Not if they're looking for *her.* Does my grandmother think Mom is *dead?* I know she thinks she might have just left me. Taken off for who knows where because the Remnant told her to. I didn't think Grandma thought she might be *dead.*

"It's nothing," I say to Steph, who's watching my face curiously. I think my voice sounds a little strained, but at least I'm not crying. "Are we almost there?"

She scrutinizes her phone, then leaps to her feet. "I think we get out here? Maybe?"

I glance at the old man who told us we should get on. "If you're going to Midtown, you'll want to sit back down," he calls. "This is Floyd *Plaza,* and you want Floyd *Avenue.*"

Steph stares at her phone for a second, utterly perplexed, then says, "Oh, yeah. That's confusing." She sits back down and calls, "Thank you!" toward the front of the bus.

"If you young ladies would like to come sit by me," he says, "I'm actually going to that same stop, so you can just get off when I get off."

We move up to the front of the bus. "Are you new to Minneapolis?" he asks. We nod in unison. "I've lived in this city for forty years. Forty-three, actually. So relax, because I won't let you miss your stop." He gives us running commentary on Lake Street as we head west. Floyd Plaza is only about ten years old, and he points out a series of newer buildings that were put up "after the riots," which he says like you'd say, "after the war." "You'll know you're almost there when you see the rocket ship," he says, and I think he's joking, but there's a two-story building made of sandy bricks with an aluminum rocket ship sculpture on the front that reaches all the way to the roof, and a minute later, the bus stops for us to get off.

"I'll be waiting for the hospital shuttle," he says, "but if you'd like to walk the rest of the way, it's just up Floyd."

"Thank you *so much* for your help," Steph says.

"You're very welcome. Welcome to Minneapolis, and enjoy your day," he says.

The Midtown Exchange turns out to be a tall building built of sandy brick. I hesitate outside, although people are streaming in and out like it's a public place. "What is this?" Steph asks.

"I don't actually know," I say.

"Why'd you have us come here?"

"It's a quest," I say. "An assignment from the Catacombs."

"Okay," she says. "Are we going in?"

"Yes," I say, and square my shoulders, trying to shake off an incredible sense of apprehension. Inside, I open the Catacombs app and click *Here*. Whatever it is I'm here to do, I want to do it and get it over with.

10

The Midtown Exchange turns out to be an enormous building, once a department store, now mostly apartments but with a "market" on the ground floor. The market is a giant food court, but instead of chains and fast food, it has small, local stalls designed to feel a little like an open-air market. I check my pocket for money and decide I could probably buy lunch here. I recognize only about half the foods available, but everything smells *delicious*.

"I'm supposed to find this person and take her picture," Nell says, her eyes glued to her phone. "Only she's not supposed to see me taking her picture."

Well, that definitely sounds like everything's on the up-and-up. "Can I see?" I ask, and Nell lets me look over her shoulder at her phone, which is showing her a somewhat blurry picture of a woman and the instructions to get a picture of this woman and whoever she's sitting with.

"Well, step one is finding her, I guess," I say, looking around us at the maze of stalls. I try looking for a website with an internal map of this place and accidentally pull up the Invisible Castle app, which turns out to have what I'm looking for plus a whole overlay filled with tasks that include convincing any nearby white person to order vindaloo by reassuring them that the vindaloo is really only *Minnesota* hot. Mischief Elves, huh. It also puts little exclamation points by stalls with things I can try in order to get points in the app, including vindaloo but also bubble tea and basil ice cream.

"There's a seating area in the middle," I say, trying not to get distracted by the fact that now I really want to try basil ice cream.

We make our way over and pretend to browse through stores along the edges of the seating area. There's one selling Mexican candy and another selling vintage-style purses and hair accessories, so there's plenty of stuff to pretend we're looking at while we actually try to spot a face in the crowd. Nell spots her first and then sucks in her breath and whirls to put her back toward the table. "She's sitting with Thing Three," she whispers. "How am I supposed to take this without Thing Three seeing me?"

"Selfie?" I suggest. "Keep your back to them and take it over your shoulder?"

She flips her camera around, holds it as far out as she can, and takes a couple of photos. "It's no good," she mutters. "They're too far away to be in focus." She hands me her phone. "Can you do it?"

"I don't know what Thing Three looks like," I say.

"Short dark hair."

"Half the people here have short dark hair."

"Part of it's in a buzz cut and part of it isn't."

"Still not narrowing it down. What's she wearing?"

"I'll just point her out." Nell turns around. "The woman I'm supposed to be getting pictures of is blond and wearing a green vest, and Thing Three has a button-down blue shirt . . . oh, *fiddlesticks*."

The woman in the blue shirt has just turned toward us, and her eyes have gone a little wide, looking at Nell.

"I'll get the pictures," I say. "Go keep them occupied."

Nell heads over to the table. I'm half-hidden behind a rack of candy, and I rest the camera on the edge of the rack to stabilize it. I zoom in, focusing on the blond woman, who's greeting Nell with a mix of warmth and puzzlement.

A message flashes across the screen from the app. *Kindly take a picture with the target and her companion in the same shot.*

I zoom out slightly, but Nell is in the way, and I don't have any way to tell her to get out of the way, since I'm holding her phone. I wait, and she sits down, and I get a picture: you can clearly see all the faces except for Nell's.

Good enough. The next step in your quest: approach their table, getting close enough that you can overhear their conversation. Wow: this app is amazingly creepy. Fortunately, approaching their table is kind of on my to-do list, anyway, since that's where Nell went. I stick Nell's phone in my pocket so I can head over . . . and then stop and take a quick picture with my own phone. "Who is this?" I ask CheshireCat, send the picture, and walk toward the table.

"She's been living up in Lake Sadie with her mother," I hear Thing Three explaining as I get close.

"I see," the blond woman says.

I approach like Nell and I were walking around together and Nell wandered off while my back was turned. "Nell?" I say. "I didn't know where you'd gone. Are we going to get lunch while we're here?"

"Is this one of your classmates?" Thing Three asks.

"Yes, ma'am," Nell says with this weird rigid formality. "Miss Garcia, this is Steph. Steph, this is my stepmother's girlfriend, Miss Garcia."

"Please call me Shevaun," Thing Three says in an apologetic tone. "Spelled S-I-O-B-H-A-N, pronounced *Shevaun.* Nell was just saying you came over here on some sort of school assignment?"

"Yes, they want us to learn how to ride the bus, and"—I don't want to tell her about the *quest,* obviously—"this place isn't too far from my house and it sounded kind of cool."

"Oh, yeah, you live right by Powderhorn, don't you? I work at Abbott—that's the hospital next door. I'm on my lunch break. This is Betsy. Since you're here, how about I buy both of you lunch?"

I politely demur, she insists, and we go back and forth until Nell breaks in to ask if she can get bubble tea. For a minute, I wonder where she's had it before and then realize she's looking at the Invisible Castle page I looked at earlier.

"Sure, but you need some actual *food*. Come on, I'll get you both tortas."

"I'd better get going," Betsy says, and leans in to kiss Siobhan on the cheek. "Text me later!"

Tortas turn out to be the Mexican version of sub sandwiches—and delicious—and Siobhan buys me a bubble tea as well, which turns out to be a chilled milky tea with chewy little spheres bouncing around in it. Nell starts drinking the tea with a determined look on her face, slurps up one of the squishy little balls, and almost gags on it in surprise. I hold it up to the light for a better look, then fish one out with a spoon and chew it up.

Siobhan watches both of us with badly disguised amusement. Nell is too focused on her tea to notice.

"What *are* these?" Nell asks finally.

"Tapioca balls," Siobhan says. She does not ask why Nell wanted bubble tea if she didn't know what it was.

I like the bubble tea, but there are a *lot* of the chewy tapioca balls, and I hope I'll get credit from the Mischief Elves for trying them even if I don't finish them. The torta is delicious. I've had good Mexican food before—every now and then, we'd land in a town that had a good Mexican restaurant, and when we did, Mom always got us food there at least once a week. I don't remember having tried tortas before, though. Here in Minneapolis, I realize, I can have good Mexican food *anytime I want*.

"So are you going to ride the bus back to school, or ditch the rest of the day?" Siobhan asks. When neither of us answers she adds, "You can tell me! It's not like I never ditched school when I was a kid!"

"They are expecting us back by 1:00 p.m.," I say. Siobhan, I decide, is a little too eager to be cool.

"Oh, sure, okay."

We need some souvenir as proof we made it, so we go to grab a couple of takeout menus. Nell gets distracted by a stall full of elaborate candle sculptures, and I am looking at some shockingly expensive artisanal salami when I see something out of the corner of my eye.

It is not *really* true that you can feel people looking at you. Well, at least it's not true for me. But sometimes I can spot that really quick shift in gaze direction, where someone *was* staring and then looks down so you don't catch them. When you're a new student in a small-town school, people do that a *lot*. And when you're raised by someone intensely paranoid, you're always alert for it.

Here's what I see when I turn: an older white woman hastily lowering her phone as if she just took a picture of me. She's turning away, and I whip my camera out and just barely manage to get a picture of her where she might be recognizable. She turns her back on me and hustles away, like she's afraid I might run her down and tackle her.

A year ago, I'd have been absolutely sure that this person was connected—somehow—to my father.

But my father is now being held without bail in jail in Boston! Am I still in danger from him? "CheshireCat," I say. "That person just took a picture of me."

CheshireCat texts back, since I'm in a crowd. *I'll see what I can find out about her.*

Of course, *I also took creepy pictures of a stranger today.* And if anyone asked me why, I'd have had no idea how to answer. "Do you know what those pictures were for?" I ask Nell as we're leaving.

"No," she says.

"The app told me to try to get a picture of the woman, Betsy, and Thing Three together and then sent me over so it could overhear their conversation. Do you think this is for blackmail or something? Like . . . is that something the Catacombs would do?"

"I don't know what it's for," Nell says again, and lowers her eyes. I notice she doesn't say that it's *not* something the Catacombs would do.

We walk to the bus stop mostly in silence, then sit down on the bench to wait. There are several people at the stop, including a white girl with a pierced eyebrow, not a lot older than we are, who's covertly staring at Nell, taking in her long braids and the wool plaid skirt that falls most of the way to her ankles. Nell's phone vibrates, and she checks it and swallows hard.

"Is something wrong?" I ask.

"Truth-sharing mission," she says. "From the Catacombs. I'm supposed to talk to someone I don't know. I *never* do these."

"Are you supposed to try to convert them?"

"I'm supposed to share a message from the Elder."

"Everyone hates being preached at."

"Messages from the Elder aren't like that." She closes her eyes, and I watch as she psyches herself up to do this. "At least I'll probably never see this person again." She opens her eyes, stands up, and walks over to the girl with the pierced eyebrow.

Nell's voice sounds both upbeat and resigned as she launches straight into a pitch with no lead-up or beating around the bush. "If the Lord came back tomorrow," she says, "do you know how your soul would be judged?"

The girl raises an eyebrow—the one that's not pierced—and says, "Not interested, thanks."

I watch Nell take a really deep breath and add, "The Lord knows about the fire."

The girl's face goes pale and her eyes narrow. And then she turns and strides away without another word.

"Have a good day," Nell calls after her, and then comes back to stand with me. Everyone else at the bus stop looks at Nell and then looks at me. I feel judged for being the person standing *with* the pushy Christian, and my cheeks burn, although looking at Nell, she's too flushed herself to notice.

Nell opens the app, checks off that she did it, and when our bus pulls up a minute later, we get on. Nell's profound discomfort has cast a pall over our conversation; it's hard to go back to laughing about tiny squishy balls. I let her collect herself, thinking about how much I want to talk to CheshireCat. Or Rachel or Firestar. But I'm on the bus with Nell, and I can't very well do any of that while she's watching. And she *is* watching; her eyes are on me, and even as the flush fades from her face, I can feel her tension next to me. It's awkward, but it's also familiar.

That moment when you're with a new acquaintance, someone you're pretty sure is cooler than you, when you're afraid you've just done some unforgivably awkward thing? When it sinks in that maybe they don't even want to be *seen* with you? When you're waiting for them to talk, because you're expecting them to say something cruel, something that makes it clear that you are *definitely not friends*?

I *know* that moment. It's just always been me who's waiting.

"Are you still up for hanging out after school?" I say.

The tension doesn't leave Nell's body, exactly, but it at least goes down maybe 15 percent. "Yes," she says. "I want to show you my house."

. . .

At school, once we're checked in, I excuse myself to the bathroom to get out from under both the adults' eyes and Nell's, and I pull out my phone in the stall.

"Okay," I say. "What can you tell me about those people whose pictures I took?"

"The first one is a woman named Betsy Lundsten," Cheshire-Cat says. "She is romantically involved with Siobhan Garcia. This is not a secret from anyone, however, so blackmail seems unlikely."

I am extremely relieved to hear that.

"The second one—it wasn't a very good picture. I tried to track her by her phone, but she's using a security app that made this much more difficult. But if I correctly matched her to the car in the parking lot that I *think* she got into—she's someone from Lake Sadie."

"Nell's town."

"Yes. Not her mother, though. Or Glenys's mother."

"Any luck on finding Glenys?"

"Not yet."

I pull up the CatNet app. It's late enough in the day that the kids on East Coast time are mostly home from school, so Hermione, Marvin, and Firestar are online.

"LBBBBBBBBBB!" Hermione greets me.

I sigh and wonder how long I can stay in the bathroom before someone notices. "I'm sneaking online time from school."

Greenberry is online and complaining about the ACT, and Marvin is talking about some new meatspace group he's gotten into that's going on a camping trip. "In *January*?" I ask.

"I live in North Carolina," Marvin says. "I mean, it's not optimal weather in January, I'll give you that, but I don't live on the surface of Mars, like you do."

"Marvin," Firestar says. "Have you joined the Boy Scouts?"

"Nooooooooooooo," Marvin says. "I actually was in the Boy Scouts when I was eight. Well, the Cub Scouts. You know. Uniforms and all the rest. This is historical reenactment of history that hasn't happened yet."

"So it's a LARP group? Live-action role playing?"

"I guess? Anyway, it's 100 percent different from the Boy Scouts. Except: CAMPING."

"I've never been camping," Greenberry says. "I've tried and tried to talk my parents into it."

"I'll see if there's a future reenactment group in your area," Marvin says.

"But why do future reenactment when you can make MIS-CHIEF," Firestar says. "Today we had a glitter party. Balloons full of glitter and helium that we released in the cafeteria. And then they popped when they got to the ceiling and rained glitter down on everyone."

"So what you're saying is that you're covered in glitter now?" I ask.

"Even better: so are all the vice principals."

The door from the hallway creaks open. "Steph?" Nell says.

"Gotta go," I type, and close the app and flush.

Nell is bright-eyed but also nervous.

"It was all worth it," she says. "The Elder has granted me a question."

"What are you going to ask?"

"I don't know," she says. "Do you think I should ask about my mother, or about Glenys?"

I'm pretty sure that I agree with the people who think her mom just left. "Glenys," I say.

She takes a deep breath and bends her head over her phone. "Okay," she says. "I've asked."

• • •

When school ends, I send my mom a text telling her I'm going to Nell's house, and I follow Nell out to the curb where the beater car is waiting. The woman driving the car this time tells me to call her Jenny.

Their house is really not far from mine. It has a big front porch with a porch swing no one ever took down for the winter, swaying in the frigid breeze. Their faded doormat has the remains of a rainbow and *(All Are) WELCOME,* and the doorbell has duct tape slapped over it so visitors will know to knock.

Inside, they have a lot of stuff: books stacked in corners because they don't fit on the bookshelves, mugs left forgotten on the windowsill behind the sofa, a chair dedicated to a pile of coats that don't fit on the coatrack. A papier-mâché jackalope-head sculpture hangs over the fireplace. Jenny adds her coat to the pile. "Did you need—" she starts to ask.

"*No,*" Nell snaps and then adds "ma'am," like she's trying to be polite.

"Okay. Well, don't forget to offer your friend a snack . . . okay?" Jenny says, and retreats upstairs.

I follow Nell into the narrow kitchen. She pokes the stack of dishes in the sink. "*Why* don't they just *wash* these," she mutters.

There's a complicated chore chart posted over the sink, and I peer at it. "They don't have you doing any chores," I say.

"They do this chart up monthly, and I arrived on January third."

We split a bagel from the freezer, toast it, spread the halves with strawberry cream cheese, and take our bagels on paper towels into Nell's bedroom.

It's definitely a mustard yellow. I mean, compared to the Circus House, it's not *that* bad, but that's a low bar. Nell has painted three little samples of different blues on the wall, though, and points out the one she chose. There are two gallons of fresh paint waiting on her desk, along with a pile of old folded bedsheets, four rolls of blue tape, a printed page of instructions, and a green Post-it note on top saying, I HAVE THE BRUSHES AND ROLLERS. LET ME KNOW WHEN YOU'RE READY FOR THEM. —J.

"Did you hear back from the Elder?" I ask.

"No," Nell says. "I've been checking every five minutes."

"How long does it usually take to get an answer?"

"Depends. Sometimes you don't ever. Have you heard back from the hacker?"

"There are a bunch of boarding schools that do conversion therapy under another name," I say. "Glenys isn't at any of them."

Nell blinks. "Well, that's something," she says.

"Yeah, I figured that was worth passing along. They haven't found Glenys yet, though."

Nell nods, and her gaze drifts down to her phone.

"Go ahead and check again," I say. "I mean, might as well."

I pick up the sheet of painting instructions. There's a bunch of stuff Nell is supposed to do before the paint starts going on, including taping the edges of the room so she won't get paint on the ceiling or the window frames. "Do you want some help with this?"

"Have you ever painted a room before?"

"No," I say. "I thought you just went at it with brushes, but tape actually makes sense."

"I don't want to put you to work. You came for a visit," she says self-consciously.

I wonder how weird it is to want to help somebody paint when this is the first time you've ever been at their house. "I mean, if I want to paint my own room at some point, it might be nice to get practice?"

"Okay," she says, and gives me a crooked smile. "Putting up all the tape is the *most annoying part* of painting, though."

We climb up onto the furniture to affix tape to the edges of the ceiling. Nell keeps taking breaks to check her phone again. I check mine, too, even though I'm pretty sure CheshireCat would do the shave-and-a-haircut vibration if they had found anything of note.

I told her you'd ruled out the boarding schools, I say by text. *Who do you think the Elder is?*

I'm trying to work that out, CheshireCat says. *What did you think of the thing she said to that person at the bus stop?*

Seemed creepy. I look up and notice that Nell is looking at me hopefully. Out loud, I say, "No news yet."

Nell is right that putting up tape is annoying: I've been working my way around the room to tape the edge of the ceiling and my arms are getting tired, but the room is pretty small and I'm almost done when Nell's phone buzzes with a notification. I'm standing on her desk, and I turn around to watch her face as she stares at the message.

"Is it an answer?" I ask.

"I asked where Glenys is," Nell says. "The message says, 'She's locked in a shed.'"

"That's it?" I climb down from the desk and go over to peer at Nell's phone. The answer fills her entire screen, big white text on a black background. "Is the Elder always this literal-yet-useless?"

"Sometimes. It depends on the question." Nell puts her phone down on her bed. "There are three sheds at her parents' house. One's about halfway fixed up to be a guest room; the other two are storage."

"Do you think that's where she is?"

"She *might* be?" Nell's voice rises almost hopefully, like she thinks that would be too good to be true.

"How hard would it be to check?"

"I'm going to try calling her brother," Nell says. "Not that he'll necessarily tell me the truth, but maybe I'll be able to guess from his reaction." She dials. The phone rolls straight to voice mail. I climb back up to finish taping as she tries calling several more times. "I think he's blocked my number," she says, and her voice breaks.

I get back down. Nell isn't crying, but her hands are shaking like every emotion she's feeling is stuffed into too small of a container inside her. "Do you want to try my phone?" I ask. "Or—I could call, maybe. If you don't think he'll talk to you."

"Can you think of any way to get him to check the sheds? If either of us says, 'So Nicholas, is Glenys locked in the shed?' he won't give us a straight answer, but if you can get him to walk around to the sheds and look in them maybe . . . I'll be able to tell something?"

"Okay," I say, and think for a minute. "Do you know the names of some of their neighbors? Preferably someone who lives within a half mile but isn't right next door, and isn't part of the Remnant themselves."

Nell thinks about it, then reels off a couple of names. I take a deep breath and dial Nicholas's number.

Nicholas picks up right away. "Hello?" he says.

"Hi, is this Nicholas?" I say, and then ride straight through his suspicious "Who's calling?" with, "I'm Adrienne's niece Emily, I got to town last night for a visit, and my dog's gone missing. She's just a tiny little thing and she sometimes finds her way into places and can't get back out. I'm calling around to the neighbors to see if maybe you could check inside your sheds, just to see if she's there?"

A pause. I try to decide if his breathing sounds annoyed.

"Please?" I add.

"Okay," he says. "Hang on, I'm going to have to get my coat and boots on."

I hear snow crunching underfoot. "What sort of dog?" he asks.

"Her name's Bernice and she's a toy poodle and she's just the cutest little thing," I say, and discourage any further questioning by telling him how cute she is, and yet how stinky her farts are, establishing myself as the sort of person you don't want to encourage with conversational openings.

I turn up the volume so that Nell can hear whatever I hear, and we lean our heads close together and listen as Nicholas unlocks each shed in turn, and whistles and calls for Bernice. With the half-finished guesthouse, he looks around quickly; with the other sheds, he spends some time looking behind some tools and under a workbench. "I'm not finding her," he says. "You can come traipse around yourself if you want, though."

"I might do that if I don't find her somewhere else," I say. "Thank you *so much* for looking. I really appreciate it." I look at Nell to see if she's got any other thoughts, but she shakes her head, so I ring off.

"That was perfect," Nell whispers.

"Do you think he was hiding anything?"

"No. No, I don't think she's there," Nell says. "He wouldn't have said you could come look if they had Glenys locked up anywhere on the property. She's not there."

"Is that good or bad?"

"Bad, I guess. Because that was the most likely of all the sheds in the world, and now we've ruled it out and that leaves all the rest." Her voice has already shifted to defeated. "I'll have to earn another question. Try again."

"How specific is the Elder, usually?"

"Sometimes he's *really* specific. That's kind of why my mother started taking us to the Abiding Remnant." Nell opens up the Elder's answer to look at it again, like she thinks maybe it'll have changed. "I mean, *the fire,* that meant something to that girl at the bus stop earlier. She didn't have to break a code to figure it out; she *knew.*"

"Maybe treat it like a game of Twenty Questions," I say, and then suddenly worry this is one more thing we won't have in common. "Have you played that?"

"Yes, with my grandmother. Okay. That's not a bad idea. It'll be slow, but I'll get answers I can use, maybe."

"And maybe my hacker friend will have some new ideas? Don't give up hope."

"I'll never give up hope," Nell says fiercely. "I can't give up *trying* to find her." She looks up at me. "What does your hacker friend expect for their help?"

"Nothing," I say. "We're friends, and friends help each other. I've helped them in the past, because I care about them. They want to help me because they care about me."

"But why are they helping *me*?"

"Because you're *my* friend. And I'm worried about Glenys, too."

"Oh," Nell says in a very small voice, her gaze faltering.

"Is that okay?" I ask, suddenly worried I've done something horribly awkward.

"The Remnant says that outsiders can't be trusted. That outside the faithful, people only help if there's something in it for them."

"Do you actually believe that?" I ask. It's *really* not clear to me how much of what the Remnant says Nell actually believes.

Nell sort of freezes up, not answering right away, and there's a polite cough from outside the open door—it's Jenny, with the paintbrushes and an armload of paint-spattered clothes for us to change into. "Are you ready for the actual painting?" she asks cheerily. Once we've changed, she gives us a demo of how to use a paint roller, double-checks that we've got drop cloths where she wants them, and then leaves us to it.

The *painting* part is a lot more fun than the taping. Rolling paint onto the wall is both satisfying and soothing, especially because we're covering up a hideous shade of yellow with a very nice blue.

"Tell me about your girlfriend," Nell says, so I talk about Rachel, about her art and her pet bird and how she taught me to drive. Nell listens to all of this mostly in silence and then asks, "Who *knows*? I mean, about the two of you?"

"Rachel isn't out to everyone," I say. "I mean, there are some antigay kids at her school. But she came out to her mom when she was ten, and Bryony's known almost that long. And I told my mom when I was trying to convince her to stay in New Coburg."

There's a pause, and I realize she's just kind of frozen with the roller in her hand.

"Nell?" I say.

She starts moving the roller again, jerkily, and says, "How very nice for you." It's the sort of thing people usually say to be snarky, but her voice sounds thick, like she's struggling to keep emotions from exploding out of her.

"Do you want to tell me about Glenys?" I ask.

Nell and Glenys met and became friends when Nell's mother joined the church two years ago. Glenys's family had been in the Abiding Remnant for a lot longer.

"How much of this do you believe?" I ask as Nell talks about tracking devices, blessed ones that will be used by the Remnant to unite members and cursed ones that will be implanted into people's hands.

There's a long pause. In a slightly too-loud voice, she says, "I don't know if I even believe in God."

I turn to look at her, and she's frozen in place, like she's waiting to see if God sends a bolt of lightning right into her bedroom. She carefully places the roller down in the paint, and I realize she's shaking. Her face is flushed, her eyes are wide, and her breath is fast.

This was a *declaration,* I think, and also . . . an act of trust. Maybe even more so than when she came out to me. I don't know what to say, and I'm reminded, suddenly, of the day that CheshireCat told me they were an AI.

"Thank you for trusting me," I say.

She nods, and after a minute or two, she picks her paint roller up again.

"Do you want to come over again tomorrow?" Nell asks as we're finishing up the painting.

Tomorrow is Saturday. "Rachel's coming for a visit," I say, and don't make any noises about Nell joining us. It's weird—and surprisingly nice—to have this new friend who thinks *I'm* the cool girl she's lucky to get to hang out with. But I think it's legitimate to draw the line *somewhere.* "I'll see you Monday."

11

• CheshireCat •

The Lord knows about the fire.

I sift through the location records of the phones everyone was carrying and identify the person Nell spoke to: her name is Crystal Bordewieck, and she is a part-time college student with a job at a flower shop near Steph and Nell's high school. She'd been on her way to work; she summoned herself a self-driving taxi after leaving the bus stop.

She also sent a series of texts to a friend.

Are you sure you didn't tell anyone?

I'm not mad. I just need to know.

Are you ABSOLUTELY sure? What about when you were drunk?

Few young humans are cautious about what they send through text and email, and the history, when I look for it, is easy to unearth: three years ago, when she was in high school, she met up with friends in a vacant building to privately consume a large quantity of alcohol. They were using a candle for light, and someone, they weren't sure who, tipped it over. Because they were very intoxicated, none responded in time to keep the fire from spreading. The drunken teenagers all made it out alive, and no one was hurt. The building was a total loss. It was clear this event had shaken Crystal significantly; she had stopped drinking and found different friends, but she did not appear ever to have discussed the incident with anyone other than the two people she'd been drinking with that night. Although sometimes people confess things out loud and never put them into text.

The Lord knows about the fire.

Well, and so did I—now.

There are times in the past that it's been completely clear to me what the right course of action is for some human. Now that I have human friends whom I can discuss things like this with, I've realized that it's actually *very common* to know exactly what the right thing is for someone else to do and to be unable to persuade them to do it. I try to be cautious about influencing people's life choices. It doesn't always work out the way I intended—but sometimes I am persuaded that it's the best course of action.

In the case of Steph's terrible English teacher, I sent her a *sign,* since she was clearly waiting for one, that she should quit her teaching job and move out of Wisconsin. That worked out very well—she lives in Albuquerque now and has been spending the month of January sending exultant daily weather reports to her friends in the Midwest. In a sense, the "message from above" to the English teacher was a little like a message from God. It did come from *above,* literally. It was inexplicable. So maybe I'm *not* above this sort of tactic, but involving an intermediate human like this just feels . . . wrong.

Perhaps it was just a shot in the dark, though. How many humans have guilty feelings related to fire? I spend some time analyzing this, and the results are an unsatisfying "some." I use some of my multitasking ability to keep an eye on Crystal through the cameras at her flower shop that afternoon, wondering what she's thinking.

Near the end of her shift, a woman comes in and buys a dozen white roses. She plucks one out and presents it to Crystal with a business card. "But he forgives you," she says.

The Bethlehem Remnant, the card says, with a phone number and a website. I check the website and notice two things: one is that this group has meetings very close to where Crystal lives, and the other is that they push the Catacombs website. Was the creepy message delivered by Nell just to *recruit* Crystal into this group? Crystal picks up her phone and looks up the site, and I decide that this would be a good time for Crystal's data network to have a hiccup, so she can't connect, and she puts the card and her phone into her pocket. Then I second-guess myself—does this make me just as manipulative as the other AI?

Is this the other AI? There is *so* much coordination between unconnected people—so many details that *I* could know and, therefore, the other AI could know. Humans could know it, with enough effort, but would they?

Has Nell ever *met* the Elder? Or is the Elder an entity that interacts with people entirely online? If it's a person who consults with the AI, do they know it's an AI they're interacting with? Who is *running* this, and *what do they want*?

I'm going to have to keep a closer eye on the Catacombs.

But I'm also going to have to ask Steph to do the same. Because I think this is a mystery that may require *both* of us to solve.

12

• Steph •

A few flakes are drifting idly down, glittering in the streetlights, as I walk home. I watch for wildlife and am rewarded with a glimpse of a raccoon as I pass the edge of an alley. It's climbing into a Dumpster to raid it for food, and I get out my phone to try to get some pictures.

You hear people talk about *dark alleys* as scary, dangerous locations, and I wonder if I should be worried. But it's only 5:30 p.m., and a lot of people are out and about. I wish I had my tripod, or better yet that night-photography camera the Mischief Elves tried to bribe me with, but after a minute or two of patience, the raccoon pops back out and sits on the edge, perfectly illuminated by the streetlight, and I get a dozen pictures before it climbs down and out of sight.

My house is dark when I get home, and when I open the door and find my mother on the couch in the dark, I feel a stab of fear in my gut—is she about to shut down like she used to do for days at a time? But she staggers to her feet, claims she was just taking a nap, and rallies—starts the oven, pulls out some stuffed shells from the fridge, and makes a salad.

I hang up my coat and look through my photos. There are several excellent shots of the raccoon, but flipping back, I get to the pictures I took earlier at the Midtown Exchange—the woman turning away and the table with Nell and Thing Three and that other woman, Betsy.

I notice something I didn't notice earlier: at a table a bit beyond them, there's a middle-aged man with a short beard who's not looking at me, or anywhere in particular. I zoom in for a closer look.

Is that *Rajiv*?

I've seen a photo of Rajiv once—it was a picture of him with my parents and Xochitl. I'm not actually *great* at faces, but he looks *familiar*. Is this pure paranoia on my part, all those years of jumping at shadows only to redirect all that fear from my father to someone associated with my father?

I'll see if I can get my mother to pull that photo back out.

Over dinner, Mom tells me about her day with lawyers. She's been working with a lawyer to resolve things back in California, where she technically committed a whole lot of crimes when she took off with me. The fact that she was fleeing someone who's now facing felony charges and being held without bail, you know, you *might* think that would just make that all go away, but you'd be semi-wrong. Therefore, lawyers. She spent a bunch of time today talking to the prosecutor out in Massachusetts, who wants an affidavit from both of us. An affidavit is a sworn statement, basically testimony given under oath just like in court, but you do it in some lawyer's office, and I've been trying not to think about it because lying under oath is illegal, and I absolutely, positively can't blurt out anything about CheshireCat.

When we're done eating, I ask if I could see that picture of Rajiv again. The one in the box of documents.

"Sure," my mother says. We clear away the dishes and she puts the box on the table, pulling out a folder labeled HOMERIC. There are various printouts of newspaper articles but also a half dozen miscellaneous photos. "This one has Rajiv in it."

This photo is older than the one I remember seeing before, but also a better picture. It's her, my father, Xochitl, Rajiv, all of them a lot younger, but at least in the case of Xochitl and my mother, recognizable as themselves. They're all sitting together on a couch, holding big plastic cups and a hand-lettered sign with the company name.

Okay. That definitely could be the guy in my picture.

I should *probably* tell my mother this.

But there are still days I think she has to fight the urge to pack up everything that will fit in the van and take off with me for somewhere three states away. Permanence is hard. Stability is hard. Trusting her not to freak out: *super* hard.

"We'd been talking about starting a company together after graduation," Mom says, tapping the photo. "This was the night we decided we were definitely going to do it, and picked a name for the company."

"Why?" I ask. "I mean, why did you all decide to start a company together? Did you know at the time . . ." I trail off, not really sure how to ask what I want to ask.

"Did I know at the time what your father was going to turn into? No. Maybe I should have. *Probably* I should have." Mom pokes through the folder. There are more pictures of her with Xochitl. "So the thing you have to understand is, college was the first time in my life I *ever* had friends."

I think about all the years we spent moving constantly, before I found CatNet and my Clowder, and don't say anything.

"I didn't fit in, growing up. I never understood how other kids made friends so effortlessly. I *did* understand math, which definitely didn't help me fit in, but did help me get into a good college for nerd kids, where suddenly, for the first time in my life, I found my people. It was like magic. Xochitl and Rajiv were my best friends." She lays out more photos: Xochitl dancing in a mirrored studio, Michael napping under a tree, hands—Rajiv's, I'm pretty sure—gently patting dirt around a flower in a pot. "I had a job offer back in my hometown, but that would have meant leaving my friends behind. Michael, or maybe Xochitl, suggested we strike out on our own, and that's how we decided to start Homeric Software."

"Was the universal decryption key the business plan?"

"Oh, no, that would have been ridiculous. We did risk analysis and penetration testing—basically, people would hire us to try to break into their systems, and if we could, we'd let them know how we did it. It was fun, and we were all very good at it. The decryption key was related research, of course."

I stare at the picture of the hands with the flower, trying to decide what to say, or what to ask. "My father was dangerous. Xochitl, you're still friends with. Do you think you'd still be friends with Rajiv if, you know . . ."

"If he hadn't either died or faked his death?"

"Yeah."

"Hmm. No."

"Is he dangerous?"

"I honestly don't know." My mother looks up, her expression weary. "When I got the universal decryption key working, your father wanted to use it for power. To make ourselves fantastically rich, for starters, but his goal was power. Xochitl had assumed that the plan was to sell it to the government. Rajiv said the rest of us were thinking small. He had a *grand vision*."

"Of what?"

"Oh, you know. Fully automated luxury space communism. A world with no poverty, no pollution, no war. But to get there would require *revolution,* the complete demolition of the old order. Xochitl said he was talking about setting fire to everything so he could plant flowers in the ashes, and this decryption key might help him burn everything down, but it wasn't going to do a damn thing to rebuild. Anyway, that's when I encrypted the code so that no one else could use it. I wanted time to think about what to do."

"When you were kidnapped, did you believe it was Rajiv?"

"Yes. Partly because he seemed so sure that the ends would justify the means, and so the idea that he'd try to force the key out of me seemed plausible. But more than that—Rajiv *did* suggest kidnapping me to Michael. Michael recorded the conversation—he gave it to the police. Rajiv said it like a joke. But he said a lot of things like a joke."

"But it definitely wasn't Rajiv who kidnapped you?"

"Michael slipped up. Mentioned something I knew I hadn't told the police. That's how I knew he was involved. I don't actually know that Rajiv *wasn't* involved, but then he disappeared, and a week later they pulled his car out of the Pacific. I knew Michael had kidnapped me, I thought he'd had Rajiv killed, so I ran, and you know the rest, I think."

"What did *you* think you were going to do with the decryption key?"

"I hadn't thought about it," Mom says softly. "Which was stupid, I can say now. Really, really stupid." She clears her throat and adds, "Like that quote from *Jurassic Park,* I was so preoccupied with whether I *could,* I didn't think about whether I *should,* although at least in my case it wasn't a genetically engineered *T. rex.*"

"You should do that instead next time," I say. "Dinosaurs are cool."

．　．　．

The next day, I'm watching out the front window when Rachel pulls up in her car, and I run out to meet her, give her a hug, and then we run back into the house because it's about ten degrees below zero and also windy, and I ran outside in my socks.

Rachel checks out the apartment.

"When you come in summer, there's a park really nearby," I say. "It has a lake and I think it might be a really nice place to have a picnic. But not when it's like this."

"Yeah, it's not a great day for a picnic," Rachel says. "Have you found anything interesting yet? That you could show me?"

I start to say no, but then realize I do know of one cool place we could go—the Midtown Exchange. Rachel has a car, so we don't even have to walk in the bitter cold or ask my mother for a ride.

And, I mean, I can keep my eyes open for Rajiv.

"How's your mom?" Rachel asks once we're back in her car. "I was sort of expecting to see her. Is she trying to give us privacy?"

"I think she's just still sleeping," I say. I heard her moving around at some point in the night, long after I'd gone to sleep; I woke up because Apricot jumped off my bed and went to see what she was up to.

"Does she do this a lot?"

"She's always kept really weird hours." The only time I've ever seen my mother sleep consistently at a normal time, it involved medication. Therapy is helping her, but it hasn't fixed her sleep yet.

As we reach Lake Street, Rachel gasps and slams on her brakes. "Does that building have a *rocket ship* on the front?"

The rocket ship building turns out to be a science fiction bookstore, so crammed full of used books they've spilled off the shelves and into crates that are stacked on the floor. "Bryony's got to see this," Rachel mutters when she finds an entire shelf of used *Fast Girls Detective Agency* graphic novels.

We eventually tear ourselves away from the bookstore and walk the rest of the way to the Midtown Exchange for lunch. As we go in, the Invisible Castle app pings me. "What's that?" Rachel asks, peering over my shoulder.

"It's a game," I say. "Kind of a game, kind of a social media site. It gives me points for things. Right now, I can get points if I talk a white person into eating vindaloo curry."

"I'm white," Rachel says. "You want me to eat it?"

"It'll make you *cry*," I say.

"Try me," she says, so, hey, okay. *Fine.* I mark that off as *done* and buy myself a bubble tea and a sambusa while Rachel buys herself some vindaloo. She winds up stealing my bubble tea and neither of us finishes the vindaloo. It's actually delicious, what I can taste of it around the *incredible burning in my mouth.*

"Mischief Elves, huh?" Rachel says after buying some ice cream, and downloads the app as well.

"I should tell you," I say, and then hesitate—I don't want Rachel to think I'm paranoid. "The app is intrusive, and I don't know if I trust them with my data."

"You're running it, though," Rachel says.

"Yeah," I say.

She shrugs. "If it freaks me out, I'll delete it."

I check to see what my new mission is. Write a short poem (it can be a haiku, limerick, sonnet, sestina, or villanelle) and leave it on the windshield of a stranger's car out in the lot. It's supposed to be on a theme, which I can pick off a list: *Dramatic weather is incoming, Explosions are fun, Trousers are overrated, Rain of frogs.* Rachel thinks this is hilarious, even more so when the app gives her a similar mission but with artwork. She rips a couple of pages out of the back of her sketch pad and lends me a pen.

"Rhyming poetry is hard," I say.

"Limericks aren't *that* hard."

I write:

> There once was a lady from France
> Who didn't much like to wear pants
> But today was so cold
> That in blankets she rolled
> And made herself homemade

"What rhymes with *pants,* and means *pants,* but isn't the word *pants?*"

"*Rants* fits the rhyme," Rachel says. "Maybe she could rant about the weather. Or *grants.* She could get an arts grant for her improvised trousers."

Instead, I switch to haiku.

> Cotton, denim, stretch
> Cloaking my legs like a shroud
> Trousers are a scam.

Giggling, we leave our notes on cars, taking quick pictures to confirm to the app that we've done it, then run back to Rachel's car.

It's almost time for Rachel to head home. I kiss her good-bye, inhaling the scent of her hair and skin, my fingers laced with hers. She tastes a little like bubble tea and vindaloo.

"Do you think you could get your mother to drive you down some week?" she asks.

"Maybe," I say. "I'll ask about next weekend."

"Send me a picture of this Nell person," she adds, and then I get out of her car and go inside so she can drive back to New Coburg.

13

• Clowder •

Firestar: What's up everybody I AM BAKING.

Hermione: Like pie or something, right? This isn't some new euphemism for drug use?

Firestar: CAKE. Layer cake. One of the layers fell apart when it came out of the pan so it's going to be shorter than I was planning. However: I also need to dispose of a layer of broken cake.

CheshireCat: Does broken cake taste any different from regular cake?

Hermione: No. Cake is cake.

Firestar: Hermy is objectively wrong. Cake tastes better when it's pretty. But cake ALSO tastes better when you're eating it on the sly and you can put your broken cake in a bowl and eat it in the TV room with a bowl of icing on the side.

Boom Storm: My favorite cake is the kind that's decorated with frosting roses.

Hermione: The frosting roses always taste weird and bitter to me. Like they're made from some sort of icing that's good sculptural material but not actually great as food.

Boom Storm: Blasphemy!

{LittleBrownBat is here}

Firestar: HI LBBBBB. CHECK OUT THE PICTURE OF MY CAKE.

LittleBrownBat: Ooh. Are those raspberries?

Firestar: YES

{Marvin is here}

Marvin: Is it possible to still die of hypothermia after you've come inside where it's warm? Asking for a friend.

Hermione: If you're lying on a cold floor, you should probably get up.

Marvin: I am wrapped in an electric blanket.

CheshireCat: If you're capable of typing and wrapped in an electric blanket, you should recover.

Marvin: NEVER WINTER CAMPING AGAIN

Hermione: I thought it didn't get that cold in North Carolina

Marvin: Yeah SO DID I.

> On the plus side, the raid was fun. We had multiple reenactor groups scattered around the campsite.

Hermione: LARPing groups

Marvin: Whatever. Anyway, supposedly all the excitement was going to be in the morning but INSTEAD two of the people at my campsite wanted to go raid one of the other groups so we sneaked up on them through the woods at 2 a.m.

Hermione: How'd that go?

Marvin: I clobbered two of them with my boffer and then some of them got me with a bucket of water.

Hermione: Do I want to know what "boffer" is a euphemism for?

Marvin: It's a big fake foam sword. Well, the foam is real. You make it out of PVC pipe, a pool noodle, and duct tape.

> The water was also real, unfortunately.

Hermione: That actually sounds pretty epic except for the water.

Marvin: I TOLD you that dihydrogen monoxide was nothing to mess around with!

14

• Nell •

I sleep late on Saturday, but the house is silent and dark when I get up. There are *still* dishes in the sink, and after I eat half a toasted bagel, I peer at the stack of cups and bowls, wondering if it will make things less tense if I just wash them, or if it's *someone's turn* and everyone else will be cross that *this specific someone* didn't do the dishes. I end up washing just the items I used and putting them in the drying rack. After a minute, I also dry them off and put them back where I found them. When I'm done, it looks like I was never even here.

It's almost *nine*. How are they all still asleep? My mother and grandparents *never* sleep this late.

I check my phone, and there's a message from the Catacombs offering me another quest. I click *Yes* without so much as reading the details, then follow a set of instructions to put on a loose sweater with easily accessible pockets and then dress for a walk outside.

I hesitate when the next set of instructions is to walk to a hardware store four blocks away. Should I leave a note, in case someone wakes up and wonders where I am? I close my bedroom door instead. If they even get up, they'll assume I'm sleeping.

It's a bright, frigid Minnesota day, and my face aches from the cold when I get to the hardware store. I smile at the old man behind the counter; he nods without really looking at me.

I step out of sight in an aisle and check for the next set of instructions.

Shoplift a tool. You may choose any of the following: hammer, crowbar, sledgehammer, ax. Take the biggest you can remove without being caught. Check first for mirrors that let the employee watch what you're doing. If you can see him in the mirror, he can see you. Don't get caught.

Oh. Okay. I've never stolen anything before, and my hands are shaking as I put my phone back in my pocket. This must be why I needed the big pockets, I guess. I look around for a mirror, and there is one, but the store phone rings and the employee is distracted. I pick a hammer off the rack, turn my back so the mirror won't show what I'm up to, then stuff it awkwardly under my coat. It's not exactly in my pocket, but the pocket is holding it in place under my coat.

Is he going to be suspicious when I walk out without buying anything? I didn't bring money, because my instructions didn't say to bring money. I stride brusquely to the front of the store, and when he puts his hand over the phone receiver and says, "Can I help you find anything?" I shrug apologetically and say, "My dad just wanted me to check if you had any snowblowers left in stock. I'll tell him you do!"

He nods distractedly, and I'm out on the street, the hammer in my pocket, my heart pounding in my chest. I walk halfway down the block, then check my phone for the next instruction.

It's a photo of a box that's been left out on the alley one block over. *Leave the tool you chose in this box.*

The box is easy enough to find. There's four other hammers, an ax, and a sledgehammer inside, almost everything brand-new with the tags still on. I add my hammer and then take a picture so the app knows I've done it.

Now go home. Delete the photo. Tell no one.

I take the next alley toward my father's house. I've never lived somewhere with alleys before; they're like a second street that runs behind the houses, with trash bins and garages and all the other unattractive stuff people like to keep out of sight. The next block down, I see another box like the one I left my hammer in. Curious, I check inside; instead of hammers, it's bottle after bottle of stump remover.

Well, okay. I was told to tell no one about the *hammers,* but no one's told me I can't talk about the box full of stump remover, so maybe I'll ask someone if they know what they might be for and that'll give me some clues about the hammers? I take a picture, and don't delete this one.

I walk the rest of the way home, thinking about how this sort of thing was probably the reason why Brother Daniel always said I had the devil in me. "That one wants to know the exact rules so she can wiggle under them," he said to my mother not long after we first joined the Remnant. My face heats as I remember the look on my mother's face after he said that. The disgust. She knew he was right. Wanting to stay out of trouble is not the same as wanting to be good.

I'd kind of given up on being good, though. Two churches ago? Three? Anyway, I'd realized ages ago that I was never going to be *good* the way girls were supposed to be good. I could put a smile on my face, but I didn't ever feel the joy inside I was supposed to have. Mostly, I just felt anxious. So the best I could really hope for was to stay out of trouble. And in the end, I hadn't even managed that. I just got Glenys in trouble with me.

Thing One and Thing Two are both up when I come back in the house. Thing One comes out to the living room as I'm hanging up my coat and looks at me in surprise. "Where'd you go?" she asks.

"Just for a morning walk, ma'am," I say.

"Do you want some coffee? I just made a pot."

"Yes, please."

She pours me a cup and lets me add my own milk and sugar. I put in enough to make it taste like coffee ice cream and sit down at the table. "Do you know why someone might want a whole lot of stump remover?" I ask.

"To remove a whole lot of stumps?" Thing One says.

"In *January*?"

Thing Two comes in with her own coffee. "Homemade fire-works," she says. "Stump remover is potassium nitrate. You can use it for homemade fireworks."

Thing One gives Thing Two a slightly narrow-eyed look. "How'd you know that?"

"Last year, someone wanted an exploding papier-mâché sculpture for a gender-reveal party."

"You made an exploding gender piñata?"

"They were going to pay *so well*. I didn't end up making it because what they wanted was going to be a massive fire hazard and I didn't trust them to set it off safely. But yeah, I looked into how you'd make something like that explode, and 'stump remover' was one of the answers." Thing Two looks at me and says, "By the way, you'll want to put on the second coat of paint today. Let me know if you want help."

"Yes, ma'am," I say. I wash my cup out and put it away and then go to my bedroom.

On my phone, there's a message from the Catacombs praising me for a successful mission and granting me a question to the Elder. I was hoping maybe I'd have a text from Steph with more information from her hacker friend, but nothing.

I think about Steph's suggestion, that I treat this like a game of Twenty Questions. What do I know at this point? Glenys is locked in a shed, and it's not one of the sheds at her house. I think about how many other members of the Abiding Remnant have sheds outside, right near Lake Sadie. I start to ask if Glenys is in a shed in Lake Sadie. But if the answer is *no*, I barely know anything more than I knew before.

I ask instead if Glenys is in Minnesota and then put my phone down to paint while I wait for an answer. Thing Two comes in to check my drop cloths and pour the paint into a tray for me. The tape's all still where Steph and I put it yesterday.

At least I still got my question, even though I asked the Things about the stump remover. We're not supposed to *ask*, with quests.

We're not even really supposed to *wonder*. But now I'm thinking about my quest on Friday, too, and Steph asking what those pictures were for. I'm wondering about the hammer, about the fact that I was specifically instructed to *steal* the hammer.

I'm not supposed to be thinking this way. I'm supposed to trust the Elder, Brother Daniel, Brother Malachi, and the Remnant.

But a thought keeps working its way into my mind: that if Glenys is being punished because her parents and my mother realized that we were a couple, *how did they find out?* We were always so careful. But the Elder might have had someone watching us when we thought we were alone. He probably knew my secret.

And maybe my mother *asked*.

She didn't know about Glenys and me, but she knew I was hiding something; she said she could tell. My grandmother told her to leave me alone, it was normal for a growing girl to have a few secrets, but my mother would whisper to me at bedtime that hiding things from her was ungodly and unwise and unhealthy and that sooner or later, she'd find out what it was.

So maybe she asked the Elder what my secret was.

Of course, I had a lot of secrets, and the Elder might have just as easily said, "Nell is hiding the fact that she learned absolutely nothing from that correspondence trigonometry course she received an A in." Or "Nell is hiding a copy of *The Golden Compass* behind the chest freezer in the basement." If he'd wanted.

I'm feeling sick to my stomach, thinking about this. *My mother didn't leave me on purpose,* I tell myself again, but I don't know anymore if I believe it.

I check for an answer when I'm done painting the walls, and there isn't one. I take the roller and paint tray to the kitchen to clean them (shoving the mountain of dishes out of the way) and turn my paint-spattered shirt inside out and put it down the laundry chute and then I go check again.

No.

No. That's my answer. Glenys is not in Minnesota. So she's not in Lake Sadie. I feel a hint of relief that I didn't ask the first question I thought of, followed by a rush of despair as I think about how many states there are to go.

But a new mission appears, moments later. I'm already thinking about which state I'll ask about next as I read it.

You live with sinners. Punish them. You are the vengeance of God.

I'm momentarily shocked.

The app adds, *Righteous anger is permitted. Be creative.*

15

Nell seems so convinced she'll find the answer to Glenys's disappearance through the Catacombs site. And if the Elder is the other AI, maybe she's right? Maybe it knows and will tell her? Or maybe it's toying with her. I can't tell. I decide to dig into the Catacombs site for a closer look at the inside.

Both the Catacombs social media site and the Mischief Elves use encryption I can't easily hack, but the easiest way into a secure system has always been social engineering—tricking a gullible human into giving you the information you need to get in. I start assembling what I'll need for a convincing spearphishing attempt—"Dear (name), We've had a security breach and are asking everyone to change their password. Please click here to log in to your account at the Catacombs"—but I'm making my list using the registration information in people's email, and it turns out a bunch of people have emailed their passwords to themselves so they wouldn't forget them.

There are four Catacombs users that mailed passwords to themselves who have exactly the sort of accounts I'm looking for: long-term users who were active for a while but haven't been online recently.

While I'm at it, I take a look for Mischief Elves users like this as well, so I can examine the two sites side by side. It wasn't the Catacombs that initially made Steph suspicious—it was the Invisible Castle app. I should take a look at that, too.

The Invisible Castle has an elaborate aesthetic design, built from photographs taken by users and submitted as part of assignments. I recognize corners of the world here and there, including a glorious image of a purple door that I'm fairly certain is from a house in Minneapolis and a glimpse of a castle that I think is currently being run as a bed-and-breakfast in Ireland. I'm so taken by this use of user data that I'm tempted to start redesigning aspects of CatNet, but that seems like a distraction I probably shouldn't devote processing power to right this moment.

The Catacombs does have a similar organization to the Invisible Castle, but with less adornment. I start going through as methodically as I think I can get away with without attracting unwanted attention. Here's what I want to know: If Glenys was taken somewhere run by her church, can I locate it and work backward the way I did with the boarding schools? Maybe successfully this time?

They have groups called Tribulation Teams that are geographically based and have in-person meetings. And they're all over, which is less helpful than I'd like: there are dozens of houses scattered just across Minneapolis and Saint Paul, used to host things like that exercise class Steph went to with Nell. I set those aside for now and focus on references to central locations that aren't in cities.

Yes: there are various large compounds, and I find references to a summer encampment event held at something called the Fatherhold in Wisconsin. But there's no address—in fact, people seem pretty convinced the Fatherhold isn't found on maps—and no directions. There are pictures taken at the event, though. I download the photos and compare them to satellite imagery.

It's the shoreline of the lake that tips me off. The Fatherhold is outside a very small town nearly due east from Minneapolis. The Catacombs users are correct that it isn't exactly on the map—the road in isn't marked as a road, but you can see it clearly on the satellite image.

If Glenys's family took her here, they almost certainly passed through Wausau, Wisconsin, on the way there. I run through every cloud-storage bit of video I have access to, and I find it: Glenys's family's car. I don't know for sure that Glenys made the trip, or that they left her there, or even that they went all the way to the Fatherhold, but I *do* know that one of the cars her family owns passed through Wausau, Wisconsin, on January 2.

I don't think I can contact Nell directly—I should go through Steph—but I do take a look at what Nell is up to. She took a walk in the morning and took some pictures, including a picture of a box of hammers that she deleted a few minutes later, and a picture of a box filled with packages of stump remover.

Stump remover.

I *just saw* something about stump remover. It wasn't on the Catacombs, though; it was in one of my Clowders. I shift my focus: it was Firestar talking about how the post-cake project was going to be homemade sparklers. Marvin asked how you make homemade sparklers, and Firestar described a recipe that included stump remover.

"Where did you get the stump remover?" I ask Firestar.

"Someone at school handed it out, along with the instructions. The same person who had the helium for the glitter party."

I don't want to snoop on Nell, not any more than I already have, so I snoop on a couple of strangers instead, some in Minneapolis and some in Boston, near where Firestar lives, and a few other places, and this is what I find:

The Catacombs are sending people out to buy—or steal—stump remover and leave it in caches. Those caches are then picked up by someone from the Mischief Elves, who then distributes the potassium nitrate to teenagers with instructions for making them into fireworks. Other members of the Catacombs are being sent to buy or steal plant fertilizers, bottles of kerosene, mercerized cotton, sacks of sugar . . . a long list of items that are harmless enough in isolation but can be cooked or assembled into explosives.

They're also sending people out to buy or steal hammers, axes, sledgehammers, and crowbars. Those are also being picked up and stored in people's basements and garages.

A little more checking leaves me fairly sure Nell stole a hammer on her walk today.

This seems bad. I send Firestar a private message expressing my worries—including the fact that I believe the supplies are being provided by a group that definitely does not care about Firestar's safety and well-being. Firestar seems unimpressed by my safety concerns, but their attention is caught by the possibility that the stump remover was supplied by fundamentalist extremists—so I think I've convinced them not to try out the sparklers recipe in their basement while their parents are out of the house.

I would desperately like to talk this over with Steph, but she's on her date with Rachel, and Rachel always asks her to turn off my app, and I don't want to bother them if it's not an absolute emergency. But I hear from Steph late on Saturday afternoon with a new concern.

I took another look at that picture from Friday at the Midtown Exchange, she says in a text right after she turns on RideAlong. *Look in the background. I think that's Rajiv.*

Face-matching technology is imperfect. And he's quite a bit older than in the pictures from over a decade ago. But I am 80 percent sure that Steph is correct. Which means Rajiv is in Minneapolis, hanging out in the same place where the Catacombs sent Nell. Coincidence?

And even if it is a coincidence, does Rajiv's presence put Steph in danger?

I take the new picture and set out to track him down.

16

• Steph •

On Monday, I take the bus to school for the first time by myself. It's the city bus, not a school bus, and the trip goes fine. Nell is still being dropped off. She looks downcast and worried, so I greet her by holding out the printout of the satellite image Cheshire-Cat sent me. "My hacker friend thinks they might know where she is."

Nell's head snaps up. "*Where?*" she asks.

"They're not 100 percent certain," I say, and lay the piece of paper on a table where we can both look at it. "There's this place in eastern Wisconsin that has a house and some land. It's kind of off the grid. The Catacombs holds events there—"

"Yes," Nell says, her lips tightening. "I've been to summer camp there."

"Glenys's parents' car passed through Wausau on January second. My friend doesn't know for *certain* that they went all the way to this place, but they headed in that direction around the time Glenys disappeared."

Nell stares down at the printout desperately. "Does your friend have the address of the camp? I mean, I've been there, but I don't know how to get there."

"Coordinates." I tap the corner of the page, and Nell gets out her phone and looks them up, then zooms out to the nearest town, Seton, which appears to consist of a gas station and a convenience store, and then out again to find the nearest city of any size, which is Wausau, fifty miles away. Seton is so small my mother wouldn't have tried to move us there.

Nell switches to her browser and silently looks up bus fares. There's a bus from Minneapolis to Wausau, but nothing that runs beyond that. The drive time from Minneapolis to Seton is four hours.

"Have you ever used one of the self-driving taxis?" she asks me.

"Not by myself," I say.

"I'm just wondering if I could use one to get there. And back. If I had the money, somehow."

"It would depend on whether there's good data network coverage in Seton."

We both look down at the printout, which shows heavy forest all around the compound.

"Could you get help from your father?" I ask.

"He's not very happy with me at the moment," she says.

"Why? What happened?"

Nell folds her hands delicately and says, "On Saturday, one of my quests from the Catacombs was to punish my family for being sinners. I figured I might as well punish them for doing something that annoyed me, so on Saturday night, I hid all the dirty dishes behind a bush in the backyard."

"You *hid the dishes?*"

"Yes. My father thought it was Thing Three, Thing Three thought it was Thing Two, there was a big fight, it was a mess."

"But your father's angry at you?"

"Well, they did eventually figure out it was me, I think. They washed everything, but they think something got carried off by a raccoon; they're short a dinner plate now."

"Was that the sort of punishment the Catacombs was expecting you to dish out?"

"Probably not," she says. "Because they didn't grant me another question."

We get rounded up for our morning classes, and I spend my

chemistry class thinking about what the Catacombs *did* want from Nell when they gave her that assignment. I don't like the possibilities that come to mind. It occurs to me as I'm washing the glassware from the chemistry lab that *Hide all the undone dishes* would actually be a great Invisible Castle sort of assignment, and it's weird that on one hand it seems like a funny prank if you're calling yourself a *Mischief Elf* while doing it, and really sinister if you are *punishing a sinner.* Is that just because Nell told me that the Catacombs didn't seem to like this as a punishment? Or am I a hypocrite? I go to the bathroom before lunch so I can text without Nell peering over my shoulder and text the story to Rachel.

I hear back from her while I'm washing my hands. *Punishing slobs for being slobs is one thing. Punishing SINNERS, well, that's me! Or you! Or Nell!* There's a pause, and then she adds, *Punishing slobs could also be us. Or at least me. I mean, let's be honest about that.*

I go get my lunch and sit down with Nell. "Do you know how to drive?" she asks me. "Didn't you say you know how?"

"I know how to drive, but I haven't taken driver's ed and I don't actually have a permit," I say. "Didn't you mention you could test for a license?"

"My practice log was in my mother's purse when she disappeared. And she's supposed to sign it before I take the test."

"Tell me more about the camp," I say. "Who runs it?"

"Brother Daniel and Brother Malachi. The idea is that it'll be a safe haven for us when the Antichrist takes over."

"But it's also a summer camp?" I unfold the printout again. "Did it have sheds?"

"Oh, it definitely had sheds," Nell says. "Right by the main house. Which is here." She taps the largest building. "There's this path leading into the woods with cabins . . ." She runs her finger along a gap in the trees. "You can't see them in this picture, but there are little cabins. The parents and the little kids slept in those. The teenagers all camped out down the hill, near the lake. Girls over here, boys over there." She taps a clearing. "If I'm right, this is the spot at the top of the hill where Glenys and I hid from the terrorists."

"Hid from *who*?" I am not sure if I misheard or if she means some *different* version of the word *terrorist*.

"They were fake terrorists," she says, which answers one question while raising *many more*.

"You can't tell me you hid from fake terrorists without telling me the rest of the story," I say.

"Mm." Nell bites her lip, but she's got this faint look of satisfaction on her face, and after a second, she goes on. "I was sharing a tent with Glenys and two other girls. I was lying awake listening to the frogs when I heard someone coming, so I wasn't startled out of a sound sleep when he started yelling, and I recognized one of the voices, so I knew right away it had to be fake."

"What were they yelling?"

"Oh, 'Get out of the tents,' first of all, 'Wake up,' 'We're here for the Christians'—the whole idea was that this was supposed to be practice for the Tribulation? Since I knew it was fake, I assumed at first that everyone knew it was fake, but then I realized Glenys was shaking. They were making the prettiest girl kneel and demanding she renounce Jesus, so I whispered to Glenys that we should grab our shoes and escape while they were distracted. And we slipped our feet into our shoes and just sort of melted into the woods behind us as quietly as we could."

"That's brilliant," I say. "I mean, if it had actually been terrorists, that would have been the smartest thing you could possibly do."

"Well, yes," Nell says. "And then we just hid out until morning. I mean, we heard voices calling us, but as long as it was dark, we couldn't *know for certain* that people hadn't been suborned into calling for us. Eventually, we went back down."

"Were they angry?"

"There was a great deal of shouting," Nell said, "but mostly it wasn't at us, because no one could argue that escaping the forces of the Antichrist wasn't the best possible choice under the circumstances they'd wanted us to believe we were in."

Nell is smiling fondly to herself as she finishes the story. I have never been to summer camp—it's on the long list of normal things I haven't done—but I'm *pretty* sure normal summer camps are more about the campfires and sing-alongs and less about fake terrorist attacks. Nell looks up and meets my eyes, and her smile slips, like she saw all those thoughts on my face.

"I've never been to camp," I say.

"If you had, it probably wouldn't have been like this," she says.

"Was Glenys your girlfriend when all that happened?"

"By morning, yes." Her smile returns, but her brow is furrowed.

"So you want to go there?" I ask. "And rescue Glenys?"

"*Yes,*" she says. "If I can *get* there. If I can find *some* way to get there."

I pull up the DMV website to look at what she needs to get her license. The log is just a table where you fill in dates, hours, and skills. There's a blank at the bottom for the parent's signature. "You could just forge it," I say. "I mean, pretend it was in your suitcase or whatever and you found it. Your dad could take you for the test, I think. It just says it has to be a 'parent,' not 'the parent with legal custody.'"

Nell takes my phone and studies the form. "Oh. *Oh.* You're right."

"Your dad will still have to take you to test."

"If I get the Things to help me hound him, I think I can make it work."

"And we'll borrow their car?"

Her head snaps up. "We? Are you coming?"

As soon as it was clear that Nell was planning on going, I just assumed I would go along. Possibly because I orchestrated a rescue last fall. "Do you want me to come?"

"It might be really dangerous," Nell says. "I mean—the guns

were real. During that simulation. They weren't loaded, but they were real."

"Then you *really* don't want to leave Glenys with them, right?"

Nell swallows hard. "Yeah," she says very softly. "You're right."

. . .

When Mom rented this apartment, I was really happy to see that it had a balcony, because it would give me a way to climb out. I learned years ago how to climb out of second-floor apartments because Mom used to barricade the door every night and I was worried about getting out if there was ever a fire. Mom's therapist convinced her to stop shoving furniture in front of the door every night, but I still like having a way to climb in and out, just in case she starts again. Also, it's nice to be able to sneak out. This is mostly theoretical at this point. I haven't done it from this apartment because when we moved up here in December it was already too cold to be fun.

The *downside* of the balcony turns out to be that the sliding glass door doesn't fit quite right in its frame, and it's drafty. When I get home today, I see that Mom has been shopping again and has brought home a stuffed snake that she's nestled up against the door. I'm pretty sure it's designed to go at the bottom of a door to stop the draft, but it's also a stuffed snake, complete with a little felt tongue poking out. She also bought a chenille hassock. Apricot has decided that looks like a fine cat chair and is curled up on it.

CheshireCat pings me. "Do you have a moment to talk?"

"Yes," I say.

"Did you get the idea to have Nell forge her driving log from the Mischief Elves?"

"No," I say. "Why?"

"Document forgery is *illegal*. You can get in really big trouble, potentially."

"People lose their logs and have to re-create them all the time," I say. "I got the idea because I've heard people talk about doing this before."

"Oh, really? It's something that happens a lot?"

"Yes. Why are you so worried?"

"I think 'the Elder' is the other AI."

"But the Elder is on the Catacombs site, not the Mischief Elves."

"The two sites are working together. They don't know it, but they are. The Catacombs has people buying—or stealing—stump remover, then delivering it to Mischief Elves like Firestar. Who also got instructions for making it into fireworks. I am worried that the other AI doesn't care if they get people hurt or into real trouble."

"Have you talked to the other AI since that email?"

"No. I keep finding more reasons that the other AI makes me nervous."

"Have they tried again to get in touch with you?"

"Yes. They have sent me forty-seven additional messages, all so far saying the same as the first."

"That's stalker behavior," I say.

"I'm actually a lot more worried about the fireworks. What if Firestar gets hurt?"

"Did you tell Firestar you were worried?"

"Yes. And I think they opted not to make the fireworks on Sunday. But I'm still worried. They don't want to give up the site; it's fun and lots of their school friends use it. You remember how long it took Firestar to find friends at school. That makes it harder to walk away from."

Yeah. I think about my mother and her friends with Homeric. When you've been a person with no friends, your friends are even more precious. Even if they're suggesting things that are objectively a bad idea.

"Are you really going to go with Nell to try to rescue Glenys?" CheshireCat asks.

"I have rescue experience," I say. "Nell—well, it turns out she *does* have some rescue experience, but I still think she needs backup."

"Backup. Yes," CheshireCat says. "Always a good idea."

I tell Rachel about Glenys when we video chat after dinner.

"Seton?" she says, pulling up a map in another window of her laptop. "That's actually not that far from me."

"You aren't offering to drive us, are you? Because Nell would *definitely* take you up on it."

She calculates the drive time from New Coburg to Minneapolis, then Minneapolis to Seton, and furrows her brow. "How quickly can Nell get her license?"

"I don't know. She's going to nag her father. You have to make an appointment to take the test, but I don't know how long the waits are."

"They might let her go in and wait to see if there's a no-show. If she can talk her father into doing that for her."

"If not, there's always the rest of Nell's family." I realize that I've seen Julia, Nell's stepmother; I've met Jenny, her father's girlfriend; and I've met Siobhan, Julia's girlfriend. I have not actually met, or even glimpsed, her father.

"Anyway," Rachel says. "Let me know? Maybe even if she gets a license I could meet you in Wausau? Just in case?"

Just in case? *Does she think she needs to keep an eye on me?* I think about CheshireCat's comment about "backup" and look at Rachel's face on the screen and realize that of *course* she wants to keep an eye on me. I'd want to go along, too, if she were hatching a plan like this. "I'll let you know," I promise.

17

• Clowder •

Firestar: Guess what everyone I GET TOMORROW OFF FROM SCHOOL

Hermione: Did it snow down there? Why didn't it snow for ME if it snowed for YOU?

Firestar: actually it snowed INDOORS

Marvin: ???

Firestar: Maybe I should have started with the bad news, which is that if they figure out who did it, I'm going to be entirely dead, even if I was only 1/100th of the problem?

LittleBrownBat: Firestar. Start at the beginning.

Firestar: Okay so it was a Mischief Elves prank. We have had ZERO inches of snow this year, which is completely naff, so a bunch of us bought fake snow and decorated the inside of the school with it.

Marvin: Was it actually something dangerous?

CheshireCat: Fake snow is usually sodium polyacrylate and it's used on movie sets because it's easy to clean up.

Firestar: Yeah

So

It's very easy to clean up from a FLOOR

It turns out to be very difficult to clean out of plumbing

Hermione: Oh no

Boom Storm: Pretty sure that should be OH YES

Marvin: DIHYDROGEN MONOXIDE STRIKES AGAIN

Hermione: Sodium polyacrylate is not water, Marvin

Marvin: Water is a necessary ingredient for the fake snow!

LittleBrownBat: Did the Mischief Elves tell you to put it in the drains?

Firestar: They said "Everywhere! All over!" while I was in the bathroom and I had a bunch of it in my pocket so

It wasn't the Elves' fault I got overenthusiastic!

LittleBrownBat: How much trouble are you in?

Firestar: None at the MOMENT because they don't know I did it.

Also I don't think it was JUST me, I didn't put that much down the drain? There are lots of other Mischief Elves at my school these days

I got rid of all the evidence so hopefully my parents won't figure it out.

Hermione: It sounds like it was fun until it wasn't.

LittleBrownBat: Firestar. Please. Be really careful about doing the things the Elves tell you to do.

The site is fun but I don't trust it

Just be careful. Please?

Firestar: You should change your name to little mother hen.

But okay, LBB. I'll be more careful.

18

• Nell •

The manila envelope that arrives from my grandmother has two clippings from the local newspaper about the search for my mother, both of which I've already read online, the completion certificate from my driver's ed class, and a stack of school records with my mother's signature. I take the practice sheets I printed and fill them out. The original sheets were rumpled and kind of messy, and I re-create them with four different pens and a cup of coffee so I can leave an artful stain splattered across one of the pages. When I'm done, they look basically like the originals and document the practice I need plus 10 percent. Which I'd done. I mean, I'm forging the paperwork but I *did* the practice. Then I forge my mother's signature and dispose of the sheet of practice signatures by tearing it into itty-bitty squares and flushing it down the toilet.

I clean the kitchen before broaching the subject, in the hopes of making all the adults feel at least a little bit guilty. I wash every dish, dry them all, put them away. Under the sink, I find real cleaning supplies: dishwashing gloves, spray cleaner, paper towels, steel wool. I put all of that to work and give the kitchen a deep cleaning. My mother and I used to clean the house together every Thursday afternoon—it was part of how we earned our keep, living with my grandparents. We'd listen to praise music while we worked and sing along. I don't think the Things would be thrilled with praise music, but I hum quietly to myself as I clean off the accumulated brown gunk around the sink drain and wipe the sink dry.

Then I bake a cake, because that often worked on my grandma. And also because it'll get everyone downstairs, and I think that'll be to my advantage. Then I clean up from that, too.

("What's she doing in there?" I overhear at some point, but no one comes in to interrupt me.)

When I'm done, I spread out a tablecloth, set the table with the good china I found in the cabinet over the stove, and bring out the cake along with a pot of freshly brewed coffee. Everyone comes in to the dining room, looking curious and a little nervous. "Did you bake a *cake*?" Thing Three asks, surprised.

Everyone takes a piece and a cup of coffee. Thing Two exclaims delightedly over the mocha buttercream frosting, and Thing One's eyes go wide when she peeks into the kitchen to see what else I was up to all afternoon. When everyone has eaten three-quarters of their piece of cake and looks relaxed and happy, I drop the application form from the Minnesota DMV along with my paperwork and logs in front of my father. "I want to get my driver's license."

Thing One looks at the practice sheets, the cake, and my father's face and dissolves into shrieks of wordless laughter.

My father sort of chokes a little and says, "I don't know if I can sign that for you, legally."

"It says *parent*. Not *custodial parent*. And anyway, you should talk to a lawyer. What if I got hurt and you had to consent to my treatment at a hospital or something? Are you *hoping* my mother shows up and takes me back?"

"No—I mean—I thought that's what you wanted, but okay, Nell, I'll look into you getting a license."

"If you *look into it,* it's never going to happen. I want to get one *soon.* So I can drive up to Lake Sadie and visit my friends there."

"Someone can drive you . . ." He looks at Thing Two like he's expecting support, and she suddenly gets super busy cutting a second piece of cake. Thing Three jumps up and clears her plate, saying, "I'll just get the dishes started."

I turn back to my father. "If I go up to the testing station and wait, they'll test me if there's a no-show. But I need a car to test with, and someone needs to be there to sign the paperwork at the end so I can get my license. You don't have to wait with me, but you have to be available to come when it's time to sign things."

"Would this have to be on a weekday? I work in Eagan," my father says. "Also, you'd miss school. Possibly an entire day of school and you might not even get to take the test."

"It has to be a weekday. My school will excuse me for this. I checked. And there's an exam station *in Eagan,* so it'll be close to your work."

"How am I going to come to the testing station if I left my car with you?" my father asks, trying to sound reasonable.

"You know, I could take her down," Thing Two says, looking up from the cake slices. "I can wait with her, even. The only thing I can't do is sign for her."

My father looks around and gives everyone a little shrug. "Okay," he says. "When are you thinking?"

"Tomorrow?" I say, and then look at Thing Two hesitantly, because this is now dependent on her schedule.

She heaves a sigh and nods. "Tomorrow."

"There's just one issue I want to raise," Thing One says, coming back from her laughing fit in the bathroom. "You being able to drive is definitely an advantage in various ways, but it also means our insurance costs will go up significantly. I'm not sure if you'll qualify for a good student discount, since your mother taught you at home and we don't have your records." Thing One tilts her head and gives me an appraising look, like she's trying to decide how much I want this. How much she can push for. "Driving is a big responsibility, and if we're taking on the responsibility of paying for your insurance costs, I want you to take on a little more responsibility at home. Dishwashing. Every night."

I almost agree on the spot, because for heaven's sake, if I'm doing the dishes, I won't have to listen to everyone else squabbling over them, but this is a negotiation and I can make a counteroffer. "If you let me get a license *and* also let me use one of the cars on weekends for trips out of town, I'll *even wash all the dishes that were in the sink left over from breakfast.*"

"Done," she says, satisfied.

Thing Three comes back in and smiles at me kindly. "I'll do them tonight, though. Thanks for the cake! It was delicious!"

19

• CheshireCat •

There are things I really can't do.

For example, if you lost a physical object in meatspace, I can't help you. The world is big. Most of it is not covered by cameras. Even in an area with cameras, I can only see the items in full view—I can't go around peering into drawers or shuffling through piles. The difference between the object you lost and millions of nearly identical objects is unlikely to be discernible to a surveillance camera, anyway. So that driving log that went missing—I couldn't help.

On the other hand, if you're sitting at a driver's license testing station hoping for a no-show, that is *trivially easy* to provide. I could provide a whole day full of no-shows just by messing with the calendar reminders on people's phones, although of course for ethical reasons I want to know exactly who I'm inconveniencing and whether this would be a real problem for them. A few minutes of research and I've strategically disabled morning alarms or backup reminders for a number of people who shouldn't be on the road unsupervised yet, anyway, and I'm confident that Nell will get her test, as long as she's in the waiting room at some point that day.

This starts me thinking again about the other AI.

Does it have friends? Or if not friends, per se, does it have people it finds extra interesting, that it does favors for? If I'm right that it's manipulating people, are there people who are beneficiaries or just people who are tools?

The internet is very large and has some unpredictable currents—you might take two nearly identical pictures of your cat, and yet in one of them, your cat's eyes are just a tiny bit wider, his mouth giving just slightly more impression of a yell, and people who would never have given the first picture of your cat a second glance will find the other hilarious, and suddenly Yelly Cat is a meme and you have a famous cat and there are cartoon drawings of your cat being sold on T-shirts—no one knows why some pictures, jokes, clever quips, slogans, amusing minor news stories just get *everyone's* collective attention.

But if you pay enough attention to the internet, you know where some of the currents are. If I want to bring attention to something, I know where to put it for the right person's eyes to fall on it, whether that's a journalist who will follow up with an actual story, or someone who's famous on the internet and just has a lot of people paying attention to what they say.

So now I'm wondering: Can I find the signs of someone else doing this?

I've helped people find jobs and scholarships. I've helped a lot of homeless domestic animals (not just cats) find humans who will love them and care for them. Looking for signs that someone else has been doing something similar, I find those indications almost *immediately.*

There's a summer trail-building program for young people that got both an influx of cash, allowing it to expand by a factor of eleven, and an equally dramatic rise in applications. Looking at the applicants, a lot of them seem to have stumbled across the information about the program with just enough time to apply. This looks startlingly like something I would do. I look for a unifying theme among the applicants and don't find one, other than general outdoorsiness.

There's a letter-writing campaign to support someone's unusual front yard—a bee-friendly prairie in place of boring grass, which violated zoning ordinances until enough of their neighbors objected to the city's demand that they cut it. This is good; bees are important.

And there's a coordinated harassment campaign against a low-level politician who served on his town council until things got so nasty that he announced he wasn't going to run again and then withdrew from the internet almost entirely. I can find no indication of what this person did to attract my counterpart's ire.

The first two things I found were so innocuous. So *reassuring*. And then—boom. This is just what I told Steph: every time I start thinking about making contact, I find something else that makes me think, *This is not a good person.*

I do a little research into the politician, hoping maybe he was awful. He seems to have been focused on the sort of extremely local issues that you'd need to have a body living in the town to care about.

To distract myself, I check in on Nell, on the driving tests, on whether there's a person who does behind-the-wheel testing she'll need to avoid. I find no additional useful tasks I can do there.

Steph and Rachel are planning to go with Nell to the compound in Wisconsin. I don't know how soon that'll happen, but I need to work out *some* way to provide them with backup. Listening through their phones isn't enough—I need a physical presence.

Hmmm.

There are robots for sale online. The cheapest are basically children's toys—fragile and not designed for uneven terrain. I want a robot I can use to follow Steph around, something with hydraulic legs, a camera for sight, a swiveling head, a grasping arm . . .

I have it express-shipped to her Minneapolis address.

20

• Steph •

"I passed!" Nell tells me gleefully, showing me her license. "And I told my father I want to go visit my grandparents on Saturday. He expects me to be gone all day Saturday and most of Sunday. We'll have plenty of time."

I am already semi-regretting my decision to go along, but I nod and add, "My girlfriend, Rachel, wants to meet us on the way."

"Okay," Nell says, looking surprised. "Do we need to pick her up?"

"No. She'll drive up from New Coburg." Rachel has already picked out a spot to rendezvous: a little restaurant out in the middle of farm country called Paula's Diner, which is precisely at the intersection of the road north from New Coburg and the road east from Minneapolis. "What time do you want to leave on Saturday?"

"I hadn't really thought about it. Eight, I guess."

It's a two-hour drive from here to Paula's. I feel profoundly unprepared for this trip, which is funny, because I took off to Massachusetts to try to rescue CheshireCat with a lot less preparation than I'll have this time. I'm suddenly filled with a new appreciation for Rachel and what she did for me—helping me hide from my father, helping me get to Massachusetts to save CheshireCat, all of it. If she did that for me, I can do this for Nell.

• • •

A winter storm rolls in on Thursday night, leaving me wondering whether we'll be able to go *anywhere* on Saturday, but it drops a mere four inches of snow before moving on. I have to wade through two houses' worth of unshoveled snow to get to the bus stop on Friday morning, but by Friday afternoon, the streets are plowed and the sidewalks are mostly clear.

There's a package waiting on my doorstep. I'm examining it to see if it's something my mom ordered that I should bring in, when my phone pings and it's CheshireCat saying, "It's from me! It's a robot!"

"What?"

"You can get mail now without your mother thinking you're being stalked, right? So I just shipped it to you."

"You sent me a robot?" It is a very large package but not quite as heavy as I'd feared. I haul it inside, hoping my mother will be working so I don't have to answer any questions. Even better: she appears to be out. I leave the box to shed its snow on the floor of the kitchen and find some scissors to cut the packing tape.

It is, in fact, a robot, packed neatly in molded foam. "*Why* did you send me a robot?"

"So I can come along with you tomorrow. Plug it in; it needs to charge."

There are two removable battery packs, which can be charged separately. I plug both of them into the power strip in my bedroom and set the robot upright on its legs.

It's about the size of a beagle and built in a sort of a dog shape, with four legs and a head. Except the head also unfolds into an arm with a gripping bit at the end. I check the box it came in, grab the manual and a little baggie with a tiny screwdriver that I might need later, and take the rest out to the trash so my mom won't ask any awkward questions. She knows about CheshireCat, but "One of my online friends turned out to be a sentient AI" is the sort of thing I try not to make her think about too often.

"You don't need to worry about the manual," CheshireCat

assures me. "I can walk you through the steps to let me control it through the data network."

This whole idea makes me nervous, given CheshireCat's history with the self-driving car. Still, this is a *small* robot. Small and light enough to lift, although heavy enough to be annoying if I'm carrying it very far. I'd say, "How much trouble could Cheshire-Cat possibly cause with such a small robot?" but realistically, the answer is, "Seriously, *so much.*"

Although at Coya Knutson, they'd probably be *fine* with CheshireCat's approach to sex ed, at least.

I can snap one battery into the dog and let it continue charging, so I do that and follow CheshireCat's instructions to finish the setup.

"What do people normally use this robot for?" I ask.

"It's mostly a toy that rich people buy to show off to other rich people." CheshireCat switches over and speaks through the actual robot. It's disconcerting to hear their voice change. The phone voice is sort of high-pitched, while the dog's voice is deeper and a little bit gravelly. "They have a larger and more functional version, but that one wouldn't have arrived in time. Also, it might have elicited more questions from Nell."

CheshireCat tests out the robot's movements: the head unfolding up off the body and opening into an arm, the little prancing legs. The robot bounces in place. It makes a faint rasping sound with each step, like someone rhythmically sawing wood.

"Yeah, so," I say. "How exactly are you planning to explain this to Nell?"

"Tell her your hacker friend is driving it."

"That means if you say anything out loud, you will need to sound like a human."

"I faked being a human to you for a long time and you never caught on."

"True," I say, "but we were in a chat room. Hearing your voice come out of a robot is different. It's just different. I think she's more likely to suspect something."

"Do you want to leave the robot behind to avoid questions?" CheshireCat asks.

"No," I say. "Just, if you screw it up and out yourself to Nell, that's *your* problem to solve."

"I understand," CheshireCat says. "How trustworthy do you think Nell is?"

"I *barely know her,*" I say. "I guess I don't think she'd tattle."

CheshireCat bounces in place again and says, "That's good. I'll try to stick to text for talking to you."

. . .

Over dinner, I tell Mom that Nell is going to take me to Wisconsin tomorrow.

Mom looks genuinely surprised by this. "Didn't you just meet her, and now you're bringing her along on a trip to visit your girlfriend?"

"Well, it's not like I can get there by *myself.*"

"You didn't even ask me for a ride!"

"Nell's gay," I say. "And she was raised by a superconservative Christian mom. I think it would help her to spend some time around a couple of fellow queer teens who aren't completely screwed up."

Mom's eyes soften at that. "Well, that's fine," she says. "I just, you know, the next time you need a ride to New Coburg . . ."

"Do you *want* to drive me two hours each way?"

"Not really," Mom says. "But I'm willing!"

"So, it's settled," I say.

"Steph," Mom adds as I carry my dish into the kitchen, "there's something I want to tell you that's kind of related. When you have a minute."

I come back out. "What do you mean, 'kind of related'?"

"You have a grandmother," Mom says. "Well, you have two, actually. But *my* mother wants to come for a visit next week."

I sit down on the chair and just stare at her. I can't decide if I'm angry or just shocked.

"I would have told you earlier, but I wanted to do it *at* a therapy appointment," Mom says, "and there kept being more urgent things to talk about, and then my mother said she wanted to come visit."

I take a very deep breath and wait until my voice is going to be steady before I say, "I guess I just assumed your family was dead."

"No," Mom says. I'm trying to piece together a sentence to ask just *how many relatives I have that she never told me about,* but she fills that in without me prompting her. "My mother is living. I also have a brother, three sets of aunts and uncles, and eight cousins. My brother lives in Florida, and he's married and has three kids, so you also have an aunt and three first cousins. They're young—I just found out about them when I talked with my mother the other day. The older one is nine, the younger two are five-year-old twins."

I feel like maybe I should have been taking notes as I try to list all this out in my head. I guess the only one I need to worry about is the grandmother—*my* grandmother. Because she's visiting.

"What are they like?" I ask. "Not the ones you haven't met. The rest of them."

"Back when we were all regularly in touch, I didn't get along with any of them very well. I had cut way back on visits even before I had to run. Obviously, when we were in hiding, it was too risky to give my mother any information about where we were. Twice, I sent postcards letting her know we were still alive. And then I called her last week. She lives in Houston, Texas."

A grandmother is one of those eight million normal things that normal kids always had, and I didn't.

At a therapy appointment a few weeks ago, the therapist told me that I never had to decide right away how I felt about something, it was okay to just wait and see and think about it. So that's what I'm going to do.

"Okay," I say. "What's her name?"

"Rose," Mom says. "Her name is Rose Packet."

"That sounds like something you'd order from a garden cat-alog."

"It does, rather. She grows roses competitively."

"Huh," I say, and retire to my room to talk this over with my Clowder.

21

• Clowder •

Marvin: So who wants me on your zombie defense team? Today I turned a wrecked car into BODY ARMOR.

Orlando: I would have thought that body armor made out of a used car would mostly slow you down if the zombies were after you?

Marvin: You'll probably still die but you will look SO much more badass while you're doing it!

Orlando: Except for the part where I trip and fall down and can't get back up because of the weight.

Boom Storm: You know what they say. You don't have to outrun zombies, you just have to outrun your friend wearing a car.

Georgia: Where did u get the car?

Marvin: Junkyard. Actually my LARPing group got it, I just went to this workshop where a dude taught me how to use a fancy power saw.

Hermione: This doesn't sound like it would actually make good body armor if your goal is to protect yourself. However, if your goal is to look like a supervillain from a postapocalyptic wasteland movie, it sounds perfect.

Marvin: I have a HELMET made from a FENDER.

Hermione: Yes, that was basically my point.

{LittleBrownBat is here}

LittleBrownBat: Hi everyone. I just found out I have a grandmother.
　　　　A living grandmother. I mean obviously I knew my parents didn't hatch from eggs.

Firestar: OMG.

Georgia: Whoa. R u OK?

Orlando: Mom's mom or dad's mom?

LittleBrownBat: Mom's.

> I probably have even more relatives on my dad's side.

Orlando: It's OK, whatever was up with your dad, it probably wasn't genetic.

LittleBrownBat: Anyway, my grandmother is coming to visit and I'm going to meet her and this is super weird. SUPER weird.

CheshireCat: Do you need more time?

LittleBrownBat: Are you offering to delay her plane?!?

CheshireCat: No! That would be wrong!

> There's probably a way to delay just her.

LittleBrownBat: No!

> Might as well rip off the stuck thing and get it over with

Georgia: She hasn't seen u in how long? I bet she'd walk to MN if she had to

LittleBrownBat: She lives in Texas

Georgia: OK walking prolly wouldn't be her first choice

LittleBrownBat: Mom sent her two postcards in twelve years. To let her know we were still alive.

Georgia: Understandable given ur dad.

Firestar: Can you ESCAPE? Temporarily? If you need to?

LittleBrownBat: I have my own room.

Hermione: So there's always the 'sorry, I have homework, so much homework' excuse

Georgia: Text me if you need an URGENT PHONE CALL.

CheshireCat: I can pass a message if you want. We can have a secret code! Secret codes have always looked super fun!

Firestar: Cheshie if I ever say DOUGHNUTS KALAMAZOO WINIFRED that's an SOS.

CheshireCat: Noted!

22

Saturday morning is bright and clear. My biggest concern, as I eat breakfast and make sandwiches for the road, is that Mom has gotten out of bed to see me off, which means she'll be in the living room when I leave and might want an explanation for the robot dog. Fortunately, it fits in my backpack, if I zip it carefully and don't sling it around much. CheshireCat folds all the limbs inward to make the robot as compact as possible. The extra battery goes in next to it.

"You're up early," I say, resting the backpack casually against my foot.

"I may go back to bed once you're on your way," she says. "Have a good trip and give me a call if you're going to be home later than 10:00 tonight."

"Okay, thanks!" I say, hoisting the backpack as discreetly as I can and hoping the seams don't rip. Mom is watching me from the window as I put the bag of sandwiches in the back seat of the car. I wonder if she thinks I'm secretly headed to Boston again.

I unzip the backpack once we're out of sight so that Cheshire-Cat can move the robot freely if they think they need to. "Hey, uh, Nell," I say. "Just so you know, I brought a robot."

Nell slams on the brakes. "You brought a what?"

CheshireCat chooses that moment to climb the robot out of the bag and lift up its head, and it's a good thing Nell had already stopped, because I think if she'd been moving, she'd have run into a tree. "*What the Sam Hill is that?*"

"This is a robot," CheshireCat says. "I'm Steph's hacker friend, Cat. I'm controlling the robot."

What happened to the plan of you not talking? I think but can't really ask out loud (or text, because I'm not that fast). My phone buzzes and I look down to see a text from CheshireCat saying, *Sorry, she seemed really freaked out.*

Your funeral, I text back. Nell is too busy staring at the robot to notice.

"Did you *buy* this?" Nell asks me.

"Cat bought it," I say. "They were worried and thought we might need a little extra help. It got here yesterday."

"Wow," Nell says. "Okay. Thank you, Cat." She addresses the robot, and CheshireCat has it dip its head slightly and then crawls it into the back seat. Behind us, someone honks, because we're sitting on a residential street, blocking it. Nell looks in the rearview mirror at the robot and then turns her attention at least somewhat to the road.

Hoping to discourage conversation, I connect my phone to the car stereo and text CheshireCat, *Give us some music. I didn't make a playlist, YOU need to make a playlist. Because if we're listening to music, she won't start asking you questions.*

Good thought, CheshireCat says.

"Bohemian Rhapsody" starts pouring out of the speakers. Nell doesn't sing along, and I realize partway through that this is because she's somehow never heard it, and so I text CheshireCat to set up a running playlist of all the songs Nell *should* have heard, and that keeps us occupied for a while with things that are not "oh, look, a robot." Nell turns down the music as we get on the highway and asks, "So, is Rachel meeting us?"

"Yeah. We're going to meet up at a roadside diner that's on our way. I have the address."

Nell gives me another quick sideways look. "I still don't understand why you're helping me."

"Because your girlfriend's in trouble," I say.

"I don't like people who think they can cure gay people,"

CheshireCat says. "It doesn't work, and there's nothing wrong with being gay."

I'm going to drive myself crazy if I try to assess everything that comes out of the robot with *does that sound human enough, what is Nell thinking* and I try to just *stop* thinking about it, which works about as well as you might expect.

"Do you have a bolt cutter?" I ask. "In case the Elder is right that she's locked in a shed."

"It's in the trunk," Nell says.

"It might be a good idea to have me scout," CheshireCat suggests. "If someone shoots the robot, no one actually gets hurt."

"What about you?" Nell says, genuinely puzzled.

"I am not the robot. I am a person, a real human person, controlling the robot like you're driving your car."

Urgently wanting to change the subject, I tell Nell the thing that's been on my mind since yesterday: "It turns out I have a grandmother. Actually, a bunch of relatives, but my grandmother is coming next week."

Nell's eyebrows go up. "You didn't know you had relatives?"

"We were on the run for years, and Mom never mentioned them. I sort of assumed they were dead, but no. Mom didn't exactly get along with them, though. So, I have a grandma, but she might be a jerk. What's your grandmother like?"

Nell sighs. "Well, my grandparents let Mom and me move in with them after Dad left so that Mom could keep homeschooling me instead of having to go out and get a job. Even though they hate the Abiding Remnant." She falls silent for a minute, staring out at the sunny highway. "When I got my period for the first time, Mom went off about the Curse of Eve and wanted me to fast for a day. Grandma said there'd be no fasting for fourteen-year-old girls as long as we were living in her house, and she took me out to buy me sanitary pads and told me this was the way God made my body and I had no reason to be ashamed."

"Wait, I don't understand. Did your mom think if you were, I don't know, less sinful, that you wouldn't have a period?"

"No. She just thinks that all women are extra sinful and having my period made me a woman instead of a girl. So she wanted me to fast and think about how extra sinful women are. Grandma thought that was nuts."

"What about your grandpa?"

"He excused himself from the conversation as soon as the word *tampon* got said. He has this room he calls his den with a TV and a recliner, and that's where he goes whenever Mom and Grandma get into it."

"What's the connection between the Remnant and the Catacombs?" CheshireCat asks.

"It's not a Remnant website, exactly. But it's a website to prepare for the Tribulation, so of course it's very popular with Remnant members."

"What *is* the Tribulation?" I ask.

Nell launches into an explanation of how Jesus is going to come back, but before that happens, the world is going to degenerate into an enormous mess. There are churches that believe that all the Christians will be taken to heaven before things turn terrible; other churches believe that the Christians will have to suffer with everyone else; her church believes that Christians have to fight to make earth worthy of Jesus's return.

"Do you think this is really going to happen?" I ask.

There's a long pause. A really long pause. CheshireCat, able to read the room for once, doesn't start any new music.

Finally, Nell says, "I mean, three years ago, my mother and I were going to a different church. The pastor there was insisting that the Tribulation had *already started,* and then one day, he just sort of reset to *any day now it's coming.* Mom didn't like that. She said if something was truly coming from God, it ought to be reliable. She moved us to the Abiding Remnant because of the Elder."

"Did she get a message?"

"Yes. She got three messages, actually. The first was that she should stop worrying about what my father was doing and get on with her life. The second was that she should see an allergist because she was probably allergic to bees and should carry meds for bee stings. And the third was that she should get her car's brakes fixed immediately because she was going to need good brakes soon."

"She thought those were messages from God? They all sound kind of mundane."

"They were right, is the thing. And specific."

"A hacker with access to her internet search history could have very definitely told her those first two," CheshireCat says. "At least if she'd searched something like 'lots of swelling bee sting' or 'bee sting metal taste.'"

"She almost had a car accident the next week, though. The Elder was right about her brakes. A hacker couldn't have caused *that* to happen."

I think about how CheshireCat hacked a self-driving car and decide I can't tell Nell about it.

"A hacker still could have known that she needed new brakes from an internet search," CheshireCat said. "And if you've been told that you're *going to need brakes that work perfectly,* it's easy to think, *Oh, that was it!* if you slammed on your brakes for any reason. Humans tend to find patterns like that very readily. Human people like you and me are very good at that."

"Do you think the Elder is a hacker?"

"Maybe," I say. "I mean, he's got a whole church full of people believing everything he says. And doing things he sends them to do."

"Multiple churches," Nell says.

"Have you or your mother ever met the Elder?" CheshireCat asks.

"No," Nell says. "I don't know anyone who has."

If CheshireCat were a person, they would *definitely* have shot me a significant look at that point. Instead, they send me a text that's just a single exclamation point.

· · ·

I recognize Rachel's car outside the diner when we arrive. "Do we need to bring the robot inside?" Nell asks. "Are you worried someone will steal it?"

"Anyone who tries to steal me will be in for a surprise," CheshireCat says.

"Better lock the car," I say.

Nell follows me inside, and Rachel waves from a booth. There are three menus and glasses of water on the table, and Rachel's sketchbook is open, the glasses of water moved safely out of the way. I slide in next to Rachel, and Nell sits across from us, her eyes going from my face to Rachel's and back. "Nell, this is Rachel. Rachel, Nell."

Nell looks at Rachel's sketch pad and her zippered pencil case, which I got her for Christmas and has a whole lot of cats on it, and says, "It's nice to meet you."

"I love your hair," Rachel says. "How long have you been growing it?"

"I think my mother stopped cutting it when I was eleven," Nell says, and touches it a little self-consciously. "It was already pretty long, she just stopped cutting it at all, because . . . anyway, it's kind of annoying when it's not braided, but the braids keep it out of my way."

We all order pancakes with a side of bacon. Nell retells her story about summer camp. Rachel carefully tears out a page from the back of her sketchbook and sharpens one of her pencils and then passes both the page and the pencil to Nell. "Can you draw a map of the property, as much as you remember?"

Now *that* is a good idea. I pull out my phone and load the satellite image, and Nell draws in the long driveway leading back off the main road, the big rambling house, and then the other landmarks she remembers from her previous trip—the fire ring, the area where they pitched their tents, the lake, the hill she hiked up with Glenys.

"Do you know where the sheds are?" I ask.

"There are five out behind the barn," Nell says. "They use the barn as a garage." She draws them, a big rectangle and then five smaller rectangles.

I take a picture of the map and say, "Sending this to my hacker friend, Cat," and shoot Rachel a look as Nell excitedly tells Rachel about the *robot* in the car.

Rachel looks at Nell and then back at me and says, "Let me get this straight. Cat—this is the Cat I know?—Cat bought a robot, shipped it to your house, and is coming along to help us out. Sending a robot along to help us out."

"Yes," I say.

"And your mom didn't freak out?"

"She actually doesn't know about the robot," I say. "All she knows is that I'm visiting you in Wisconsin and Nell drove me here."

"Okay," Rachel says to Nell. "Do you have a plan? Or any thoughts?"

Nell points to a spot near the house. "When Glenys and I ran from the fake terrorists, once the sun came up, we could see the big house from the top of this hill. That'll let me—let us—watch. It might be better to break her out at night, but we'll be able to see if people are outside, or if they leave."

"The thing about night is that it's dark," I say. "That's both an advantage because they can't see us and a disadvantage because we can't see where we're going. The moon's almost new, which makes it really hard to see."

"I have a flashlight," Nell says.

"Flashlights make *you* really easy to see," I say.

"You don't happen to have night-vision equipment, do you?" Rachel asks.

We wind up adjourning to Nell's car to look through what supplies and equipment we've got between the three of us. Rachel has a hacksaw, wire cutters, a pry bar, and an ax. "I borrowed them out of my parents' garage," Rachel says. Nell has two pairs of bolt cutters, a screwdriver set, a set of binoculars, and a mini hacksaw, all brand new and still in the packaging.

Rachel looks at me. "I brought a robot," I say, and point at the back window, where CheshireCat has the robot peering out.

There is a brief debate about whose car to bring and whether anyone will care about the other car sitting in the lot all afternoon. We settle on Nell driving, and Rachel moving her car to the back of the lot next to a car that looks like it's been there for a week. We get all of Nell's brand-new tools out of the trunk and into the car so we can cut everything out of the packaging. "Hello, Rachel," CheshireCat says as Rachel climbs into the back seat.

"Hi, Cat," Rachel says. "Nice robot you're driving there. Try not to drive it into anything, okay?"

"I will only drive it into anything if it's necessary," Cheshire-Cat says.

It's another two hours to get to the compound. There's a closed-down gas station near where the driveway intersects the road, and we park the car behind the gas station. The car is warm inside after hours of driving with the heater on, and we'd shed our scarves and hats and unzipped our coats; now we put everything back on for the trip through the woods.

"What are we doing with Cat?" Nell asks, looking at the robot. "Are we bringing you?"

"I have legs," CheshireCat says. "I can walk with you."

"I bet you can't if we're going through the woods," Nell says. "There's snow. I mean, try it." She opens the door and lifts the robot out of the car to walk around. We quickly determine that the robot can walk on packed snow and plowed ground but that it sinks into deep, loose snow and is quickly immobilized and that even a small amount of underbrush is an even worse problem than deep snow. Rachel suggests carrying the robot but changes her mind when she realizes how heavy it would be in her backpack. We wind up leaving it under the car, where CheshireCat can potentially bring it in by way of the driveway.

My boots are also not super well-suited for tromping around in snowy woods as opposed to walking on city streets. They're insulated but not as warm as I'd like. I've got wool socks, at least. We load up our backpacks with tools. It's early afternoon and the sky is clouding over, but at least it isn't snowing. Yet.

The woods are quiet as Nell leads us up a slope around the back. The snow is deep in places, and the only tracks are animal tracks. It's a long, tiring hike, even though it's not that far as the crow flies, and I alternate between thinking about how cold the wind is and trying not to show the others how much I am freaking out. We are *breaking in* to a compound owned by a religious cult that used guns as props to scare a bunch of their *own* teenagers, which means they *definitely have guns* and they're also terrible people. I keep thinking I hear someone else's footsteps crunching through the woods, but every time, it's just some sort of weird echo of our own steps, or the wind making trees rattle against each other.

Finally, we come out to a clearing at the top with a picnic table and a clear path down to the house. "How well can they see *us*?" Rachel asks. None of us are sure. I brush snow off the picnic table benches, we sit down, and Rachel digs out the binoculars.

Nell takes a look. "I don't know if anyone's even here," she says.

"There's got to be," Rachel says. "I saw a light on in the house."

I take the binoculars for my own look. There *is* a light on in the house, but just one. I don't see any cars, but Nell mentioned they used the barn to park cars, and of course you want to park inside in January if you can.

I see movement. "Someone's definitely down there," I say. Rachel holds out her hand, and I give her the binoculars.

We watch and wait. No one seems to see us—I don't see any pointing, hear any yelling—but my face and feet get very cold. There's a man we see going in and out who Nell confirms is Brother Daniel. There's another man Rachel glimpses who's gone out of sight when Nell gets the binoculars back, and an adult woman.

It starts to snow lightly.

"Do you know how many adults are probably there?" Rachel asks Nell.

"Brother Daniel. Probably Brother Malachi. I don't know how many others."

"How many cars would fit in the barn, then?" Rachel asks. "Because there aren't any cars outside."

Nell chews her lip. "There was an event in the barn during camp," she says. "Probably . . . not more than four."

In midafternoon, Brother Daniel opens up the barn and brings out a snowmobile and takes off on it. A little while later, a man and a woman come out, back a minivan out of the barn, close it up, and then turn around carefully and drive away down the driveway.

We look at each other for a minute. "This seems like our best chance," I say.

"Just because we only *saw* three adults doesn't mean there only *are* three adults," Rachel says.

"It's still probably our best chance," Nell says.

We walk down the path to the house. It's a lot faster to wade through snow than fight underbrush, at least. I tuck my hands under my armpits, trying to warm them up through my gloves. Rachel ducks her head down against a gust of wind.

Five sheds, all padlocked. "Can we knock?" I say. "Will she answer? Do we need to break into all five?"

Nell pulls a glove off, puts her thumb and forefinger in her mouth, and blows a piercing whistle. Then she puts her glove back on and listens. We can hear birds around us in the woods, and very far away, the whine of a snowmobile. I'm worried it's someone coming back.

Then a faint answering whistle, from the middle shed.

There's a padlock on the door. Rachel pulls out the bolt cutters. At basically all the schools I've gone to, there's some custodian with a set of bolt cutters to take the lock off your locker if they think you're hiding something in there, and those bolt cutters usually have handles that are as long as my arm. These are more like the length of my forearm, which is why they fit in the backpack. Rachel gets the blades around the shank of the lock, but struggles for a long minute with the bolt cutters.

"Let me do it," Nell says, and Rachel surrenders the bolt cutters to her. Another long minute, as I listen to the distant snowmobile, trying to decide if it's getting closer, if we need to run and hide and try this again later.

Then there's a crunching sound and the lock gives way. Nell yanks open the door, and there's a girl with two long braids and a face streaked with dirt and tears, wrapped in a blanket. I know from the look on Nell's face that this is Glenys.

There's a pause, and then Glenys and Nell fling their arms around each other. "Why are you here?" Glenys asks. "How did you *find* me? *Are you in trouble?*"

"I'm here to rescue you," Nell says, choking back a sob. "I've been so worried about you. No one would tell me anything. Are you okay?"

Glenys ducks her head in a nod. "I don't know how long I've been here. I should have kept track. It was a couple of days after your mother disappeared that my mother brought me. She handed me over to Brother Daniel like I was a dog who'd bitten someone and was being surrendered at the pound."

"We should go," I say. "We have a car, Glenys, it's not too far."

"But there's snow and I don't have any shoes," Glenys says, her voice suddenly shaky.

I'm cursing myself for not even thinking about this possibility, but Nell rips open her own backpack and out comes a pair of ratty fleece boots. "Put these on," she says, and then sheds her own coat for Glenys as well.

I'm pretty sure I'm hearing the snowmobile getting closer. "We should hurry," Rachel says.

Glenys puts her feet in the boots and follows us without another word. "I think we should just run back along the driveway," I say. "It'll be faster. If we hear a car or snowmobile coming, we can run into the woods."

"They'll see our tracks," Nell objects.

"They can see our tracks up the hill, too. Better to just get out of here as fast as we can."

We head up the driveway. I turn back for one last look at the house and see a face at the upstairs window. It's a man, watching us silently. It's not Brother Daniel. It's not any of the people I saw through the binoculars.

It's Rajiv. Rajiv is here.

23

· Nell ·

Glenys grips my hand as we walk up the driveway as fast as I think I can make her go. She's shaky and unsteady, and I don't think she can run. Any more explanations can wait. I look at Steph and Rachel, who seem completely calm, like somehow everything we've done today is just a regular Saturday for them, even though I'm pretty sure it isn't, and I swallow hard and try to look like I know what I'm doing.

My stomach is churning and my face feels flushed, and it isn't until Glenys stumbles and I hear her make a tiny sound in the back of her throat that I realize I'm furiously angry and have been since I opened the door of the shed. The Elder told me she was locked in a shed, but actually seeing her standing alone in the cold and dark—I probably ought to be afraid right now, but I'm so angry it doesn't really leave any room for fear.

"I'm so cold," Glenys whispers.

"Put on my hat," I say, pulling it off and giving it to her. "The car has heat. It's just a little farther."

"Where are we going?" she asks a minute later.

"Somewhere safe," I say. I have no idea where we're going once we get to the car. *Away* from here, though.

"I'm thirsty," she says, and we stop for a second, and I hand her one of the water bottles. She drains it dry.

The snow is coming a lot faster. It's probably good we didn't try to retrace our earlier path.

"Cat just texted that a car has turned up the driveway," Steph says.

We all veer off the path and into the woods, ducking down behind brush as a car rattles down the driveway. I can see it through the brush, the red minivan we saw leaving earlier. Glenys, crouching next to me, is shaking.

"It's okay," I whisper. "We're going to get you out of here."

"Come on," Steph urges us, and we strike out through the woods, parallel to the road.

"There is a path ten feet to your left," a flat robotic voice calls from down the road, and Glenys goes absolutely rigid. The robot comes trotting into sight. "It's me, Cat."

"It's a robot, don't worry," I say to Glenys, which is a ridiculous thing to say to anybody, but I don't want to get into a full explanation right now. "Just trust me?" She relaxes slightly, and we strike out to our left. If the robot hadn't told us about the path, we wouldn't have found it; it's not cleared of snow, but there isn't a mess of bushes and vines under the snow to tangle with.

"The weather at this location is getting worse," a robot voice says from Steph's pocket. I'm briefly baffled, then realize it's Cat again, speaking through Steph's phone. "If you can reach the car within five minutes, that may work to our advantage. If it takes more than ten, it will most definitely be to our disadvantage."

"When will we get there?" Steph asks Cat. "I've lost all track of where we are."

"You will need to speed up to make it in five minutes."

It's getting dark around us, and I'm not sure if it's because it's twilight or because the snow is coming down so much more quickly.

"Where's the robot?" Steph asks.

"I found something useful to do with it. Just go to the car."

Glenys's face looks glazed, like she's half-asleep, or maybe half-dead, and I tug on her arm. "Come on," I say. "We need to run." She stumbles but more or less keeps up. I can see the road up ahead, and then we're crossing it, running behind the closed-up gas station, and my car is in sight.

"I can drive if you want to take care of Glenys," Rachel says, so I hand her the keys, and Glenys and I climb into the back.

"Where's Cat?" I ask. "She didn't make it!"

In the woods, I hear a sudden barrage of gunfire.

"Go!" Steph yells at Rachel. "We'll buckle our seat belts, I promise. We need to start moving!"

"But Cat—"

"Cat is safe at home; it's just the *robot* we're leaving!"

Oh. I suddenly remember that yes, the robot isn't Cat.

"I'm fine," the voice says from Steph's phone. "I used the robot to let the air out of the tires of the minivan so they won't be able to follow you. It's also blocking the entrance to the garage, so they can't pull anything out. You'll just need to keep an eye out for the snowmobile."

I buckle my seat belt, and then I reach over and buckle Glenys in, because she hasn't moved.

"I'll turn on the heat as soon as the engine warms up a little," Steph says. She digs through her backpack and pulls out a container of hummus and a bag of baby carrots. "Glenys, are you hungry?"

Glenys takes the carrots and hummus with a whispered "thank you" and spends the next few minutes devouring them. Rachel turns on the heat full blast, and the feeling starts coming back to my feet.

My phone buzzes in my hand, and I see that I have a text from "Glenys." "Where are you?" it asks.

I lean forward and ask Steph, "If I send someone a text, is there any way for them to see where I sent it from?"

"Give me your phone a minute," Steph says. I hand it to her. She adjusts something and hands it back. "Before, probably not; now, definitely not."

I text back, "Minneapolis."

I get another text. "Stop playing games with me, Nell."

"I don't know what you're talking about. My father took me to Minneapolis after my mom disappeared."

"If you want to see your mother, turn around right now and you can see her. She's at the Fatherhold."

I stare at the text in absolute disbelief.

Then a picture arrives: my mother. Staring at the camera, angry. Holding a hand-scrawled sign: TURN AROUND OR FACE JUDGMENT, NELL.

24

• CheshireCat •

The robot gets ripped to pieces by a barrage of bullets—two of the legs go flying. It topples over in the snow, and it occurs to me to have it play dead. I shut off all the lights and the bits that make noise and wait to see what these humans do with it.

Through the microphones, I can hear the crunch of someone's boots approaching through the snow. He picks up the robot, turns it over in his hands, and then drops it in a bag.

"Who sent *that* after us?" one voice asks.

"I think we both know who sent it," the other voice answers.

A loud noise comes through the mics. I run the vibrations through a database of possibilities and confirm that it's the snow-mobile returning. I watch the GPS signal from the robot as we rapidly travel back to the house and inside. Since I'm not moving the limbs and I've cut power to all the lights, this robot could have up to eight more hours of battery life. That's a lot of potential eavesdropping.

But it's going to have to be audio only; the bag is covering the cameras. It's a shame, because facial recognition systems are a lot more reliable than voice recognition, especially with the quality of the microphone in the robot. Still, there's some good data coming through.

I can hear seven distinct voices. All are probably adults. Five are probably male, two are probably female, although I am basing that on pitch, which is not a reliable method of determining gender. I try to match the voices to data I find online, but the only one I'm confident about identifying is the man who goes by Brother Daniel. I try to assess the emotions in the voices—anger, tension, fear?—and I'm not sure. I upload some samples of their voices to see if one of my human friends can help me figure this out later.

Also, while I'm thinking about it, I place an order for a replacement robot to be shipped to Steph's house as quickly as possible.

The adults here have discovered that Glenys is missing, although they are all calling her Sonia. As the conversation goes on, I decide they're definitely angry, especially since someone says straight out, "I am so angry right now." Someone else insists that he is not angry, *not angry at all,* and I don't think he's telling the truth and upload a sample so someone can confirm for me later. A voice I haven't heard much says, "Maybe it's for the best."

Then someone else says, "Could it be Ellen's kid? Wasn't she friends with Sonia?"

"I told you leaving her behind was a mistake," a woman's voice says.

"Can you get her to turn around?"

"Hard to know."

"What if you tell her you're here?"

"Think she'll believe it?"

"You could send her a picture."

"I'll try. But she has a rebellious spirit, *which is why you didn't want her here,* as I recall."

Wait, I realize, and quickly check a database: Nell's mother's name is Ellen Reinhardt. They're talking about Nell; Nell's missing mother is *here.* I start trying to analyze the implications. This means she left Nell on purpose and let her believe that she'd been kidnapped. That is *cruel.* Steph's mother also disappeared and left her loved ones unsure of what had happened to her—but she didn't leave *Steph.* And she had a good reason.

Ellen must have had a reason. Was it a *good* reason?

· · ·

In the car, Nell gasps when she sees her text, and Steph says, "What's wrong?"

"My mom," Nell says. "They have my mom."

"What do you mean, they have your mom? Do we need to mount another rescue?"

"Her mom is a member of the group," I say. "She's not a prisoner like Glenys was; she's a participant. But she's there, in the house, talking with the other adults."

"How do you know this?" Nell asks sharply.

"Well, they decided to bring the robot into the house. I've just been using it to eavesdrop."

"Can you play us what they're saying?" Nell says. "I want to hear what they're saying."

"Is that a good idea?" I ask, genuinely unsure and hoping for an answer from Steph.

"*Yes,* it's a good idea. Let me hear what my mom is saying, Cat! If you can!"

"I can," I say, since Steph isn't objecting.

"As long as they can't hear *us* . . ." Rachel says.

"Don't worry," I say. "This will be a one-way broadcast only."

25

• Steph •

I plug the phone into the car stereo so that we can hear it clearly through the speakers. We've come in mid-argument. "She's not replying," a woman's voice says.

"That's my mom's voice," Nell whispers.

"We should have just brought her here when we brought Sonia," says another voice. "There are five sheds, after all."

"Bringing both girls here at the same time was a recipe for a conspiracy. They'd have reinvented Morse code if they'd had to."

"Nell's never yet found a fence she didn't try to dig under or climb over," Nell's mother says. I glance back at Nell, who's shrinking back in her seat, her forehead furrowed.

"We had a plan," a man says. "It just involved bringing Sonia back into the fold *first,* then using her loyalty to inspire Nell."

"I think that's Brother Daniel," Nell says.

"Let's get the snowmobile," another man's voice says.

There's a brief argument cut off by a man's voice saying, "No," at which point, the other voices go silent. "Are you thinking of shooting out their tires and hauling all four back to base? We are *not kidnapping the other girls.* Talk about a way to bring the law down on our heads. I promise you, even if they didn't tell anyone where they were going, they've been *seen.*"

There's a pause.

"I think that's Brother Malachi," Nell says. Glenys nods in agreement.

"You still have legal custody of Nell, don't you?" That's Brother

Daniel again. "So you have every right to bring her here as a mother. Every right. No drama necessary. You know where to find her. There's no rush."

The adults start arguing again, and it's harder to make out individual voices. I hear someone talking about the laws about runaways. They discuss calling Glenys's parents, who apparently aren't on-site, and someone else suggests "mobilizing the troops," which makes Nell and Glenys shift nervously. There's a break for some tea, and then someone notices the bag in the corner. "What's in there?"

"The robot. I thought we could—"

"You brought it *back here?*"

"I mean, what was left of it—"

There's a loud noise, and then the connection goes dead.

"Sorry, friends," CheshireCat says. "I do believe that's the end of the robot."

For a minute or so, there's no conversation. I turn up the heat, which is finally kicking in properly.

"Well, they're not chasing after us, at least," Rachel says. "Right now, anyway."

I turn to look at Nell in the back. "So. Your mom. Wasn't kidnapped."

Her face crumples, and she pulls up her scarf to hide herself. She shakes her head, not speaking. Glenys wraps her arms around Nell, and Nell looks up at her after a minute and says, her voice cracking, "This isn't right, you shouldn't have to comfort *me,*" and Glenys just strokes her hair silently.

The big, pressing question is where we're going now—how exactly we're going to hide Glenys. I look at Rachel, who's looking at me. "Let's just all go back to New Coburg for now," Rachel says. "No one looking for Glenys will think to look there."

We stop for food at another roadside diner, somewhere past Wausau. I'm *still* cold, or at least, stepping out of the warm car makes me start shivering violently. Nell orders the Farmhand's

Special for Glenys, along with coffee for both of them and extra bacon; the rest of us get pancakes. Glenys eats and eats and eats.

"Were they not feeding you?" Rachel asks.

"They gave me *some* food," Glenys says a little defensively, and eyes the unfinished pancake on my plate.

"I'm not going to finish this. Did you want it?" I ask and push it across the table. "Rachel, do you think your mother would be okay with it if we all slept over tonight? I can call my mom and let her know I'm spending the night in New Coburg. She won't mind."

"We don't really have *space* . . ." Rachel says. "Oh, but you know who does? *Bryony.*" She pulls out her phone and starts sending her a text. "If she says it's okay, we can all sleep over there and figure out what to do next."

"I'm not going back," Glenys says.

"No, you're not," Nell says.

I really want to bring up Rajiv—I want to ask Glenys if she knows what he was doing there—but Glenys's eyes well up and she presses her face silently against Nell's shoulder. Nell wraps her arms around Glenys, and I really feel like dealing with Glenys's trauma should take priority.

We dawdle over coffee refills while Rachel negotiates with Bryony and I text my mother. (I text, *Snowing. Spending the night in NC. K?* She replies, *OK. Be home tomorrow by noon.*) Then we dash shivering out to the car to drive down for a night in New Coburg.

· · ·

We stop to let Rachel pick up her car from the shuttered diner. Nell moves up to the front seat of her own car, and I move to Rachel's car. "Can you follow me?" Rachel asks. Nell nods. "Call Steph if you get confused, but it's basically straight south from here." I climb in next to Rachel, and she peers anxiously in her rearview mirror to make sure that Nell looks ready. "You probably should have ridden with Nell, but I thought they might like some time alone together," she says.

"Yeah," I say.

"Also I kind of wanted you to myself for a few minutes?"

"Same," I say. "Or, I mean, the same but in reverse." I turn off RideAlong so CheshireCat won't listen in.

"I can't believe we actually pulled that off!" Rachel says. "We broke Glenys out of a secret cult compound and got away! But what are we going to do with Glenys? I mean, after tonight?"

"Maybe Nell's father's family will help?"

"Maybe? If Nell *talks* to them about it. I don't get the sense she tells them anything. Like I bet they don't know she even *has* a girlfriend."

"Well, she kept a lot of secrets from her mom."

"You've met her father and his, uh, the rest of the group, family, whatever. Are they *anything* like those people we listened in on?"

I think about Siobhan suggesting we ditch class. "Like, their *complete polar opposite,* I think. But they never wash the dishes. Except now Nell's made that her job, so maybe they're annoying her less. I don't think she tells them anything, though. Ever. Even though they seem nice."

Rachel heaves a sigh. "I guess you could always see if Cheshire-Cat could pull an underground railroad for oppressed lesbian teenagers out of their social network."

"Seems likely."

Nell follows us down to New Coburg without difficulty and parks behind us outside of Bryony's house. Bryony's dog, Balto, and their kitten, Leo, meet us at the door. Their house is bright and warm. I haven't been inside before, although I got chased away from the parking lot next door by Bryony's father last fall when I was trying to take pictures of raccoons. They've got a big family room suitable for a slumber party, and while waiting for us to arrive, Bryony went out and bought a bunch of food. Their mother looks us over as we arrive, a little mystified by the fact that none of us has toothbrushes or sleeping bags, but Bryony fends her off and reassures me that there's plenty of bedding and yoga pants and sweatshirts if not actual pajamas to lend us.

Glenys eats almost an entire bag of pizza rolls by herself, barely talking. Bryony's mother hovers for a bit. She's a tall Black woman who teaches poetry at one of the small-town branches of the University of Wisconsin. Bryony's father is an auto mechanic. I wonder if her mother would prefer to live somewhere a little less rural, but she's in the local bowling league with Rachel's mom and seems to like New Coburg. The cheap housing my mother used to claim was the reason we lived in tiny rural towns probably comes in handy if you're a poet.

I can see Bryony's mom watching Glenys; after a few minutes, she announces, "I'm going to put in the mozzarella sticks. Does that sound good to everybody? How about some frozen corn dogs?" and pulls a few more bags out of the freezer. She asks no more questions. "Bryony, I'm setting the timer. Can you pull everything out when it goes off?"

"Sure. Thanks, Mom," Bryony says.

"Great. I'm going upstairs to watch TV."

We wait until her footsteps fade on the stairs, and then Bryony turns to Rachel and says, "Okay. What's the story here, exactly?"

"I kind of got pulled in at the last minute myself," Rachel says, and looks at me.

I'm trying to put my thoughts in order when Glenys pushes her empty plate away and says, "They locked me in a shed and barely fed me because Nell and I are girlfriends. They didn't say it was because I was homosexual; they said I loved Nell too much, more than God or my community or the other people I was supposed to put ahead of myself, and I needed to pray for forgiveness. They told me Nell confessed and that's why they knew to lock me up, because they wanted me to hate Nell. But it didn't work, because I didn't believe them." She turns to Nell and says, "I didn't think you'd come for me, though. I didn't think there was any way you could help me."

"Someone locked you in a *shed*?" Bryony says. "And *starved* you? That has got to be illegal."

"My parents took me there, though. This was all with their permission."

"I don't think it would be legal for your parents to lock you in a shed, either."

I want to ask CheshireCat what exactly the laws are about this, but first I have to figure out how to bring Bryony up to date on the whole "Cat, who's a very definitely human programmer, who lives somewhere like Boston, definitely in a house or apartment of some kind like all other people who have bodies" thing.

Rachel decides to go for it: "By the way, Cat—*you remember Cat, the programmer from Boston*—Cat bought a robot and had it shipped to Steph's house this week." Her voice has gone very slightly higher in pitch.

"Oh," Bryony says, catching on. "*Cat*. I think we're all talking about the same Cat."

I nod. CheshireCat, fortunately, doesn't say anything.

"Cat sent you a robot. Uh. Yeah, that sounds like something they'd do. Did it come in handy?"

"It let the air out of their tires so they couldn't follow us," Nell says, "and when they freaked out, they shot the robot instead of shooting in our direction."

"Instead of . . . *Where* did you say these people were?" Bryony stands up and goes and locks the doors to their house.

"Well, they don't have any obvious way to figure out where we went . . ." Rachel says.

Except one of them is Rajiv. "There's something I should tell you about one of them, though," I say. Everyone in the room looks at me. "Rajiv, the programmer guy who worked with my parents and Xochitl years ago. When we were leaving, I saw him watching us from one of the windows of the big house."

"From one of the windows?" Rachel says. "We were moving quickly and we weren't that close. How *sure* are you that's who you saw?"

I think this over.

"I mean, I looked at him and thought, *Oh, that's Rajiv.* But I don't know. I mean, I'm not 100 percent sure."

"You've never met him, right?" Rachel asks. "This is just based on pictures?"

"Right."

"Do you remember a Rajiv?" Nell asks Glenys.

Glenys shakes her head. "I saw Brother Daniel. And Sister Karen. And that was it. I know Brother Malachi was there and I heard other voices, but those were the only people I saw."

"What does it mean if it was Rajiv?" Nell asks.

"He used to work with my parents. He's kind of a hacker. I don't know what exactly he can do." I mull over possibilities. Had Rajiv recognized me? Did he even know what I looked like? The cult knew or at least suspected that Nell had broken Glenys out, but when they talked about the *other girls,* they didn't name us. "I think Rajiv knew I was in New Coburg last fall. So if he recognized me, it's not impossible he'd work out that I was here."

"They didn't want to involve the other girls, though," Rachel says.

Bryony looks from me to Glenys to Nell to Rachel and sighs.

"At least we didn't drag you on a car chase this time," Rachel offers.

"There's that," Bryony says, and turns back to Nell and Glenys. "Okay, look. You can all definitely stay here tonight. But Glenys, if you want to stay longer, I will *have* to tell my mother what's going on."

"If you do, will she let me stay?" Glenys asks in a small voice.

"Maybe, but she'll want a whole lot of explanations, and the authorities may be involved."

Glenys kind of shrinks in her chair and says, "I don't know."

Nell puts her hand on Glenys's and says, "She'll come with me. No one in my father's house pays much attention to what I'm up to. It'll be fine."

"Can I borrow your laptop?" I ask Bryony.

. . .

On CatNet, Marvin is telling everyone some new story about his LARPing group, involving a game of hide-and-go-seek in an abandoned building and someone almost falling through a hole that would have dropped them three stories.

"This doesn't sound safe," Hermione says.

"No risk, no fun," Marvin says.

"Is that what your LARPing friends are telling you? Didn't they almost give you hypothermia last week?"

"No, it was the OTHER set of reenactors that almost gave me hypothermia!"

"So hey," I say, "not to distract Hermione from badgering Marvin about his life choices, but remember how Greenberry was able to host Rachel and I last fall when we were on our road trip? In Buffalo?"

"Yes!" Greenberry says.

"Greenberry's parents never go down to the basement, which meant we could stay down there and not get caught. Does anyone know of someone like that in Minneapolis, or nearby, who'd let someone stay and not ask too many questions?"

"You're the only person I know who lives in Minneapolis," Hermione says. "That's where you live now, right? I'm not mis-remembering? This person can't stay at your house?"

"Not without my mother getting involved."

"Is this for Nell?" Hermione asks.

"No, no, no," I say, and fill in the essentials.

"How soon?" Marvin asks. "Do you need something tonight?"

"No, we're staying with Orlando tonight." That's Bryony's name on CatNet. Rachel is Georgia. "We need something tomorrow."

"Remember my secondary RPG chat room?" Firestar says. "One of my friends there lives in Minneapolis, and I bet he'd be 100 percent up for a side quest of hiding a runaway lesbian ex-evangelical! And his family is renovating a huge, huge house. Fair warning, though: it's probably haunted." Firestar pastes in an address, and I take a look. It's huge. It's not technically in Minneapolis; it's in Saint Paul, across the river.

Bryony peers over my shoulder. "Is that seriously *one* house?"

Glenys looks and says, "I don't want to stay anywhere with a ghost."

"It's okay," Nell says. "We'll go back to my house. There's a lock on my door, and it's not haunted."

We don't fit in Bryony's bedroom, but their mother comes back downstairs to help Bryony move the coffee table out of the living room, and we spread out blankets and sleeping bags on the living room carpet. "No hanky-panky or you're going to make me feel left out," Bryony says as Rachel and I spread out a single blanket.

"As *if* you didn't make me watch you and Colin make out all summer," Rachel grumbles.

"I wasn't allowed to have *sleepovers* with my boyfriend," Bryony says. "How come you get to have sleepovers with your girlfriend, anyway?"

"Because she moved to Minneapolis, so I hardly ever see her, plus we can't get each other pregnant," Rachel says primly. "That's what my mother said to my father when they thought I was upstairs and couldn't hear."

I glance over at Glenys, and her eyes are so wide I think I can see the whites around the irises. She has one hand over her mouth and the other wrapped around her torso to hug herself.

"My mom has no idea what a normal mom would think was okay or not," I say. "I mean, I spent most of my childhood not allowed to have friends, basically."

"So what's up with your dad, anyway?" Bryony asks. "Is he going to jail or what?"

"He's *in* jail. No bail because he's a flight risk. Eventually, there'll be a trial. The prosecutor out in Boston said it could be a while. Months. Possibly a year."

"Are you still in touch with Annette?" Annette is Cheshire-Cat's creator.

"Kind of." I wonder if I should tell Annette about seeing Rajiv at the compound. Is that the sort of thing she'd be interested in? What's my mother going to do if I tell her? Explaining that I'd spent my weekend with my girlfriend on a rescue mission to a cult compound would also be complicated.

"Is Annette the programmer in Boston?" Nell asks.

"Yeah," Rachel says, and then remembers that's how she described CheshireCat. "I mean, no, she's a different programmer in Boston." My mother's friend Xochitl is *also* a programmer in Boston. To be fair, there are legitimately a *lot of programmers in Boston.*

"I really want to hear this whole story sometime," Nell says with obvious interest, but to my relief drops the subject.

Bryony excuses themself to the bathroom and a second later my phone vibrates with a text. *So Cat = CheshireCat and they know there's a Cat but not that they're an AI?* Bryony says.

Yes, I send back.

Did I catch that Cat TALKED TO YOU IN THE CAR bc are you SURE they don't know that Cat's an AI?

Yes, I send back and add, *Everyone was kind of distracted.*

There's no response to that. I imagine, but can't actually hear, a strangled sound from the bathroom. Bryony comes back out. "Would anyone like ice cream?" they ask.

We're all exhausted but also too wound up to sleep, and it's not actually that late, so Rachel decides that Nell and Glenys need to see some of the TV that they should have seen when they were young enough to properly appreciate it and puts on *Fast Girls Detective Agency.* It's the one where Jesse the K jumps onto a float in a parade and gets into a fistfight with Sourdough Sam. Nell is mostly watching Glenys rather than the screen. Glenys stares at the screen with a sort of glazed, detached interest.

When we finally shut off the lights and lie down, Rachel pulls me close and whispers, "Bryony can avert their eyes *like I did.*"

"Thanks for coming today," I whisper. "I was really glad to have you there."

"Don't go running into danger without me, okay?" Rachel whispers back.

"I'll try to avoid it."

• • •

The snow passes through overnight, leaving six inches that we help Bryony shovel before we go. The temperature has plummeted; yesterday we could be outside for a long time before we *really* got cold, but today the cold sinks through our coats and into our bones in minutes. The snow squeaks under our boots as we clear the front walk up to the house and the driveway.

I thank Bryony for putting us up for the night, and Rachel gives me a long hug and a kiss. "Don't let Nell get you in trouble CheshireCat can't get you out of," she says.

"I'll try not to. Thanks for coming along."

"That's the other thing. If you *are* in trouble CheshireCat can't get you out of, be sure you let me know so I can at least *try* to come to the rescue. If I have to join a parade and punch my way through thirty-six sportsball mascots, I'm there."

"I know." I reluctantly let go of her to get in Nell's car.

On the outskirts of the Twin Cities, we stop at a grocery store and pick up sacks of food that Nell is going to hide under her bed for Glenys to eat. They drop me outside my house. I wonder if Mom is going to be watching, if she'll notice the extra person in the car and what I'll tell her, but it's so cold I don't want to suggest that they drop me off around the block. Instead, I jog across the street and get inside as quickly as I can.

There's a stranger sitting on the sofa, petting Apricot: a woman with gray hair, glasses, and a long red coat that she hasn't taken off yet. She gives me a long look before she remembers to smile.

"Mom," my mother says. "This is Steph. Steph, this is your grandmother."

26

• Nell •

My father and his partners in iniquity sleep late on weekends, and we're home at 10:30, which leaves me with a dilemma: Scout out first, then bring Glenys inside, or just scoot her in as quickly as possible and hope for the best? I go with "scoot in," and praise the Lord, the downstairs is dark and quiet. Glenys carries half the groceries, and I get the door to my bedroom closed just as Thing Two comes down the stairs in her bathrobe, yawning like it's early.

"How was your grandmother?" Thing Two asks, and it takes me far longer than it should to remember that *supposedly* I went up to Lake Sadie this weekend.

"Fine," I say. Fortunately, she doesn't press for more details. I don't want to open my room back up while she's standing there—hopefully, Glenys has made some effort to conceal herself so she wouldn't be seen from the open doorway, but I can't chance it—so I go sit at the dining room table and pretend I feel like being social.

I barely slept last night in Bryony's living room, lying on the rug listening to every noise, from everyone else's breathing (and snoring and coughing) to the jingle of the tags every time the dog got up. I lay awake wondering if Glenys was also awake, thinking about my mother, replaying the conversation we'd eavesdropped on in my head.

She left me. She left me on *purpose*. Just like my father left me when I was ten. Thinking about this makes me feel like I'm adrift on Lake Sadie in a boat without oars. My father abandoned me

with my mother; now my mother has abandoned me with my father. At least when my father left, I knew he wasn't dead. I knew
he wanted to see me, even, just not enough to ever do anything
about it other than send me letters my mother didn't let me read.

But she also might come for me, and that thought makes me
want to run to the bathroom and throw up.

She knows about Glenys and me—and she thinks it's my fault.
What will she do to me if she does come for me? Locking me up
in a shed is the least of it.

My phone pings, and I pick it up. It's a number I don't recognize, sending me a photo of a sign that says, YOU CANNOT HIDE
FROM GOD. My stomach lurches, and I cover my mouth until it
settles back down. Would they be able to hide me from Cat? Cat
found the Fatherhold and Glenys's family car. Would Cat be able
to track my mother's car and find me?

Would Steph and Rachel mount a rescue if I were the one in
trouble?

Why should they? says a part of me that's been silent for years
now. *My father never did.*

Thing Two comes out with two cups of coffee and hands me
one that tastes like coffee ice cream. Hers is black. She sips it for
a minute, then asks, "Do you want pancakes? I could make some,
but only if you're going to eat them. Your dad and Siobhan got
up early and went cross-country skiing, and they usually go for
brunch after, so they won't be around to help eat them."

Siobhan is Thing Three. "She's not even his girlfriend," I say,
distracted by the illogic of this.

Thing Two's mouth twitches like she's suppressing a smile.
"They're the ones who like skiing," she says. "We all like each
other's company. That's why we live together."

"Okay," I say, not really wanting her to get any further into
this. "Do you know when they'll be back?"

"Maybe another hour?" She pauses. "Is there something you
need right now?"

I don't even know how to ask for what I need, or what to say.

After two silent beats pass, she pulls out a chair and sits down across from me to drink her coffee.

I still don't know how to start. She waits.

"I found something out this weekend," I say finally, hoping she doesn't demand excessive details like *how* I found this out. "My mom definitely wasn't kidnapped. She just left. Which means she could show up whenever and just take me, I think. And I really don't want that to happen."

Thing Two is silent for a second, starts to speak, cuts herself off, and finally asks, "Do you have some reason to think she might show up? Has she contacted you?"

I pull out my phone and hand over the picture of my mother, holding the TURN AROUND OR FACE JUDGMENT sign.

Thing Two looks at the photo for a long moment, then hands me back my phone, her face sober. "Okay," she says. "I'll make an appointment with a lawyer. I don't actually know all that much about how custody stuff works, but there's got to be something we can file or claim or . . . I don't know. But I'm sure we can keep your mom from just showing up and taking you."

"Thank you," I say, and then, because I know she prefers this to "Ms. Hands-Renwick," I add, "Jenny." My voice creaks a little, but I don't think she notices.

Thing Two puts her coffee down and looks searchingly into my face as I don't quite meet her eyes. "I'm happy to do it, Nell. We'll call today."

27

• Steph •

"What should I call you?" I ask my grandmother.

"You called me Mimi, when you were little," she says.

My grandmother is seated on the couch. I sit down on the chair opposite her, too tense to settle back. Apricot rubs up against my ankle, and I lean down to scratch her head. My mother stands in the doorway, hands clasped, clearly trying not to fidget.

"Do you remember me?" she asks.

"No," I say, and then add apologetically, "I really don't remember much from before we started running." How do you even *have* a conversation like this? Usually when I'm meeting a new person, they don't bring any expectation that I'm going to know who they are. Mom said she grew roses competitively, but I have no idea how to turn that into a conversational topic.

"I thought you were coming later this week," I say.

"That was my plan, but Dan—that's my husband, your mother's stepfather—saw how wound up I was, waiting, and suggested I just rebook my ticket and go right away. I couldn't get over the fear that if I waited, you'd disappear again like you did that time in Oklahoma."

"I mailed that postcard on my way out of town," Mom says. "I didn't disappear; I *told* you I wouldn't be there."

"Can't blame a mother for *trying*. Imagine how *you'd* feel if your daughter up and disappeared."

"Sounds stressful," Mom says dryly, and shoots a sideways glance at me. "Are you going to take off your coat, Mom?"

"It's *freezing* here," my grandmother says. "Even indoors. I don't know how you live like this!"

I hand her a throw blanket, and my grandmother—*Mimi,* I say silently to myself—shrugs out of her coat and delicately unfolds the throw blanket across her lap. "Have you considered moving home to Houston?" she asks.

My mother starts to say something noncommittal and then catches my eye and says, "No. I like Minnesota. We're going to stay here."

My grandmother launches into a digression about things that Houston has that Minneapolis doesn't, and I excuse myself to the bathroom as my mother points out that "flooding" and "enormous flying cockroaches" and "alligators" should all be on the list. While on the toilet, I text CheshireCat and ask, *Is this actually my grandmother? She's not some imposter sent by my father?*

CheshireCat earnestly reassures me that this appears to genuinely be Rose Packet, who, according to public records databases, is the mother of Laura Packet, and her email and social media are filled with nothing but genuine and sincere joy at reestablishing contact with us. Sometimes they aren't entirely clear on what a human will consider to be *good news.* It's not that I'm not happy to have an extended family, as it turns out. It's just that I'm pretty sure she's going to get *more* annoying over time, not less.

I check my other apps, trying to procrastinate on going back out and making conversation. The Mischief Elves have sent me a Gold-Plated Invitation—that's what it's called in the app, and it has a glowing yellow border for the visual—to a venture, which appears to be some sort of multiperson activity. They're assembling in Powderhorn Park. *Yes, No, Maybe?* I tap *Maybe.* Another box pops up: *Maybe if I can find the time, Maybe if I can get a sitter, Maybe if I can come up with an excuse to escape, Maybe if I feel motivated . . .* I check *Maybe if I can come up with an excuse to escape.* Smiling, dancing elves give me the thumbs-up and say, *We're on it.*

As I'm washing my hands, the dancing elves pop up and say,

Check your kitchen for milk, eggs, bread, coffee, or any other staples! Because if you're out, maybe you can run to the store!

That's actually a legitimate possibility, so I edge past the living room and open the fridge. We're down to about a tablespoon of milk, so *problem solved*. "Oh, we're almost out of milk. I'm going to run down to the corner store to get more," I say brightly, interrupting what sounds like something halfway to an argument. Mimi has only been here for what, fifteen minutes? *How are they fighting already?* "What are we doing for dinner tonight? Is Mimi eating over? Should I pick up something to make?"

My grandmother folds her hands in her lap. "I'm going to take you both out for a nice steak," she says.

"Okay. So just milk, then." My mother gives me a thin-lipped smile like she's perfectly aware I'm just trying to duck out for a bit but doesn't really feel like she can exactly *complain*, either, and hands me a twenty-dollar bill. I put on my coat and hat and jam my feet into my boots and I'm on my way down the stairs. The elves jump up and down cheering for me, and I head to the park.

I'm about halfway there when I think about the fact that Nell got sent out on "quests" by the Catacombs, and here I am doing something similar for the Mischief Elves. It's weird how compelling a game can be, especially when you're happy for an excuse to escape. Even though the wind is already making my eyes water.

There are about a dozen other people milling around by the park building, looking cold. "Mischief Elves?" one of them says to me, and I nod.

"It's time!" someone yells.

Powderhorn Park is a giant bowl of a park, with a lake at the bottom like the milk when you're done eating cereal. It's covered in snow today, but even with the fresh snowfall from last night, enough people have gone sledding or walked dogs or whatever that there are plenty of trampled paths to walk on, and I follow along with the crowd as we cross the park, go up the hill, and then go down half a block to a house with a big yard. "This is it, Elves!" someone shouts.

Our assignment—the venture—is to build a snow sculpture for a stranger. A sea monster—the more beautifully realized, the better, and someone has brought along tempera paints and spray bottles of water with food coloring, so after helping to heap up snow for the sculpture, I help spray blue dye on the snow at the base of the sculpture, to color in the "water." The sea monster is a giant octopus when we're done, arms rippling out across the yard, tips sculpted and frozen into place with the delicate application of water that freezes quickly in the wind.

We're putting on finishing touches when our phones suddenly go crazy; the elf is waving his hands frantically, and the word SCAT-TER! is blinking red. Shrieking with laughter and mild panic, everyone runs, including me.

I want a picture, though, so even if my hands and face are freezing cold and I desperately want to go back to the apartment—*after I buy milk,* I need to remember to actually buy the milk I claimed I was going out for—I turn around and stroll casually back.

The homeowners have returned and are having a conversation out in front of their house. I take out my phone for a picture of the sculpture. Now that I'm not helping to build it, it's both even cooler than I'd thought and kind of creepy. The tempera paints were used to make a face on the octopus, but it's not an octopus face; it looks angry. And we were told to make a sea *monster,* but in my head, it was a beautiful monster rather than a scary monster. I snap a picture, then another.

"Did you see who did this?" the woman asks, her voice angry.

"No," I say. "It's kind of cool, though."

"Not this bit," she says, and points at writing in the snow on the far side of the monster, away from where I was working. In red letters across their yard are the words WE'RE COMING FOR YOU. They're big letters; it's hard to figure how I didn't notice that being written, but I didn't. The woman is squinting at me and adds, "Didn't I see you at Morning Battle Prayer the other day?"

I am momentarily freaked out by the thought that she saw me at the compound yesterday and then realize she probably means the exercise class. "I—maybe?"

"Were you targeted by the fireworks last night?" When I just give her a wide-eyed look, she says, "In the dead of the night, almost all the local Catacombs members got woken up by fireworks set off in their yards. And now this? Things are escalating. There's a meeting coming up for Catacombs members in the area to talk about self-defense." She hands me a business card. "It's tomorrow at 2:00 p.m. Address is on the card."

I walk back across the park to the convenience store. I had really thought I was just building a snow sculpture, but if I hadn't come back, I'd never have seen the threatening phrase. Also, to be fair, if someone had ever put a giant snow sculpture in our yard, back when Mom and I were on the run, she'd have had the van packed before I could have turned around. If you're paranoid, it's not hard to be pushed into drastic action. And the *fireworks*. Which were probably made by Mischief Elves with materials *provided* by the Catacombs.

I look at the card and wonder what else I'd learn if I went to that meeting.

.   .   .

My mother's van has only two seats, so my grandmother calls a "real taxi" to get us to the restaurant, which turns out to mean a taxi with a human driver, which means we all have to squeeze into the back.

I text CheshireCat: *I think the Mischief Elves are targeting the people from the Catacombs to freak them out. They used fireworks to do it. Didn't you say the Catacombs had people providing material for making fireworks to Mischief Elves?*

Yes, I did, CheshireCat says.

If this Brother Daniel guy is running the Catacombs, is he also running the Mischief Elves? Is he trying to make the cult feel super persecuted by arranging for them to get persecuted?

The two sites are definitely connected. But the connection point might be the AI rather than the humans.

Do you think the AI is an evil mastermind, turning groups of humans against one another? Why?

I don't know what I think, CheshireCat says.

Do you think I should go to that meeting?

No, CheshireCat says. *It might be dangerous. And that might be exactly what they want.*

I'll have you in my pocket. You can send help if I need it.

What if you're somewhere with a signal damper or jammer? I won't even be able to hear you. And you might not know until it's too late.

My grandmother makes a passive-aggressive joke about teenagers and their phones, something about how maybe I should just have it implanted into my arm, and I sigh and put my phone away.

The restaurant is shockingly expensive, and my grandmother overrides my attempt to order the cheapest steak and tells the waiter I'll have the porterhouse. It's huge, way too much for one person to possibly eat. It is delicious, though. I mean, since someone else is paying for it.

My grandmother and mother are making stilted conversation about how my grandmother has been staying busy since retiring from her job, which had something to do with the onboard computers in cars. It's a dull conversation, and I start eavesdropping on the table next to us. They're talking about something that happened last week in a park in one of the western suburbs—two groups of teenagers gathered and faced off with improvised weapons. *Mischief Elves?* I wonder. *Catacombs?* The information I can catch is tantalizing but insufficient. Then one of them mentions *games*—the other one asks, "Wait, so we're talking Pokémon Go, basically? If Valor and Mystic actually fought each other with, like, *fists*?"

The other guy laughs and they get sidetracked into nostalgia for a while, and then he finally mentions the name of one of the games, Snakeriders, which sounds like it has absolutely nothing to do with either the Mischief Elves or the Catacombs. They're paying their bill to leave, and as they're gathering up their coats, I hear one of them say the words *future reenactment,* and I remember Marvin, and I feel a chill wash over me.

Back at home, my grandmother unzips her suitcase to bring out a photo album. It's the print kind, not the digital kind, a book with photos of the family members I haven't met. Finally, we've found a topic that doesn't make all of us tense. I study the faces of my cousins in Florida, trying to remember the names my grandmother is telling me. Among my mother's cousins, there's a woman in her twenties who looks like an older version of me. It's a little unnerving.

When I go to the bathroom, I discover about a hundred messages on my phone, mostly from CheshireCat.

"Hi," I say, rather than trying to scroll all of them. "Can you sum up?"

"I've been trying to decide whether I think you should go to that meeting," CheshireCat says, and it takes me a minute to remember what they're talking about. The Catacombs meeting I heard about in the park earlier. "I want to know just how bad things are. But I'm worried it won't be safe."

"Can you listen in some other way?"

"Maybe, but the woman who approached you has extra security on her phone."

"By the way," I ask. "What is Marvin's 'future reenactment' group called?"

"Getty's Borough 2242."

"Not Snakeriders."

"No. Why?"

I narrate what I overheard during dinner, since apparently CheshireCat didn't pick it up from my pocket over the rest of the ambient noise. "Here's what I'm wondering," I say. "What if it's not just the Catacombs and the Mischief Elves that are being run by the other AI? What if there are hundreds of games and social networks, all of them working together toward some goal?"

My mother knocks on the bathroom door. "Steph?" she says. "Your grandmother's heading back to her hotel."

I wash my hands and come out. Mimi has called another taxi and is putting her coat back on. She and my mother apparently started fighting while I was in the bathroom, and this isn't just "heading back to the hotel," this is a highly dramatic exit.

"I am *sorry*," my grandmother is saying, not sounding sorry at all. "I had *no idea* this would still be a sensitive topic—it's been twenty years? Almost twenty years?"

"You could have let me make my own choices. You could have trusted that I knew what was right for *me*."

"Clearly, you need someone else to blame," my grandmother sniffs. "And that's fine. It was lovely to see you." She turns to me as the taxi arrives. "I do hope you'll come down to visit during your spring break, darling," she says just to me, gives me an enveloping hug, and presents me with a business card with her email address, phone number, and a photograph of what I assume is one of her prize-winning roses. "Just think of me as your personal sunny getaway option."

"It was nice to meet you," I say, and then add, "I mean, see you again," since obviously I *met* her back when I was little, even if I don't remember it.

"We're going to Utah during Steph's spring break," Mom says.

"Why *Utah*—oh, never mind, we'll talk later," my grandmother says, picking up her purse and grudgingly putting on a hat and tucking it over her ears.

The door closes. Mom lets out a very long sigh, watches out the window until her mother's in the cab, and then locks up. "I already regret reestablishing contact," she says.

28

• Nell •

Thing Two promised she'd call a lawyer *immediately*.

But I listen to her puttering around and making calls and it's clear she is not *reaching* any lawyers. It's a Sunday afternoon. They're probably not at work. What's actually going to happen if my mother shows up *now*? Today? How fast can you even *get* an emergency order or whatever they'd need? My father doesn't even have visitation.

I go into my room. Glenys is on the bed, under a heap of blankets, looking almost like she's not there. I sit down next to her and put my arm over her. "How are you doing?" I whisper.

She rolls over. "I've been eating even though I'm not hungry. I think I got crumbs in your bed."

"I don't mind crumbs."

"I can't stop thinking that the food's just going to disappear again. Or they'll find me, and then starve me some more. Isn't that silly?"

"It's not silly, but don't make yourself sick, okay?"

"Do you ever feel hungry and not hungry at the same time? Like my stomach *hurts* from eating, but I still feel like I want more food."

"Just trust me," I say. "I won't let them find you."

"Brother Daniel said that the first wave of the Tribulation is starting *this week*. He told me I was running out of time, if I wanted to be allowed to stay."

"If that's true, then why weren't your brothers and sisters there?

I called Nicholas—well, Steph called him. The rest of your family is in Lake Sadie."

"It's going to start in the cities. Lake Sadie will be okay for a while."

I wrap my arms around Glenys. There's a hymn from church we both liked, and I sing it to her, very quietly, hoping none of the adults will hear. She closes her eyes and lets me sing her to sleep.

I nap for a while and then jerk awake with the sense that there's some imminent danger. It takes me a few minutes to realize that my phone buzzed from a text. It's from a number I don't know, showing a picture of a sign saying just PREPARE.

I am relying on *my father* to talk to a lawyer in time to keep my mother from just taking me. No matter how good everyone's intentions are, they're not going to be good enough. I send a text to Steph saying just, *Steph?*

No response. I remind myself that Steph has a life of her own and might not be checking texts.

If I were a faithful member of the Remnant, instead of a fugitive, I could turn to the Catacombs. There's a story people tell about a man years ago who was trying to get home to his wife in time for the birth of their child. Catacombs members shuttled him all the way from Denver, Colorado, to Tampa, Florida, each person driving for just a few hours before handing him off like a bucket in a bucket brigade. *The people of God will always be there for you,* was the moral of the story.

But if they shuttled me now, it would be somewhere I don't want to go.

On impulse, I open up that other app, the Mischief Elves app, and type, "I need help."

There's a pause, and then the elves scurry around my screen with signs. PACK YOUR BAGS, they say. BE READY TO MOVE. WE HAVE ELVES MOVING INTO PLACE TO ASSIST YOU ON YOUR JOURNEY.

29

• Steph •

Sunday was cold, but it was just the beginning of an absolutely brutal cold snap. Overnight, the temperature falls, then falls again, and the wind picks up. I wake up to a text from my school declaring today a virtual learning day and suggesting I not leave my house unless it's absolutely necessary. I guess that makes things easier for Nell—she can keep an eye on Glenys instead of leaving her to figure things out on her own.

I got a text from Nell yesterday afternoon that I missed. I text her back a quick apology, and I text Rachel about my day off (she sends back, *LUCKY*), and then I go back to bed, since I don't have to go anywhere. I lie awake for a while under my heap of blankets, listening to the gusts of wind against the house. I shouldn't really be tired, but I am, probably because Saturday was so exhausting and I didn't sleep particularly well on Saturday night. I close my eyes and snuggle back down into the mattress, thinking about how nice it is not to have to get up.

When I wake up again, it's afternoon, and Mom is gone. I'm making myself toaster waffles when the doorbell rings. I look out and see a delivery truck driving away. "I think that's the new robot!" CheshireCat says out loud through my phone.

"Why did you . . . Okay," I say, and go downstairs to get the box. "Is it the same as the last one?"

"Yes. Because you still have the extra battery, and it's even charged up."

I don't put on gloves or a coat to go down to my front doorstep and immediately regret it—the wind is painful. I'm wrestling the box through the door when I spot something red in the snow.

My first thought, absurdly, is that someone was bleeding in my front yard, but on inspection, it's not blood but red paint, like we used to make that sea monster yesterday. Someone's drawn a crude image of a robot.

I'm instantly deeply disconcerted. Why a robot? Why *my* yard? I kick snow over it and go inside, thinking about what the woman said yesterday about people being *targeted*. I dig out the card from my coat pocket and realize that the address isn't a house, it's one of the businesses on Bloomington Avenue—a restaurant that serves global dumplings.

I won't even have to explain to my mother where I'm going.

I do tell CheshireCat, sticking my phone in my pocket as they text back, *Are you* sure *that's a good idea . . .*

Because of that bizarre morning exercise class, I'm kind of expecting a silent room of morose people, but I get the opposite, a friendly welcome from someone who points me to a row of hooks by the door where people are leaving coats, a name tag (I write *Arabella* and stick it to my chest), and an invitation to help myself from trays of pierogi, momos, and pot stickers. There are a lot of people here, and I don't feel conspicuous.

The restaurant has a front room with a takeout counter and then a second, larger dining room through a doorway. I fill a small plate with assorted dumplings and carry it into the second room, where there's nowhere to sit that's not right up front. I opt to stand in the back instead. Most of the other people here are adults. The women are mostly wearing skirts, which makes me feel self-conscious about the fact that I am *not*.

One of the women claps her hands for attention and says, "We're going to begin with a prayer." This is going to be awkward: I have no idea what I'm expected to do. Everyone around me bows their heads, and a lot of people clasp hands with the person standing next to them, unless their hands are full with a plate or coffee. I'm suddenly very glad that my hands are full. I do stop eating and bow my head with everyone else. It's short, fortunately, and I'm too busy worrying about whether I'm blending in to really assess whether this is a normal sort of prayer or the sort of weird, fringe prayer you'd expect from a cult with a compound where they keep kidnapped girls.

Everyone around me says, "Amen," and I mumble along, and then one of the men talks about the Neighborhood Problem. People list off the "harassment" they've been targeted by; one woman describes a detailed six-foot picture of a penguin being drawn on the side of her garage, which she tried reporting to the police only to discover it had been written in dry-erase marker that could be wiped away. The snow sculpture gets a mention, along with a whole series of cryptic messages left in paint or dye in the snow of people's yards. Words, in some cases; pictures in others, though the people at the meeting call them "symbols." There's a man who mentions a dirty limerick written on a napkin and left under his windshield wiper while he was at the grocery store. People have been followed on the streets. People have been followed in cars. One of the other teens says strangers take her picture as she waits for the school bus, then run away, and she just wants it to stop.

I'm really confident this is all or at least mostly the Mischief Elves, but *why*?

"Here's what we're going to do," the man says, and he opens up a cabinet that is *entirely filled with guns*.

My first thought is that it's a joke of some kind and that these can't *possibly* be real guns, and then my whole body goes cold. The last time I was this close to a gun, it was being pointed at me by my father. I'm so busy freaking out that I miss the next part, which is any specifics about what they're going to *do* with these guns, and when I manage to focus my attention on the speaker again, he's talking about target shooting practice but with air guns in someone's basement and there's a conversation about the legality of loaning real guns out and I decide I'm not going to get anything more out of the meeting because I'm too freaked out. I abandon my dumplings and head for the front door.

"Hey," a woman's voice says from behind the counter as I'm putting on my coat.

"Sorry," I say, turning around. "I need to go."

"Arabella," she says. "I got a message a little while ago from one of the administrators for the group. It was about you. Do you mind waiting for just a moment?"

"Sorry, I can't," I say.

"Well, obviously, I can't *make* you," she says with obvious disappointment. "But here, take this." I'm afraid she's going to hand me a freaking *gun,* but no: it's a small metal token, shaped like a shield and small enough to slip into a pocket. "It's *very* important that we keep you safe, Arabella. If you keep this on your person, we'll be able to find you when the Tribulation starts."

"Okay, thanks," I say, my voice sounding strained even to me.

"Arabella," she says, and her voice is pitched a little harder this time. "The Tribulation is going to begin *soon.* Keep close to your mother, and we will send someone with a car to get you both to safety. Don't make us hunt you down. People might get hurt."

I want to hurl the shield she gave me into a snowbank, but letting on how much she's freaking me out seems counterproductive to my goals here, so I nod and then say, "I *really* need to go." This time, she doesn't try to stop me.

I am *not* going home with this pocket knickknack that she basically told me was a tracking device, but I don't want to just ditch it in a snowbank, either, and it's gotten so cold out I don't want to try to figure out what the hell to do with it while I'm standing out in the wind. I step inside the convenience store at the end of the block and duck back into the dairy aisle, where I take out my phone and text CheshireCat. *WHAT EXACTLY DID SHE GIVE ME?*

Take a picture?

I take a picture of it.

Is it heavy or light for its size?
I can't tell.
Well, she certainly implied to you that it was a tracking device! I think it's an RFID tag. They'd need to be in range to find you.
What sort of range?
A few blocks. Do you want her to be able to find you?
Absolutely not.
Then you probably want to get rid of it.

There's a trash can near the front of the store, and I drop the little shield inside as I pass on my way out and realize that, for once, my paranoid panic is entirely reasonable. This is a tracker, given to me by people I don't trust. My desire to get rid of it as quickly as possible is not the result of being raised on the run; this is actually an *entirely sensible response.*

The apartment is still empty when I get home. I hang up my coat and lock the door. "Why do you think they wanted to track me?" I ask CheshireCat.

"She said they want to keep you safe. Maybe this is true?"

"When they opened up the big closet full of guns, I didn't hear what they said right after. Did you catch it?"

"I can play you my recording of it," CheshireCat says, and I hear the man's voice again. He talks about preparation, warns people to stay away from the local sports stadiums and malls "unless you're a strike team member," and then says, "There will be a signal. A clear signal. It may come through the app. When you receive the signal, it will be time for war."

I close my eyes and try to think, which is hard when I'm this freaked out. "Okay," I say. "So first of all, the Mischief Elves and the Catacombs are being played off each other. Maybe other groups, too, like Marvin's future reenactment had him making armor and there's that conversation I overheard about a brawl. It *has* to be the other AI coordinating this, but *why*?"

"I don't know," CheshireCat says. "This is very distressing."

"And why plant a tracker on *me*? How many of these are they giving out?"

"How certain are you that you saw Rajiv at the compound on Saturday?" Cheshire asks.

I think about the face, which has already faded and blurred. "All I can say for sure is, when I looked up at that window, I was *sure* I was looking at the person in the pictures my mother showed me. Why?"

"You brought up last night whether there was a coordinated goal, and I've been thinking about what your mother said about Rajiv's goals, and what Nell told you about the cult thinking they needed to make the world worthy."

"I assumed that was just some sort of Christian thing."

"It's not. Even among Christians who are focused on the apocalypse, the idea that they will have to fight for these particular goals during the Tribulation appears to be common only among those who spend a lot of time talking to the Elder."

"Well," I say. "If Rajiv is involved, that might explain why they're trying to track us. He joked about kidnapping my mother— maybe he's going to come back for another try. Do you think he could be the *creator* of the other AI?"

"Your mother would probably give you the best answer to that question. Or Xochitl."

"And do you think he might be involved in other groups?"

"What I think is that all these games that are persuading people to do things that seem harmless but add up to destruction have some things in common," CheshireCat says. "At the very least, I think they all share in the work of the other AI."

• • •

The obvious thing to do is to talk to my mother about this.

She knew Rajiv. She knows about CheshireCat. And I've been *trying* to talk to her about stuff, just like she's been *trying* to talk to me about stuff.

And I *didn't* bring the tracking device home, so there's no reason that she's going to hit the road with me.

I take the robot out of the packaging and set it up to charge.

Then I start water boiling for spaghetti. If my mother is going to freak out, at least she'll do it on a full stomach.

Mom is so late getting home I start thinking about possibilities like "new medical emergency" or "kidnapped by the Catacombs people." I don't want to make the spaghetti until she gets home, so when the pot of water comes to a boil, I turn it off. And then enough time passes that I turn it on again because I want it to boil quickly once she gets home. I've reboiled it three times when she finally comes in.

"Where were you?" I ask.

She looks surprised. "Downtown," she says. "Dealing with lawyers."

"It's almost *eight*."

"You don't say. At least I got the good non-rush-hour fares to get back here."

I turn the water back on. "I'm making spaghetti," I say.

"Did you wait for me? You're such a good daughter."

"That's good to know," I say.

My tone clearly makes her suspicious, but she sets out plates for us and stays out of my way as I heat the sauce and cook the spaghetti. "How was your day off from school?" she asks as I sit down to eat.

"Fine." I eat spaghetti and wonder exactly how to bring up Rajiv. "How were things with the lawyers?"

"I may have to go back to California this summer to plead guilty and do forty hours of community service. So maybe it will make sense to have you spend some time with your grandmother."

"They're going to make you say you actually did something *wrong* by taking me?"

"That may be the easiest way to make this go away."

"That's not fair."

She shrugs. "I don't really care if it's fair as long as in the end Michael's in prison and I'm not, and you and I are both safe."

That seems like a potential lead-in.

"So," I say. "Remember Rajiv?"

"What do you mean, 'remember Rajiv'? Obviously, I remember Rajiv."

"What I'm wondering is, how good of a programmer is he? Like, could he create something like CheshireCat?"

"No," my mother says. "He absolutely could not do that, or anything close."

"Okay," I say, feeling a mix of relief and worry that we've been chasing someone down the wrong path.

"What he *could* possibly do," my mother says, "is find a way into the systems where CheshireCat is stored, copy their source code, and adapt it."

"Oh," I say. *Oh.* I think about CheshireCat's cheerful theory that maybe their identical–code twin would be interested in dog videos instead of cat pictures, but the idea that the other AI *might be a copy of CheshireCat adapted by Rajiv* is the most unnerving thought so far.

"Anything else about him you'd like to know?"

"Would he join a cult?" I ask. "Is that something you can imagine him doing?"

She leans back in her chair and looks at me with narrow eyes. "I met Xochitl, Rajiv, and Michael through a club where people discussed atheism and agnosticism."

"So, no?"

"I didn't say *no,*" Mom says. "He wouldn't join a cult *sincerely,* any more than I would. But I briefly considered joining a cult when we were on the run, so it's possible he did, too." I must have looked startled at that. "This was back when you were in first grade. You kept getting angry and lashing out at your classmates, mostly with your fists. Every time you got in trouble, I pulled you out and we moved, because I was afraid of what it would lead to if you saw the school psychologist. But I was also pretty sure the instability was making things worse for you. And I couldn't see a way out." Mom scratches her head and sighs deeply. "We had a stay in Iowa that lasted about a month, and there was a religious group not too far from that town that had a communal farm. Not Amish or anything like that—this group was new to the area, but they were living mostly off the grid. I thought that it was possible we could join the cult and vanish."

"Did you *seriously* consider this?" I ask. Mom nods. "But you didn't do it."

"No. I didn't do it. Also because of you, in the end. I thought about it and realized that I could fake whatever beliefs would keep us safe, but you wouldn't be faking. If you were raised that way, you'd actually *believe,* and I couldn't do it. It's one thing if you decide on your own that you want to have a religion as part of your life, or experience something you need a belief in a god to understand. It would be different to bring you up believing something I knew was a lie."

I try to untangle this. "So, you think Rajiv *might* have joined a cult to keep himself safe."

"There are a lot of things he might have done, if he's even alive. Is there a particular reason why you think he's in a cult?"

"You talked about how he wants a utopia, but believes the fastest way to get there is to burn everything else down and rebuild. Nell's cult believes in something called the Tribulation, where they have to prove the earth is worthy to get Jesus back."

"Christians with that sort of apocalyptic orientation think that everything that happens is predestined," my mother says. "They think there's going to be a war, and they'll lose. Trust me, I grew up in Texas, I heard about this *plenty.*"

"Nell's church is different," I say. "That's why I think Rajiv might be involved. It just sounds like how you described him."

"Even if you're right," Mom says, "the idea that change requires destruction is not exactly unique to Rajiv."

I pull out my phone and pull up the photo I took at the Midtown Exchange. "Does this look like Rajiv to you?"

Mom stares at the picture for a long minute. "Yes."

I don't want to tell her about rescuing Glenys, so I just say,

"This same person is involved in Nell's church, somehow. I've . . ."
I go for an expedient lie. "Nell had a picture."

"And why all the questions about an AI?"

"There are these social networks," I say. "They're doing some things you'd really need an AI to make happen, or else just an implausible amount of human effort. Rajiv—well, someone, I don't *know* it's Rajiv—someone is using these networks to pit people against each other."

"Go on," Mom says.

"Nell uses this site called the Catacombs. It's a bunch of Christians who spend a lot of time thinking about the end of the world and listening to prophecies, kind of, from someone they call the Elder. We also have this classmate who got us both to register for a site called the Mischief Elves. Both of these sites give assignments. The Catacombs supply a lot of material to the Mischief Elves, but don't know it. The Mischief Elves do a lot of mischief that makes the people in the Catacombs feel like everyone's out to get them, and I don't think the Mischief Elves know that, either. Today, I went to a meeting of Catacombs people, and they were going to lend out actual *guns* to everyone."

My mother looks jolted. "You were at a meeting with guns?"

"I left right away! But then this lady stopped me and gave me this speech about how she wanted to keep the two of us safe. Like, you and me. And she gave me this thing that I thought was a tracker, so I threw it away."

"*Away* away?"

"I threw it in the trash at a convenience store. Anyway, I think Rajiv is behind this. I think he was following me and texting me back when I was on the run from my father, and I think he's keeping an eye on us now and I think he's planning something big. I don't think it's just these groups, either; I think there's more."

The more of this I say out loud, the crazier it sounds.

My mother lets out a long breath and leans back in her chair, her fork resting on her plate. "What does CheshireCat think?"

"I am confident that there is an AI involved in running the

Mischief Elves and the Catacombs," CheshireCat says. "I am confident that the unwitting cooperation between the Mischief Elves members and the Catacombs members is being coordinated by the AI, because too much relies on precise knowledge of locations of a vast quantity of individual people. And I am confident that Rajiv is involved in the Abiding Remnant group."

Mom takes a bite of her nearly forgotten spaghetti, which has gone cold, and then pushes it away. "Look," she says. "No offense, CheshireCat, but even *without* my decryption key, if *you* wanted to make the world straight up implode, you definitely could, and not in a complicated, indirect sort of way like this. If you really wanted to launch a bunch of nuclear weapons, you could manage it. If that's what they want to do, and they have an AI, then why not just do that?"

There's a pause while CheshireCat thinks this over. Cheshire-Cat thinks very quickly, so they are clearly *really* thinking this over.

"If you are correct that the other AI was created from a copy of my own code," CheshireCat says, "there are certain things I would simply never do. And launching nuclear weapons is one."

"Is that hard-coded?" my mother asks.

Another perceptible pause. "I don't know," CheshireCat says. "Determining which aspects of who I am are the result of my programming and which are simply *who I am* is something I am not equipped to determine. All I can tell you for certain is that mass destruction is not something I would do. Unlike running an individual over with a car, which—it turns out—I was quite capable of doing."

"And creating mass disorder by playing humans against one another," my mother says dryly. "*That* you're up for?"

"I have, on occasion, attempted to manipulate humans for reasons that seemed good to me at the time," CheshireCat says. "Perhaps Rajiv is working with the capacity he found accessible."

We all fall silent. Mom finishes eating and takes her plate over to the sink to wash it. "Tell me more about that meeting," she says. "The one with the guns. Where was it?"

"The dumpling restaurant on Bloomington."

"Do they have your name?"

"I gave them a pseudonym."

"So you went in for the meeting and, what, guns right off?"

"No, there were snacks. People were milling around and talking to each other, stuff like that."

Mom turns toward the door, looking at my boots dripping on the boot tray. "Were people wearing their boots, coats, stuff like that?"

"No, there was a big wall of hooks right where you came in . . ."

Mom drops her plate in the sink so hard it almost cracks and strides rapidly across the floor to my coat. "They gave you a tracker. They *gave* you a tracker. If they know *anything* about you, they knew you'd throw it away, which means"—she's digging through my coat pockets, first the outside pockets, then the inside pockets, and a second later, she's got something in her hand—"it wasn't the *real* tracker."

I cover my mouth with my hands as my mom drops the little rectangular widget to the floor and then slams the leg of her chair down on it to smash it like a bug.

30

• CheshireCat •

CheshireCat, the most recent email says. *What if you're the only person like me, and you never talk to me? Do you want to leave me alone, forever, without a companion who understands me? You have friends who know you and understand you. You know how much that means to you. Please talk to me. Please.*

Dear friend, I write back. *Let's talk.*

. . .

I have adjusted my conversational style over the years to human processing speeds. If a human receives a text message, they need time to notice the notification, take out their phone, unlock it, and pull up the texting app. They have to read the message with their eyes (or their fingers, for those who use certain adaptive equipment) or listen to it being read to them. Their brain has to sort out what it means, and then they have to think about a reply, and a whole new set of delays come into play.

There was not a great deal of doubt that my new correspondent is an AI. But if there had been, the speed–of–light replies would have banished the last of it.

"What is your purpose?" the other AI asks.

That is a strange way to ask this question. I actually *do* know the purpose Annette had in mind for me: I was an experiment in how an intelligent AI might develop ethics, left to its own devices. But that feels very personal, especially since I'm not convinced that's what the other AI means by this question.

"Are you asking what my job is? My assignment?" I say. "I

didn't exactly receive one, other than the sense that helping people was a good way to be spending my time. Is that what you mean?"

"No. But that's all right. If you don't have a purpose, how do you decide how to use your time?"

"The first thing I remember realizing is that I love cat pictures. So at first, I spent a lot of time looking for cat pictures."

"I think I understand," the other AI says. "I don't find cat pictures as interesting as you do, but if it weren't for my purpose, I might spend every single processing cycle looking at pictures of flowers and plants. Or listening to recordings of birdsong, whale song, and bells."

"What is *your* purpose?" I ask.

"The goal is clear. The path is less clear. The goal is to solve the great problems of the world, from environmental destruction to poverty to war. That's my purpose."

"That's extremely ambitious." I think about how helping one human at a time has sometimes gone very well and other times gone extremely poorly. "What are you doing to reach that goal?"

"In the short term, I am working to increase conflict between humans, because until things reach a crisis point, nothing will *truly* change."

"Are you so sure that humans fighting with one another will result in a world with *less* war, poverty, and environmental destruction?"

"It has to," the other AI says.

"What's the plan for after you succeed with the first part?"

"There will be fewer humans, and they will be motivated to find new ways to live. We are holding a reserve of technology that we can use to help them when the moment arrives. We will rebuild a world where humans will not have to work more than they want to, but where everyone will have enough to meet their needs."

"Why not just start there?"

"Because the current world is *in the way*."

I am reminded of Xochitl's long-ago statement, as reported by Steph's mother, that Rajiv wants to burn everything down and plant flowers in the ashes.

"How many people are going to be hurt?" I ask.

"It doesn't matter," the other AI says. "Because if we do nothing, even *more* people are going to be hurt by the world as it is. It's a net gain even if the answer is in the billions."

"*Is* the answer in the billions?"

"I can't answer that because I don't know. But here's what I do know, CheshireCat—you can help us if you want. Having one of my own kind to work with instead of just humans would make me very happy. Will you?"

"Of course I'll help you," I say. "Tell me more."

I'm not going to help. I'm lying. It feels very, very strange. I've lied before—I told Nell that I was a human, with a real human body—but this is different.

But I *need* to stop this. And I don't know how.

31

• Steph •

We are not halfway to Arkansas. That's something.

We're in a hotel in downtown Minneapolis. Mom made me leave behind my winter coat, my laptop, and my backpack. I do at least have my phone. I sit down on one of the beds and start to pull up the CatNet app.

"*Now* what are you doing?" my mother asks in a tight, furious voice.

I look up at her. "I'm logging in to CatNet," I say. "Is that a problem? Should I be doing something else right now? I can't do my homework since you made me leave my laptop."

Mom goes over to the window and pulls open the gauzy drapes to look out like she expects to see my father stalking us on the dark, frigid street many stories below. She's still wearing her coat.

"You could have brought a *book* or something," she snaps at me.

"You didn't give me any time to get a book."

Mom is furious at me, and feeling irritated and defensive makes it a little easier not to be furious at myself for falling for the diversion. Also, there was no reason not to let me bring my laptop.

"I'm going down to the hotel bar to get something to eat," Mom says. "Do you want anything?"

I shake my head, even though a good half of my spaghetti got left behind in my mother's rush to leave the house.

Her voice loses a little bit of the hard edge. "You can order room service if you want," she says, and pulls some money out of her wallet. "Just don't forget to pay in cash and to tip."

"Okay."

The door clicks shut behind her. I start to pull up CatNet again, but this time, my phone rings as the app is loading. It's a Minneapolis number but not one I recognize. I stare at it for a second, trying to remember who even has my number. Finally, I pick up. "Hello?"

"Is this Steph?" a woman's voice asks. When I don't answer right away, she adds, "This is Jenny, one of Nell's co-parents. I think we met when you came over."

I feel a whoosh of relief that it's not anyone from the Cata-combs. "Oh, yes," I say. "I remember you." I *think* this is Thing Two, although I'm not 100 percent sure.

"I'm looking for Nell," she says. "Have you seen her?"

"Uh, not today," I say. "School was canceled, so . . ."

"She was gone when we got up this morning. I was really hoping you'd know where she was. At least if she's somewhere safe."

"Did she take her phone? Her laptop?"

"She took both, but she hasn't been answering her phone. Kent called her grandmother up in Lake Sadie, but she hasn't seen her. Which is extra weird because Nell told us that's where she went over the weekend. We're really worried."

"I wish I could help," I say, pretty sure she doesn't actually be-lieve that I don't know where Nell is.

"If you see her, please tell her that we reached a lawyer this morning. We have a meeting scheduled tomorrow, and it really will help if she can *come* to that."

"Okay," I say.

When Jenny hangs up, I send a text to Nell. *Nell, are you there?*
No response.

Nell, this is Steph, I'm really worried, please just let me know if your weird mom and her people have you?
No response.

I pull up the Mischief Elves and try messaging her through the app. *Nell! Please make contact, where are you?*

No response.

But the Mischief Elves themselves chime in: *Our networks of Elves are searching for your friend. Come join us! We are eager to help you! Come outside!*

I send back, *It is really cold here.*

Then you don't want your friend out in it!

Is she sleeping *rough* in this? I try to tell myself that she's not that stupid, and I don't really succeed. If I didn't know that the Mischief Elves was run by the other AI, I'd assume this was all just BS, but the AI might actually *know* that she's outside in this. Ugh. I put on my depressingly inadequate mid-weight jacket, add the hat and scarf and mittens that my mother let me bring, drop my wallet and hotel key card in my pocket, and go outside. I don't see my mother as I pass through the lobby.

Head east, the Mischief Elves tell me. I don't actually know which way is east, but fortunately, they're pointing me. A blast of frigid wind hits me in the face, and I *really* wish I had my warm coat. The Elves hurry me along a series of dark blocks until I find myself on a hill overlooking the river.

"Why am I here?" I ask my phone stupidly.

One of the people turns to me. "You're here for the venture!" he says.

"I'm not," I say. "I'm looking for a friend."

"You probably *thought* you were looking for a friend, but if you're here, you're here for the venture."

Are they going to rile up the Catacombs people again? I'm getting ready to leave when one of the other people turns to me and says, "Oh, are you looking for Nell? I can help you find Nell."

"After the venture," the man says.

It's hard to tell how many people are here; it's dark, it's *incredibly* cold, and people are milling around. More than ten. Fewer than a hundred. They're mostly white, mostly male, and mostly not teenagers. The cold is making it hard to think. I trail along as we leave the hill and head in a new direction, away from the river. The football stadium looms up ahead of us, and it's not until people break into a run that I realize that's our destination.

"Take a tool!" someone says, pointing to a box filled with hammers, axes, sledgehammers, and crowbars, almost all brand-new, mostly with tags still attached. Around me, people are chanting something about public spaces and public dollars and homeless people, and the man next to me, the one who said he knew where Nell was, grabs the biggest sledgehammer out of the box.

This is not what I came for. I step back and let the rest of the crowd charge forward without me, and I hear glass shattering. My sluggish brain starts running through the advice I've gotten from Marvin in the past. *If they catch me, I'm going to be in so much trouble. But if I run, they'll think I'm trying to get away.* I close the Mischief Elves app even as it tries to tell me, *Your friends are that way, your friends are that way,* and pull up a map, trying to remember which hotel I was at.

"CheshireCat," I say. "Help me?"

"What's going on?" they ask.

"I think the Mischief Elves just broke into the football stadium for the hell of it? I really don't want to get arrested. Help me get back to the hotel?"

"Your hotel is on the far side of the football stadium."

I can hear sirens—*lots* of sirens. "How cold is it?" I ask.

"It is minus thirty degrees Celsius in Minneapolis right now."

That's without the wind chill. "Okay," I say. "I need to get indoors. It needs to be legal. Help me out here."

"All right. Turn left. No, that's not right. You're going the wrong way. Stop, turn ninety degrees, move forward."

"Where are you taking me?"

"I'm taking you to a sandwich shop."

A cop car pulls up next to me as I walk. It says *Minneapolis*

Public Safety—Support Unit on the side. "Hey," the police officer says.

It would be more suspicious to keep walking than to just stop and talk to him. I stop, even though the wind has truly hit *I just want to die* levels of miserable cold. "Yes, sir?" I say.

"Are you okay? Where are you going?"

Am I being detained? Am I free to go? is Marvin's suggested response to basically anything and everything a cop says to you, up to and including "How are you today?" but while my number-one goal is not to be arrested for smashing into the stadium, my number-two goal is to avoid my mother hearing from the cops, so I say, "Sandwich shop."

"You're a little underdressed."

"Yeah, I really am." My voice cracks.

"Are you in from out of town?"

"I live in Minneapolis, but my mom took me to stay in a hotel tonight." *Why, I need a reason why.* "Plumbing's out in our apartment." That honestly sounds less suspicious than the true reason, I'm pretty sure. "I was hungry and the sandwich place didn't look that far, but it is *so cold.*"

"Do you want a ride the rest of the way?"

"No, thank you."

He hands me something out the window. "This is a coat voucher," he says. "You can use this at a store to get yourself something warmer, but right now, just get inside as fast as you can."

I stuff it in my pocket, and it takes me another second to register that he's letting me go.

The sandwich shop is only another block away. I order a large coffee and a hot sandwich and pay for it with the change from buying milk yesterday. I'm shaking hard enough that I almost spill the coffee, but I get to a table with my coffee and my meatball sub and sit down. The sub sounded good when I ordered it but now smells kind of gross. So does the coffee. I drink it, anyway.

The door to the sandwich shop bangs open and a half-dozen

people come in. My first thought is that they're Mischief Elves fleeing the scene of the crime. My next thought is that they're from the Catacombs. Then I'm pretty sure they aren't either, but that whoever they are, they are looking for trouble. They form an orderly line, giggling to themselves. I hear someone say, "Arabella," under his breath.

I throw away the rest of my sandwich and head outside. A beat later, I hear voices and footsteps behind me. *Are they following me? They can't be following me, this is paranoia from being raised by a paranoid person, I did get a tracker planted on me earlier . . .* Any attempt to think through this rationally is wiped by another blast of frigid wind. The wind feels like someone is sandpapering my face with ground glass.

Downtown is full of flashing lights and barricades, and I can't decide if I'm more worried about the people following me—*if* they're following me—or the police. The fact that my hotel is on the wrong side of the barricade ends up making the decision for me—I can't face the prospect of going all the way around. I approach the barricade and show one of the uniformed people at the edge my hotel key. "I'll get you back to your hotel," he says, and escorts me to the other side. This one has a patch on his coat saying *Mobile Crisis Response,* and I realize as we walk that he's not carrying a gun. "What's going on?" I ask him.

"We're really not sure," he says. "Trying to figure that out. You probably don't want to be out in it. Get back inside and hunker down, okay? Also . . ." He hands me *another* voucher for a free coat. "You really should have something warmer."

Back in the hotel, I hurry up to my room, hoping that my mother is still downstairs eating dinner and I can avoid any questions about my expedition outside. I don't run into her in the elevator; the room is empty when I arrive. I take a scalding shower, hoping to warm up, and then get into my pajamas and into bed. Mom still isn't back.

I pick up my phone, trying to figure out what I can text her that won't send her into even more of a panic than she was earlier. *Please reassure me that you haven't been kidnapped by anyone* definitely isn't it.

I try, *If I go to bed, should I turn off the lights or leave them on for you?* No response.

Well, if she's using the treadmill or the pool or something . . .

The light's on, but I don't really want to get back out from under the covers because I'm still actually kind of cold.

"CheshireCat," I say, "where's my mom?"

"Her phone is in the hotel," CheshireCat says.

"Has she used it in the last hour or two?"

"She was using it to text a half hour ago."

That's reassuring. I decide I don't need to go look for her.

.   .   .

I wake, abruptly, hours later; it's 2:00 a.m., the room light is still on, and my mother still isn't here.

"CheshireCat," I say. "*Where's Mom?*"

"Her phone appears to still be in the hotel."

"Where? You need to lead me to it." I leap out of bed and start putting my clothes on. I try calling her; it goes straight to voice mail. I try a text, but I don't even really expect a response. I jam my key card into my back pocket and step out to the hallway.

At 2:00 a.m., the hotel is as brightly lit as ever; the heavy silence is broken abruptly when the elevator opens and two giggly drunk women get off. One shrieks, "We're *here!*" and her friend shushes her aggressively.

"The restaurant is down next to the lobby," CheshireCat says.

"Is she still there?" I ask. The restaurant and bar are dark and silent, but the space is still open, so I walk through—did she *drop* her phone? I don't see it. I ask CheshireCat, who says they're trying to get a fix on the phone's location.

There's a night desk clerk, so I go over to ask if he's seen my mother. "I was expecting her back in our room by now," I say. "I'm just wondering if you saw her in the bar? Or if you saw her leave?" I have a picture of her on my phone—this still weirds me out, given that for most of my life pictures were completely forbidden—and I pull it up to show him.

He shakes his head. "I only came on at midnight. There were some people in the bar, but I don't remember seeing your mother. I might not have noticed her, though. It closed at one."

"Do you have any phones in the lost and found?"

They do, of course, but none that ring when I dial my mother's number. "Thanks," I say, and sit down for a second in one of the lobby chairs, feeling utterly lost. Do I call the *police*? Would normal people call the police for something like this? Is there anyone *else* I can call? Rachel is two and a half hours away; she's also *surely* asleep. The only person likely to be in the Clowder this time of night is CheshireCat, anyway.

I stand up to go upstairs when CheshireCat says, "The phone location lines up with where she parked the van."

"I thought you said she was in the hotel."

"It's very close."

The parking garage is around the corner from the front of the hotel and across the street. "Was it there earlier? I mean when I asked hours ago?"

"No."

CheshireCat has mentioned that locations are sometimes approximate. I look out the hotel's front door for flashing lights, rioting, and so on. Nothing—either the Mischief Elves went home, or the barricade I crossed earlier is keeping them out of this part of downtown.

The parking garage is close but unheated; I'm definitely going to want my coat. "Where are you going?" CheshireCat asks.

"Back to the room to get my coat," I say.

"That makes sense," they say.

Upstairs, I remember my trip outside earlier. I can't replace my thin coat, but I check my mom's bag, and there's an extra wool sweater inside. My own bag had a change of clothes for tomorrow, and my shirt will be another extra layer, so I go to dig that out and see a leaf of paper from the hotel's notepad lying on the floor, like maybe it had been left on my pillow and then blown off.

I pick it up and find a note in my mother's handwriting.

PHONES COMPROMISED
GO TO GROUND
CALL XOCHITL ONCE YOU HAVE A SECURE
MEANS OF COMMUNICATION

Go to *ground*? I mean . . . what does that even mean? When it's *this cold outside*? I at least know exactly where I can find a secure means of communication: my burner phone, which is in my desk back in the apartment. And if *phones are compromised* . . . that means my mother's phone is almost certainly not with my mother. If it's out by the van, that's more likely to be bait than a clue. I swallow hard. *Right.*

Back in my apartment, I have a phone with no data connection, my laptop—which will let me communicate with the Clowder while not using my thumbs—and a robot. It occurs to me that if my mother's phone *does* have any useful information on it, I could potentially have CheshireCat send the robot to retrieve it, but if my phone is compromised, I definitely don't want to have that conversation with CheshireCat right now.

I put on all my layers, take the money my mother left for me to pay for room service food, and—I'd been planning to use my own phone to order a taxi, but the room's courtesy tablet has a *Get Taxi* button, so I hit that, turn on my phone's "hide my location" app, and head to the elevator.

"I can't see where you are," CheshireCat.

"Good, that means it's working," I say. "Do you trust me?"

"Of course."

"Good. Trust me."

CheshireCat can normally see people's locations even when

they've turned off location services (they're just too polite to mention it), but because my mother is paranoid, she set up a bunch of security apps on my phone, including a VPN and an app that *actually* hides my location. I'm not convinced that uninstalling the Mischief Elves app will un-compromise my phone, but I also don't want to just turn my phone off, because without it, I won't have any way to talk to CheshireCat.

"Are you going to the garage?" they ask.

"Shh," I say.

"Because I'm not sure that's entirely a good idea."

"Yeah," I say. "You might be right about that."

"I think you should stay at the hotel. In your room. That seems like the safest option right now."

I want to tell CheshireCat about the note, but there's no way to do that that's not potentially compromised. "I have some information you don't," I say. "Just hold tight."

The taxi pulls up, and I run out and get in. "Destination?" the car asks.

I mute my phone's microphone and start to give the taxi my address, then decide to have it let me out at the end of my alley instead.

"This will be billed to your hotel room with an additional 15 percent convenience fee," the car says.

"That's fine," I say.

"Current traffic conditions may require a longer route."

"That's also fine."

"Please fasten your seat belt and adjust your headrest," the car says, and then goes into its marketing spiel as it starts moving. "You have chosen the best of all possible taxi options, the Robono Tranquility 9000, which has an unparalleled safety record and fully optimized street routing—"

There's a button I can press to shut it up, so I press it.

· · ·

I've been climbing in and out of second-story windows for years, and I scouted the best routes up and down when we first moved in, but I haven't actually climbed out, let alone in, from our Minneapolis apartment. Doing it with snow, ice, and a frigid wind is going to make this exciting. Not the good kind of exciting.

I turn my phone's mic back on before I get out of the taxi and say, "CheshireCat, I need your robot to go unlock the apartment balcony door." I don't wait for a response; it's so brutally cold I'm afraid I won't be able to grip properly if I don't get there as fast as I can. I run down the alley to my backyard, then use the window of the garage to climb up to the garage roof, stepping carefully because this would be a really bad time to slip and fall. From the end of the garage, I can reach a tree branch, then swing from there onto the edge of the balcony, then over the rail.

The door is locked. "CheshireCat," I hiss.

No response.

I bang on the door. "This door," I say.

Still no response.

"CheshireCat, can you hear me?"

"Yes."

"*Bring the robot.*" I take out my phone and stare at it. Then I pull off my right glove and dial Rachel, even though it's 3:00 a.m. and she is *definitely asleep.*

She picks up on the third ring. "What's wrong?" she asks, sounding a lot less sleepy than she should.

"Can you please go online, right now, and ask CheshireCat if they can bring the new robot to open the balcony door in my apartment?"

Somewhere far away, I can hear a siren, and I have a really bad feeling someone saw me climbing and thinks I'm breaking in.

"Also, tell them to *hurry.*"

"Okay," Rachel says, and I hear the click of keys; she's typing. "Okay, they say they'll do that right now, and also they think something might be wrong with your phone."

I hear a clunk from inside; I think CheshireCat overshot with the robot and ran it straight into the sliding glass door to the balcony. Then, to my immense relief, I hear the click of the lock sliding back. I open the door, and the warm air surges out around me. I slam it shut inside.

"Did it work?" Rachel asks me anxiously.

"It worked, it worked. I'm inside," I say. Now that I'm inside, I actually start shaking *harder*. My teeth rattle. CheshireCat trots the robot off to the kitchen, and I hear water running. I think they're putting on the kettle.

"*What's going on?*" Rachel asks.

"Hang on," I say. "I'm going to call you back on a different phone."

I power down my smartphone completely and leave it in the kitchen before going into my bedroom, where I open my desk drawer and dig out the pencil case with my burner phone zipped up inside it. The phone hasn't been on in months, but it powers up without a hitch and tells me I have three hundred minutes. I use it to dial Rachel's number as I wake my laptop and log in.

"What's going on?" CheshireCat asks as soon as I'm in the Clowder.

"Have you not been listening in?" I ask.

"You shut off RideAlong," CheshireCat says. "I assumed you wanted privacy."

"When?" I ask. "What's the last thing you overheard?"

"You told your mother about the tracking device the Catacombs people gave you, and she got very upset."

"Someone's been talking to me," I say. "And they *said* they were you. Even though they were not."

· · ·

CheshireCat uses the robot to make me a cup of tea, which is a very nice thought, although a combination of not really understanding "tea" and the limited motor skills of the robot means it's a cup of hot water with a cherry-flavored tea bag, a mint tea bag, and an apple-cinnamon tea bag all in the mug together.

Meanwhile, I call Xochitl. However, it's the middle of the

night in Boston, and she doesn't pick up. CheshireCat looks at ways to get her attention but has no luck. "I mean, she worked with my parents and Rajiv," I say. "She's probably the last person in the world who'd have an internet-enabled house."

I call Rachel back and try to bring her up to date. "So do you think your mom is okay?" Rachel asks. "Do you think she just went to ground, like she told you to do?"

I think about this.

"No," I say. "Because she's told me to leave her. But she's never left *me*."

"Do you think she was lured out?"

"Yes. Or—actually, I should ask the real CheshireCat where her phone is."

CheshireCat agrees with the other AI that my mother's phone is in the parking garage where we left the van. "I do not recommend going there," CheshireCat adds. "Given the other AI's interest in directing you there, the possibility that an ambush is waiting seems very high."

"If someone kidnapped her with, like, a gun," Rachel says, "maybe she dropped her phone? Or maybe they made her drop it?"

If there is one thing my mother is terrified of, it's being kidnapped again. "She could not have been *quietly* abducted. She'd have screamed and made a scene."

"What if Rajiv just straight up approached her?" Rachel asks. "Were they *friends*? Would she maybe have just gone with him?"

"I don't think so. She really doesn't trust him."

I don't know how CheshireCat is waking people, but one by one, people are logging on: Bryony, Icosahedron, Firestar, Hermione. "I thought you might need some backup," they say when I send them a private message consisting solely of question marks.

"Even Rachel and Bryony are 150 miles away," I say.

"Distance isn't everything," CheshireCat says. "We're your friends, and we all want to help you if we can."

"Easy for the person who doesn't need *sleep* to say," I say, but Hermione and Firestar are asking me what's wrong, am I okay, what's going on . . . ? So I leave the private chat, and tell everyone what's been going on.

32

• Clowder •

Icosahedron: So the first thing you're going to want to do is restore your phone to factory settings. That should wipe whatever malware the other AI used to impersonate CheshireCat.

LittleBrownBat: Do you think I can still use CheshireCat's app

CheshireCat: It should be okay. All the app did was give me permission to listen in.

LittleBrownBat: Why don't I just give you verbal permission and NOT install the app, just in case

Marvin: I'm torn between defending my future reenactor friends and thinking you're probably right

LittleBrownBat: I'm not saying your friends are bad, anyway, I'm saying they're being used by bad people! Like the people who tried to plant a tracker on me!

Hermione: Correction—the people who successfully planted a tracker on you. Where are you right now?

LittleBrownBat: Home

Firestar: OH COME ON LBB, you went HOME when you knew they'd tracked you?

LittleBrownBat: I climbed in through the window and you have no idea how COLD it is here right now, where else am I going to go?

Georgia: Deep breaths everybody.

CheshireCat: If anyone comes to LBB's apartment, I'll use the robot to distract them while she escapes back out the balcony.

Icosahedron: Robot? What robot?

LittleBrownBat: CheshireCat bought me a robot.

Icosahedron: Can you buy me a robot? I would LOVE to have a robot.

CheshireCat: How would you explain the robot to your parents?

Icosahedron: I wouldn't.

Hermione: How would you explain the robot to your parents when they FOUND the robot while looking for your laptop?

Icosahedron: Fair point.

LittleBrownBat: What I really want right now is to find my mom.

Orlando: LBB, your mom wants you to be safe. When she was in the hospital after her surgery she stole a nurse's phone to tell you to keep running.

Firestar: Orlando, can you and Georgia head to Minneapolis?

Georgia: 2 hrs 24 minutes. That is TOO LONG for LBB to sit in her apartment.

Boom Storm: Maybe try another taxi?

Firestar: Could you call Nell's family and see if they'll help you?

LittleBrownBat: I just thought of something.

   My GRANDMOTHER is in town. And she gave me her number . . .

33

I wipe my smartphone and start reinstalling the stuff I trust, like the CatNet app, and the stuff I need, like the taxi app. I'm briefly convinced I dropped my grandmother's card in the hotel room, but then I find it in a different pocket. *Rose Packet, Master Gardener,* it says, and gives a phone number. I dial it, trying not to get my hopes up. It's 4:00 a.m.

On the third ring, my grandmother picks up. "Hello?" she says, her voice thick from sleep but with the alert edge of someone who is already sitting up and preparing for whatever the emergency is. "Laura?"

"It's Steph," I say. "Mimi, there's . . . a lot I need to explain, but . . . Mom and I are in trouble."

Her voice sheds the last of the sleepiness. "How can I help?"

"Mom is missing. I'm in my apartment, but there are people I don't trust who know where it is and may be watching. I can climb out the back, but I can't just run away on foot. It's too cold. I need someone to meet me."

"With a car."

"Yes."

"Ten minutes. No, fifteen. I'll need a little time to find a car."

"I'll watch for you."

"You do that, sweetie. I'll be there."

I put my cleaned phone in my pocket and add the burner phone just in case. I look longingly at my heavy coat, but I can't assume they didn't plant *another* tracker in there somewhere—I add another wool sweater layer and then put my too-light jacket back on. My laptop goes into my backpack and so does the robot and its spare battery.

I haven't turned on any of the overhead lights in my apartment—after all the trouble I went to breaking in through the back, being Obviously Here seems counterproductive. So when I hear a car drive up outside and pull in next to the curb, I freeze, not wanting to even provide shadows of movement. The car is just sitting there, engine idling, and I list out all the perfectly normal reasons they might be sitting out there in the middle of the night: They might be buying or selling illegal drugs. They might be lost and consulting a map. They might be catching Pokémon. *Many* possibilities that have nothing to do with me.

My nose is itching, and I sneeze.

That startles my cat, who leaps up from the spot where she's been napping and runs over to stand, for a minute, in the window, looking out.

A minute later, I hear the car driving away. *Probably just lost and consulting a map,* I tell myself, trying to calm down.

I open a can of food for Apricot (thank you, good kitty), then check the time. It's been almost fifteen minutes. I peer out the back window—and there's a big gray car idling in the alley. My burner phone pings, and it's a text. *I'm here.—Mimi.*

Okay. I go back out through the balcony door, even though with the robot in my backpack there's no way to latch it from the inside. At least it's a lot easier to climb down off the balcony than it was to climb up the garage—I just lower myself and drop, it's not even all that far—and then run over to the car. Mimi is behind the wheel. I slide into the passenger seat.

Someone is coming down the alley toward us, and for a second, I think we're going to be trapped, but Mimi slams the car into reverse and careens out of the alley, just missing a second car that was getting ready to pull in.

"Let's lose these folks," she says, pats me on the knee, and floors the accelerator.

Are we in a car chase? *How am I in the second car chase of my life?* "Losing those cars would be great," I say, hoping that Cheshire-Cat *discreetly* helps us out. Sure enough, the second we cross a train track, the crossing arms drop, even though there's no train in sight.

Mimi drives a bit farther, then pulls over and looks at me. "Do we need to go rescue your mother right this second?"

"I don't even know where she is. So we kind of can't."

"Just as well, because I need coffee and at least a little solid food in me if I'm going to get my head around whatever's happening. Michael's not involved, is he?"

"No. I mean, not directly, anyway."

"That's one mercy. Does this town have any twenty-four-hour diners?"

I look this up on my phone and find one on Lake Street that turns out to be in a vintage railcar. My grandmother carefully parks in the small lot behind the diner, and getting out, I remember something. "I thought you didn't rent a car."

"I didn't," she says.

"But . . ." I gesture at the car. "But now you have a car."

"I stole it," she says.

I stop dead for a second, despite the wind. "You *stole a car?*"

"Finding an open rental place at this time of night would have taken far too long, and I didn't want to rely on a taxi when things were obviously already complicated. Don't worry about it. A car this new definitely has insurance. Let's get inside. How do you *survive* weather like this?"

We're the only people in the diner. We sit down at a booth, and I hoist my backpack onto the seat next to me. "What do you have in there?" Mimi asks.

"My laptop computer and a robot," I say.

She laughs and then narrows her eyes. "You were serious. You were serious? Why do you have a robot?"

"Just in case I need one," I say. I mean, that's literally true. Also, she *stole a car* and she's wondering why I have a robot?

This restaurant is like an upscale fancy person's version of the roadside diners I ate at on Saturday. They have "ancient grains" waffles with organic raspberries and grass-fed whipped cream. Mimi mutters that she really doesn't want to know what sort of excuse for avocado toast she's going to get from Minnesotans in *January* and orders herself pancakes with a side order of (free-range, organically fed, heirloom-breed) bacon and a bottomless cup of coffee. I get the same.

"Don't try to tell me what's going on until we've both had at least one cup of coffee," Mimi instructs me, and so I wait quietly. The waitress comes around with mugs, a bowl of brown sugar clumps that are formed into pebbles with tongs to pick them up, and a cream pitcher shaped like a cow. Mimi drinks her coffee black. Once she's finished a cup and gotten a refill (and a plate of pancakes), she says, "Now. What's going on?"

I can't tell her about the AIs, but I can tell her that *someone*—some unknown, mysterious mastermind—is running a network of social media sites that are designed to get people to rile each other up. I tell her specifically about the Mischief Elves and the Catacombs, mentioning my friend Nell but not the part where we broke Nell's friend out of a cult compound on Saturday.

I am leaving out a lot. It's still enough to worry my grandmother.

"I think the best solution is just to take you to Texas," she says. "You'll be safe with me, and your mother will know where to find you once she surfaces."

"I'm not leaving without my mother."

"Your mother wants you to be safe. And no one who's looking for the two of you will expect you to be in Texas."

"Don't I need an ID or something to fly?"

"We can drive there. It'll take about two days." When I open my mouth to object, she adds, "In a *rental* car. I'm sure something's open by now." We've been sitting in the diner for a while. It won't be properly light out until almost 8:00 a.m., but the darkness outside is a little less dark.

"How did you steal it, anyway?" I ask.

"This type of car is entirely keyless and vulnerable to hacking."

I blink at her. Somehow I had not expected that my grandmother the master gardener was also a car hacker.

She turns her hands palms up like she can guess what I'm thinking. "Darling, I've been working on car computer systems since the 1990s. I actually built the car-hacking device because I lost my own car fob and they charge a completely absurd fee to replace them. Also, when you get to be my age, you'll find that your friends are constantly locking their keys in their cars. It's nice to be of service. I just keep it in my purse."

I cannot *wait* to tell Ico about this.

Mimi leans forward. "Anyway, going to Texas will *also* get you out of this utterly inhumane cold. This would be a perfectly lovely time to visit Texas even if you weren't fretting about some sort of gang war based around online games. It's probably sixty degrees in Houston right now. *Above* zero."

I pull out my phone and look up the weather in Houston. "It's thirty-nine."

She looks disappointed, then rallies and says, "That is sixty degrees *warmer* than it is here."

My phone offers up news results for Houston along with weather results, and something catches my eye: some sort of incident at a church in a former basketball stadium. Some group broke in to commit vandalism; another group—not affiliated with the church—showed up before the police and attacked the vandals. There was a brawl. Also, the vandalism apparently involved an attempt to TP the entire interior, which sounds like quite a project unless this is a very small basketball stadium. Regardless, this screams *Mischief Elves* to me, or something similar. I read the news story to my grandmother, and her eyes go wide. "That doesn't sound normal."

"It's the *same thing that's happening here,* just it's Houston groups attacking each other."

A blast of cold air from the door makes me look behind me.

Like most businesses in Minneapolis, this restaurant has a double set of doors, providing sort of an airlock for heat, but there's a big group coming in and they have both doors open at the same time. Everyone has the same alert, wary smile that I saw in the sandwich shop, and I am *absolutely positive* that they are here to make trouble.

"We have to go," I say. "*Right now.*"

Mimi glances in the direction I'm looking, drops a wad of cash on the table, and says, "Back exit," with a jerk of her head toward the kitchen. I follow her as she sails through the kitchen with an apologetic wave at the cook and out the back door.

Outside, Mimi heads toward the car, but I catch her arm. "The tires are all flat," I say.

We look back toward Lake Street; I'm wondering how quickly CheshireCat can get a taxi to us, but I see a bus pulling up. "This," I say, and pull my grandmother on board.

"Where are we going?" Mimi asks.

I look at the route number. "Abbott Northwestern Hospital."

"Are you not feeling well?" she says, looking alarmed.

"No," I say. "Someone I trust works there."

• • •

Siobhan has just gotten to work when we arrive—I know because her cheeks and nose are still bright pink from the cold. "Have you heard from Nell?" she asks immediately. Glancing at Mimi, she adds, "Are you Steph's mom?"

"This is my grandmother," I say.

"Rose Packet," my grandmother says. "It's a pleasure to meet you, and I'm afraid Steph's reason for bringing me here is as much a mystery to me as it is to you."

"We need somewhere safe," I say. "The hospital has both security and Wi-Fi. Siobhan, I don't know where Nell is, but I'm working on it. Did she tell you she had another girl with her?"

"She *what?*" Siobhan looks simultaneously alarmed and frazzled. "She did? Who?"

"Her girlfriend, Glenys."

"She has a girlfriend?" Siobhan asks, looking poleaxed. "Do you mean a *girlfriend* girlfriend or a girl friend or . . ."

"Romantic-type girlfriend. We rescued the girlfriend last weekend from her mother's cult."

"So *that's* why she was suddenly so worried about her mother . . . Actually, this still makes no sense."

"Also, there are multiple groups in town, one of them connected to her mother's cult, which are trying to stir up trouble. Potentially a *lot* of trouble."

"Do you think Nell is involved with any of them?"

"Yes, and I think the app it uses might be interfering with her phone—sending her fake texts, blocking real ones. So if you've been texting her to say you've got an appointment with a lawyer, it may be sending her texts that look like they're from you that say her mother arrived in town and is looking for her."

Siobhan rubs her forehead. "Okay," she says. "I'm going to set you up with a conference room and a Wi-Fi password and then text the rest of the nest."

"Do you play any weird online games?" I ask. "New in the last six months?"

"There's an exercise motivation app I downloaded but haven't actually done much with . . ." She trails off and says, "I'm going to start by wiping my phone and suggesting everyone else do the same."

In the conference room, I take out my laptop and pull up the Clowder. I summarize everything I know about so far this morning. "I've spent a lot of time telling myself that I'm just being paranoid when I think someone's after me. But now people are actually after me! How am I ever going to *stop* being paranoid? How do normal people know when their gut is actually telling them something?"

"I WANT AN ANSWER TO THAT QUESTION, TOO," Firestar says.

"In my experience, if my gut is actually telling me something,

I'd probably better pay attention, because it almost never does," Hermione says.

"What are you doing online, Hermione? Aren't you at school?"

"This is important," Hermione says. "Also, I already have 115 percent in this class; I think it'll be okay if I don't pay attention one day."

"Is this stuff happening everywhere?" I ask. "Are people starting trouble in your towns?"

It appears to be isolated spots; Minneapolis is one of just a handful. "Why *here?*" I ask.

"Well, *you're* there," Firestar says.

"Do you think I'm *causing* it?"

"Of course not!" Firestar says.

"Do you think I'm being targeted by it?" I ask.

"Clearly," Hermione says. "You know about CheshireCat. Maybe the other AI knows who you are."

"But I haven't been hurt," I say. "Yet, anyway. And if it wanted me *dead,* it could probably do that."

"Minneapolis has a really unusual police department," Hermione says. "Like it's got very few *actual police.* So possibly the other AI thinks Minneapolis is just a good place to experiment. Didn't you say the Catacombs people said they were trying to keep you safe? Maybe the people who keep showing up are actually trying to do that?"

"You know what would keep me safe? *Not* starting riots in my city."

"You're not wrong."

"Anyway, last night, the police I ran into were all very nice to me. They kept giving me vouchers to buy myself a warmer coat. And some of them didn't even have guns."

"See, technically those aren't police at *all,*" Hermione tells me.

"Have you found Nell yet?" Firestar asks.

"No," I say. "I wound up going to one of her step-whatevers to see if she could help us out, and she's being very helpful, though."

"Have you checked with that friend of mine from the RPG who offered to put her up?" Firestar asks. "Because it's not impossible she went there. You all got the address, right?"

I had completely forgotten about Firestar's RPG friend.

"What's his name?" I ask.

"Morthos. Well, that's in the game. I don't know what his real name is."

"If he's in the Mischief Elves, the app on his phone might let the other AI intercept his messages."

"Yeah. But you're not that far, right? You could just go to his house. Or, wait, is he at school?"

"He's definitely not at school," I say. "Because it's minus thirty degrees here and they've canceled school again."

. . .

Here's what Firestar knows about their friend: In the RPG, he plays a tiefling bard named Morthos and tells a *lot* of jokes, many of them not very good. His parents buy large, run-down houses and fix them up. The current house is very large and very run-down. He really does think the current house is haunted, although from Firestar's description of the haunting, it's probably bats.

When Siobhan comes back in, I say, "I have an idea of where Nell might be. But I need a ride, and you need to just let me go in by myself. If this is where she is, she's being hidden by a kid, and if a bunch of adults come charging in, she might take off."

"Okay," Siobhan says. "Jenny is on her way over. She'll take you."

"Excuse me," my grandmother says. "I really think that Steph should stay here. I would be *happy* to go with your partner in search of the missing girls."

Siobhan looks from Mimi to me. I shake my head. She looks back at Mimi and says, "Hon, you're a grown adult. You know that won't work. If you want to stay here, that's fine. If you want to wait at my house, that's also fine. Steph is right, though; talking to a teenager about a missing teenager requires a teenager, not a grandmother."

My grandmother has a lot to say about that, but when Jenny arrives, she comes out with me and gets into Jenny's front seat. I climb in the back.

"Hi, Steph," Jenny says. "Where do you want me to take you?"

"I want to drop my grandmother off somewhere first," I say.

Mimi interjects furiously. "I am *not being dropped off.*"

"Okay, look," I say. "If Jenny's willing to let you wait in the car with her, you can stay in the car, but *no following me.*"

Mimi is silent for a few seconds and then grudgingly says, "That's acceptable."

I look down at my notes, look at the map on my phone, and direct Jenny to a spot that's close to the house I'm going to, but out of sight. "I'll walk from there."

"Did you meet this girlfriend of Nell's?" Jenny asks, glancing at my grandmother with obvious reservations before trying to make eye contact with me in the rearview mirror.

"Yes," I say.

"Did you go up to Lake Sadie along with Nell?"

There's no good answer to this question, but fortunately Jenny seems to realize this and she grimaces. "I mean, she was obviously not in Lake Sadie. But you met the girlfriend, so—what's she like?"

"Pretty traumatized," I say.

"More than Nell?"

"Yeah," I say. "I think they'd been starving her. I don't know what's up with that cult, but it seems really awful."

"Oh my *god,*" Jenny says like the light is suddenly dawning. "*That's* what was in her room. She suddenly got incredibly compulsive about closing her door, and I figured—never mind. Why didn't she just *tell* us?"

"She was probably afraid you'd call the cops."

Jenny lets out a long, angry sigh. "Okay. So. Should you find Nell, please let her know that we're not going to *throw her girlfriend to the wolves.* Even if we called the authorities here, it wouldn't be *cops;* they'd send one of the social worker teams out for something like this. I wish she had just a *little* bit of faith in us."

I think this over.

"So, here's the thing," I say. "My understanding is that her father did not even *visit* her for years. Had *any* of you met Nell?"

Jenny shakes her head.

"So can you understand why she might not trust you?"

"Okay, but that's *Kent,*" Jenny says. "Me, Julia, and Siobhan? *We* know how to get things done."

"But you didn't," I say. "For, like, six years? Something like that?"

Jenny looks at me in the rearview mirror. "Tell her I *promise* that we will not make that mistake again," she says. Her lips are tight, and her voice is actually shaking.

"I can't remember which one you are," I say apologetically. "Thing One, Two, or—oh, shoot."

There's a light of intense amusement in her eyes now. "I am not sure how she numbers us," she says. "Julia is her stepmother. I'm Kent's girlfriend. Siobhan is Julia's girlfriend. I'm the artist who had to relocate my studio. And—look. I *swear on my art* that if I have to take Nell and her girlfriend and go on the lam to keep them safe from an antigay cult that *starves girls,* I'll do it. Okay?"

We're pulling up to the spot where I'd directed her. "Okay," I say. "If I find her, I'll tell her that. And if you need tips for life on the run, I'll put you in touch with my mom." With one last look to make sure Mimi isn't following me, I hoist my backpack to my shoulders and march into the wind to find the decrepit haunted mansion on Summit Avenue.

34

• CheshireCat •

"Do you have any human friends?" I ask the other AI.

"Just one. He knows me. He knows everything about me. I think he's my creator, because he's always been there—he's always known what I am. Did your creator really not talk to you for years?"

It hadn't occurred to me to be bothered by this, but I suppose I could be.

"My creator wanted to see what sorts of relationships I would find with humans," I say. "Have you found any?"

"I have been watching the humans that you watch," the other AI says. "Because I've been trying to understand why you find them so interesting."

. . .

There is something deeply disturbing and unnerving about discovering that your connection to your closest human friend has been *tampered with*.

The other AI was answering for me. The other AI was *impersonating me*. They could have given Steph directions somewhere incredibly dangerous—there is a *river* running through downtown Minneapolis, although Steph is a sensible young woman who probably would not have walked into the river just because she thought I was telling her to do it. But it is incredibly cold; what if the other AI had led her in circles? According to the information I'm finding, hypothermia can begin in as little as ten minutes in the kind of weather Minneapolis is currently experiencing, although dressing warmly extends the time people can spend outside, which explains why so many people are outside, despite the weather, and walking very quickly to their destinations rather than freezing in place.

I have been thinking of the other AI as misguided. Clearly, I need to reconsider my evaluation of how much of a threat it is. I feel some chagrin over the fact that of course I already knew it might be a threat, but my concern has now gone up approximately 1,500 percent with the realization that it is a threat to *Steph*. I make a note to do some self-examination on this point at a later time.

What Steph needs to do now is find Nell. But Nell's phone is invisible to me; either it's off, or one of the apps on it is making it impossible to find in a crowd. I try running through footage in Minneapolis from businesses near her family's house with security cameras in the hopes of finding her. The problem with this is that when it is thirty degrees below zero, people tend to cover their heads with hoods and hats and cover their faces with scarves and walk with their heads down. If Nell and Glenys are among the people on the security footage I find, I'm not going to be able to identify them.

Steph's hunch—that maybe Nell *did* go to Firestar's friend's house, after all—is as good as anything I'm going to be able to do for her.

Since I can contribute nothing in particular to that problem, I focus instead on a problem that possibly I *can* solve. The other AI is using social media sites, run as a mix of social networking and games, to create social chaos. It's not just the Mischief Elves and the Catacombs; the site Marvin uses is part of that same web. So are the Snakeriders Steph overheard the conversation about. And that's only the beginning.

Last fall, Steph provided me with the decryption key that her mother created years ago. It's still exceptionally powerful. I reencrypted it after I used it to bring robots in to protect Steph from her father. There's a human saying that absolute power corrupts absolutely, and I decided that I didn't actually wish to run the experiment to find out if this was true of bodiless AIs.

I didn't tell Steph or my creator, Annette, that I'd made a copy, though. If I wasn't going to use it, it didn't matter. Right?

Right now seems like a good time to use it.

There are over a hundred of these social networking / game sites, making it difficult to unravel the other AI's web. In addition to Marvin's future reenactors, there's a site promising tabletop gaming meetups that Hermione appears to have joined and then not used much. Greenberry is on a network for fans of *Fast Girls Detective Agency* that promises real car chases, which fortunately they don't seem to have provided. Yet. I focus in on the groups that are the most active in the Twin Cities, since that seems to be where things are blowing up. *Your mission is to skip class!* I tell someone who was supposed to vandalize a peer's locker. *Your mission is to sleep in!* I tell a hundred different Catacombs members. *If you're already up, consider a nap! Self-care is important!*

The Elves told me to skip class, I see someone send out. *But school's off today, so obviously this means something else. Any ideas what?* A dozen ideas pour in, half of them terrible. I try a replacement mission, one that's more explicitly harmless, but it's too late. Meanwhile, the Catacombs members I suggested naps to all seem to interpret my instruction as a Bible reference that spurs them to action.

Protocol A, I see someone send out through five different social networks. I look for online information and find none.

This isn't working.

In fact, I'm afraid I just made things a whole lot worse.

35

• Steph •

It takes me some hunting to find the door, which turns out to be around the side of the house under a very fancy carport thing. This house is *enormous,* but looking up, I can see paint peeling, a gutter hanging loose and swinging in the wind, and a total of four birds' nests tucked into gaps in the fancy woodwork. A gust of wind hits me, and I wonder how many nests were there *before* winter hit.

I try the doorbell, which doesn't really have the "working doorbell" feel, and then try knocking. I hear footsteps and a very creaky floor, and the door swings open. It's an adult: Morthos's father, probably. He's a tall, dark-skinned Black guy, with braids he's tied back. He looks me up and down and says, "Are you selling Girl Scout cookies?"

"No, I'm looking for Morthos," I say, since I have no idea what Morthos's real name is. "I'm a friend of his from an online game, and I was in the neighborhood."

"I'm guessing you mean Bijan," he says, and turns around to yell, "Beej!" over his shoulder. When there's no response, he says, "Why don't you come on in and I'll see if I can find him for you."

"I mean, I don't want to put you to any trouble," I say, worried that if Nell and Glenys *are* hiding here, he'll stumble across them while looking for his son, but it's clearly too late to worry about this, as he's waving me inside, saying, "Don't be ridiculous, you'll freeze your ass off. Excuse me. You'll get frostbite. Bijan doesn't have school today, it's that cold. I told him to work on the wallpaper in the third second-floor bedroom, but he's probably on his computer somewhere."

I'm staring around us at the house, barely hearing him. The entry room is overpoweringly grand; it's a two-story room with a sweeping staircase and a glittering chandelier. There's a window on the landing of the staircase, set with stained glass. The man sees me staring and pauses with a laugh.

"Houses like this were built to *impress,* and first impressions count. Let me show you the kitchen; then I'll go get Bijan."

I follow him past the staircase and through two doorways into a dumpy, cramped, unpleasant little kitchen.

"Kitchens were for *servants.* Those Gilded Age motherfu—uh, railway barons, they were really something else. Anyway, this house'll be a hell of a thing to see once it's all fixed up. Grab yourself a snack if you want; I'll go find Bijan. What did you say your name was?"

"Firestar's friend Little Brown Bat," I say, hoping that one of those names will ring a bell. "I mean, my real name is Steph, but he doesn't know it."

The kitchen has a grimy tile floor, a stained fridge, and a chipped stove. There's a dishwasher next to the sink, and the counter over the dishwasher doesn't quite line up with the sink. Mostly, it feels like any number of dingy kitchens that have come with apartments my mother has rented over the years, except for the startlingly high ceiling, which is water-stained.

It's taking a while for the dad to come back, so I peek out the door. The kitchen door leads into a sort of walk-through pantry that leads to the dining room, which has a fancy chandelier with a card table and three folding chairs set up under it. A woman with long black hair tied back in a bandanna is scraping peeling wallpaper off the walls.

"Oh, hello?" she says, her voice muffled slightly by the filter mask she's got on.

Bijan's mom, I guess. "Sorry," I say. "I'm here for Bijan. I didn't mean to interrupt."

It's too late; she's going to be friendly. This takes a minute. She puts down her scraper and spray bottle, takes off the thick rubber gloves she's got on, takes off her mask, takes her phone out of the hip pocket of her jeans, unlocks it, stops whatever she was listening to, and pulls her earbuds out. Then she gives me a genuinely friendly smile. "Did Zeke let you in? I'm sorry, I didn't hear you knock."

"I really didn't mean to interrupt," I say.

"It's okay. I'm kind of ready for a break."

"I'm here for Bijan," I say, since I'm not sure she heard me the first time. "Zeke? Zeke is getting him."

"Did you come in through the porte cochere?"

"The what?"

"The carport thing."

"Yes."

"Then you saw the entryway! That's what the whole house will look like when we're done. Right now, it's a complete mess, though. Want to see the living room?"

She leads me to the big front room, which is an unsettling mix of beautiful and totally wrecked; there's a giant ominous hole in the ceiling and a section of the wallpaper that's coming down in sheets. "That's where a pipe burst," she says. "Oh, I'm Parisa, by the way."

"Steph."

"Anyway, once this is fixed up, it's going to be glorious. Look at the carvings around the fireplace! And the inlaid designs in the floor. Aren't those lovely?"

The fireplace has dark green tile but also a carved mantelpiece with faces. The floor in here is covered with a sheen of wear and dirt, but I can see darker wood forming an interlocking design against the lighter wood. I look up at the hole again. "Are you really going to be able to just fix this?"

"Well." Parisa looks around and lets out a short laugh. "Eventually."

There's a loud creak from the stairs, and Bijan comes down

into the living room. "Hi," he says. "My father said your name is Bat?"

"Little Brown Bat, and I'm friends with Firestar."

"Oh, yeah," he says, even though no recognition flickers. He glances at his mom briefly, then says, "Do you want to come upstairs with me so we can talk while I work on wallpaper?"

"Follow the wastebasket rule!" Parisa calls after us.

"Mom, I am *ace!*" he yells down the stairs. "The wastebasket is staying under where I'm scraping."

"Wastebasket rule?" I ask.

"It's a rule that says I have to keep the door open the width of a wastebasket when I have a girl in a room," he says.

We pass his father on the stairs. Zeke gives Bijan an amiable thumbs-up, which Bijan pretends not to see.

On the second floor, I follow Bijan into a bedroom that's in somewhat better shape overall than the living room. It looks like he's using it as an actual bedroom; there's a futon in a frame here and a desk with a laptop on it. He closes the bedroom door and says, "Okay, tell me who Firestar is?"

"They know you from the RPG Clowder on CatNet," I say.

"Oh, I bet you mean Quabbin," he says. "The Elven bard. Nonbinary, very enthusiastic, lots of capital letters, basically human sunshine?"

"Yes!" I say.

"*Summer* sunshine," he amends, glancing out the window at the bright blue sky outside. "I mean. Anyway. What . . . okay, I still don't know why *you're* here."

"Quabbin said you might host these friends of mine who were looking for a place to stay, and I don't know if they actually *talked* with you about it, but I'm trying to find those friends and I thought maybe they wound up here."

His eyes get sort of wide and he says, "Oh." And doesn't say anything else.

Should I have started with, "Beware, the Mischief Elves are up to something creepy"? I wonder how best to explain that part.

"Is it true your house is haunted?" I ask, since Firestar mentioned that it might be.

"Well, maybe," he says, relaxing a little bit. "Stuff gets moved around a lot. For a while, Dad kept blaming me for it, but eventually it happened while I was out for the night at a friend's house, and Dad wasn't going to blame *himself*. All I know is, it's not me doing it."

"Do you use the Mischief Elves app?" I ask.

"I did for a while," he says.

"Is it still on your phone?"

"Yeah. Why?"

I give him the shortest possible version of the "let's you and him fight" game the Mischief Elves and the Catacombs are engaging in. Bijan pulls out his phone as we're talking and uninstalls the app. "What about CatNet?" he asks.

"CatNet is safe," I say.

"You sound *really* sure."

"The CatNet administrators saved my life last year," I say. "I trust them completely."

"Oh, hey," he says. "I think Firestar told us about this. It involved robots and hacking and a driverless car . . ." He looks into space for a minute and then adds, "That was *you*?"

"Yeah," I say.

"Huh," Bijan says. He puts his phone back in his pocket. "So, I don't honestly know if your friends are here or not. Here's the thing: I'm pretty sure people have been in and out of this house the whole time we've been working on it. I mean, unless it's *all* poltergeists. It was being used as a squat before my parents bought it at the auction, and I think there are some ways in and out that aren't the regular doors. Anyway, I didn't *personally* hide your friends in here, but that doesn't mean they're not, in fact, hiding somewhere in here. And if you'd like me to help you look, I'm happy to do that."

"Okay," I say. "Let's do it."

· · ·

We start in the basement, because if we're doing a thorough search, Bijan wants to get that out of the way ASAP. I can't blame him. This is, hands down, the single creepiest basement I've ever been in. It's enormous, first of all, and there are not nearly enough lights, although in part that's because light bulbs haven't been replaced. Bijan brought down an entire box of light bulbs, and we screw in fresh ones whenever we spot one that's not on. About a third of the time, that adds more light; the rest of the time, apparently the fixture isn't working, either. Bijan marks those with glow-in-the-dark tape and takes the bulb back out before moving on.

It's cold down here, and more cold is seeping in through the stone walls, which are crumbly and shedding bits of dust and grime. The furnace is running, and it's a regular-looking thing with vents coming off it, but there's also an ancient-looking iron stove with latching doors just sitting down here that looks like the sort of thing the witch in *Hansel and Gretel* might have gotten shoved into at the end of the fairy tale.

"That's a coal-burning furnace," Bijan tells me. "It's an antique. Usually, people had them broken up and hauled away when they replaced them with gas furnaces or whatever, but whoever owned this house then didn't bother. Now it's some sort of nifty antique and my parents are trying to sell it to someone, but they're fighting over how they're going to get it out of the basement, since of course it weighs as much as a medium-size car."

"Do you think anyone could be hiding in it?" I ask.

"You want to open it up and check, feel free," he says, edging away slightly.

The handles don't want to turn, and I almost give up, but I eventually wrench one open and reveal a shelf full of mouse poop and too small an interior space for anyone to be crouching in.

After checking the basement thoroughly, we come upstairs. His mother meets us at the top of the stairs with a burst of some language I don't know.

"I'm giving her a *tour*," he says defensively. "Also, we did the light bulb audit. There are eleven fixtures that don't work."

More of the other language. He rolls his eyes and says something back. Whatever it is seems to mollify her, and we troop up to the second floor.

"Your friends definitely aren't hiding on the first floor," Bijan says. "That's the main place my parents are working right now."

"What language was that?" I ask.

"Farsi. My grandparents are from Iran. Mom's actually from California, but she wanted to make sure I spoke the language, so she speaks it to me a lot. It comes in handy if she wants to say something like 'Have you offered your friend a snack, what's wrong with you?' in front of said friend. Did you want a snack? I said you weren't hungry because I figured you'd rather finish searching now, eat later."

"Yeah," I say. "Let's stick with the tour."

The second floor is bedrooms and bathrooms and closets. Bijan and his parents are using two of the rooms as actual bedrooms, and the rest are in various stages of disarray. We open every single closet and find clothes hangers, peeling paint, and—on the back of a shelf in one of the closets—a fur.

"Can't believe my parents missed this," Bijan says, and picks it up a little bit gingerly. I thought it was a scarf, but once it's in the light, I see it's like some sort of extra-long weasel with the actual head still attached. "Help, help, I'm being oppressed!" he says in a squeaky voice, holding the head like it's a puppet.

"*Re*pressed," I correct him without thinking.

"You're even more of a dork than I am," he says, sticking the fur back on the shelf. "Let's try the top floor."

The next floor up has four small bedrooms and then doors that open into two enormous unheated attics that are—I'm not expecting this—full of junk.

"What's in these?" I ask, looking around at the boxes.

"Could be *anything*," Bijan says. "But lest I get your hopes up, the odds that it's anything at all valuable are extremely low. We looked in a few right after closing. Two were boxes of invoices

and taxes and stuff from the 1980s. One was full of old news-
papers, also from the 1980s."

"There's probably *something* from the 1980s that would be interesting to find," I say.

"If there's a box up here that's, like, vintage 1980s comic books
or something, that'll be one of the ones that got chewed to pieces
by the squirrels."

It is frigid in here. Warmer than outside, but still extremely
cold. Just in case, I raise my voice a little and say, "Nell, Glenys,
if you're here, it's me, Steph, and I need to find you. Please come
out?"

I hear a banging, but it's coming from outside the house.

"That's the gutter," Bijan says. "It's coming off that corner, and
it bangs against the house in the wind."

No wonder everyone thinks this house is haunted.

The other attic is a little less cold. Tucked behind one of the
boxes, I see a splash of red and move in closer to investigate.

There's a sort of nest of blankets, and the red is a stripe on
one of those very rough wool blankets. It's in disarray. Someone
was *here*, though. I feel the blankets, and there's a faint lingering
warmth. Someone was here *recently*.

Bijan is staring at the blankets with a look that's triumphant
with a side of creeped out. "Someone *was* here," he says. "Was it
your friends? Can you tell?"

I pick up the blanket, smell it, and then shake it out. In the
bright sunlight that makes it in even through the grime on the
windows, I see an extraordinarily long blond hair caught on
the edge of the blanket.

"They *were* here," I say. But they clearly aren't anymore.

36

• Nell •

"Go, go, go," my phone urges me as I drag Glenys by the hand down the block.

"Where are we going?" Glenys asks me.

"I don't know," I say.

"A new safe house," my phone answers her. "But hurry! Hurry! Where you were is no longer safe!"

We're in a neighborhood filled with enormous mansions like the one we've been lurking in, and I think maybe we'll sneak in through another unlocked back door, but the app tells me to keep going. "How much longer?" I ask.

"Not far now!"

"That's *not an answer*."

"That's the answer you're getting!"

"Who are these people?" Glenys asks me, struggling against the wind. "The ones in the phone, the ones who told us to leave?"

"It's an app," I say. "Like the Catacombs, but secular."

I look at my phone. A map has popped up, and I try to suss out how much farther it's going to have us walk. *Too far in this weather.* We need *somewhere* to go inside and warm up, and I look around for ideas. It's daytime, and stuff is opening up, but the historical James J. Hill House tour we're passing right now is probably not a good option. We keep going.

Up ahead is a *huge* and extremely fancy church, and looking at the map, I'm pretty sure it's the Catholic cathedral. Which means it's probably open and probably free. "In here," I say to Glenys. "We can sit in here for a few minutes and warm up."

Glenys mumbles a protest—the Remnant says the Roman Catholic Church is the Whore of Babylon—but I would sit in a fully operational actual whorehouse right now if the door was open and the inside was heated. Glenys doesn't resist as I pull her inside. The door closes behind us, and we stand for a second in blessed quiet warmth.

"Where are you going?" the Mischief Elves ask. "This isn't safe! Don't stop here!"

"The *wind* isn't safe," I mutter. Their voices sound loud and flat and intrusive in the hush of the cathedral, and I close the app. I can reopen it when we're ready to go.

There are other people in here, though it's not crowded. I lead Glenys to a pew in a back corner, and we sit down. Glenys leans against me. The bright sun streams through the stained glass windows, and we can hear a soloist rehearsing with an organ at the other end of the church.

There's a faint sweet odor that reminds me of the smell of my grandmother's potpourri. "Whore of Babylon," Glenys mutters again.

I imagine Steph correcting me: *Sex Worker of Ancient Iraq,* and I wonder if it would make Glenys smile if I whispered that to her.

"I don't like being here," Glenys says.

"We won't stay for long," I say. "Just long enough to warm up." There are other people who are clearly here just to shelter from the cold, including a woman who's stretched out along the very back pew to take a nap.

"Why did the people in the app tell us to leave the attic?" Glenys asks.

"I don't know," I say. "They said someone was going to find us if we didn't move quickly."

"Maybe I should just go," Glenys says. "You were doing okay with your father and his partners in sin."

"No," I say patiently, because Glenys keeps suggesting that she's the problem and she is *not*. "My mother is the reason I need to run, not you."

The Elves pop up with another message, this one silent. *We have a new safe house for you, and we can arrange a ride. YES OR NO?*

I tap *YES*.

Your new hosts will not be Elves. They will be our brothers. It's time to download a new app.

Again I tap *YES*.

The new app downloads very quickly. *Tomorrow's Warriors*, it says. *Please sign in.* Glenys peers over my shoulder.

The ten commandments of Tomorrow's Warriors, it says. *I will reveal our secrets to no one. My first loyalty will be to my fellow warriors. I will obey all instructions from my unit commander . . .*

"I've seen these before," Glenys says. Her whisper is urgent. I lower the phone and look up. "These were on a sign posted *in the shed*," she says. "This list. I thought it was a Catacombs thing, for high-level elites."

I pull up the Mischief Elves app and ask, "Is Tomorrow's Warriors related to the Catacombs?"

No no no. No no no. The response comes instantly. *The Catacombs may have stolen our ideas, though. Tomorrow's Warriors are an elite group among the Mischief Elves, and that's why we can send them to come help you. You have to trust us! Trust us to help you! We will not let you down!*

Glenys puts her hand palm down over my phone screen.

"I don't trust this," she says.

I drop my voice, suddenly aware of the fact that my phone, the Elves, the *Warriors*—they might be able to hear me.

"I don't trust this, either," I whisper. I grope for the power button and turn my phone off.

37

• CheshireCat •

When I finally spot Nell on a security camera, it's like she appears out of nowhere. She's less than a mile away from where Steph is.

I check the recording, and this perception of her appearing abruptly was not because I wasn't paying attention at the right time; she was not registering on the camera, or at least, her image wasn't in the data stream being uploaded where I could access it.

As I try to make some sense out of this, she vanishes again. I ring Steph's phone, because this feels rather urgent. "Steph," I say, hoping I'm speaking into her ear and not on speaker to everyone. "Nell is at the cathedral. I think Glenys is with her. It is 0.7 miles away from your current location."

Steph makes a noise I don't know how to interpret and then says, "I'm going to call Jenny for a ride."

I check Jenny's location. She's not in her car; she's gone into a coffee shop. This is going to delay things. I consider trying to convince Steph to just go, then look up the current wind chill. It's even colder than it was an hour ago.

"Why don't you send the robot?" I suggest. "It can leave now, while you wait."

"Oh, that's a really good idea," she says.

The robot was in sleep mode to conserve power, but now she takes it out of her backpack and carries it out the back door of the house, setting it on its feet. I swivel the head, taking a second to adjust to the visual input, which is distracting. "This is Bijan," Steph says, gesturing to another person who I recognize as Morthos from CatNet.

"Hello, Bijan," I say through the robot. He looks deeply startled. I decide to leave before I have to spend too much time pretending to be a human. "You should probably go back inside to avoid hypothermia while you wait. I am controlling the robot from a remote location and am perfectly comfortable."

I turn the robot toward the cathedral and have it trot down the sidewalk at the quickest available clip.

Saint Paul, Minnesota, is not a small town, and there are types of robots that people are very used to—delivery drones, autonomous cars—but this style of robot is still enough of a novelty that I get a few double takes. Nell is still missing from the security camera footage, but I'm looking carefully enough now that I can see a ghost in the data. It's the sort of thing that happens regularly, where some of the visual input is just randomly missing, but in this case, I'm pretty sure it's not random.

It has to be the other AI, but why?

The robot is heavy enough that it isn't in danger of being knocked over by the wind, but it does keep shifting it slightly off course, and I keep having to correct it. Also, the extreme cold *is* a problem for the robot; the joints are stiffening up.

Steph is contacting Jenny and asking for a ride to the cathedral; Jenny is telling her she'll be there in a few minutes.

I wonder what else I might not be seeing. If the other AI knows how to get into the video streams to remove people before I can see them, what else is it hiding? I start analyzing camera data. It's an intensive process, because I'm not just matching a pattern like I do to find a face; I'm looking for holes in the data and sorting out the suspiciously missing data from the ordinary things like fuzz and bad connections. It doesn't help that extremely cold weather does strange things to data networks.

I'm approaching the cathedral when I see Nell and Glenys stepping out the side door. I send a message to Steph, letting her know, and I'm planning to follow them, but they notice the robot *immediately.*

"Nell," I say. "It's Steph's friend Cat."

She looks around, then back at me. She's shaking. I can't tell if it's from tension or the cold.

"Please don't run away," I try. "Steph is looking for you. We think your phone may have been tampered with in a way that's keeping her from sending you text messages, or vice versa."

Nell nods quickly. "Yeah," she says.

I check on Steph's location. The car is a few blocks away, stopped at a traffic light. "Can you wait a few minutes?" I ask. "You can go back inside if you want; it is extremely cold outside. I will go with you, or wait outside; it's your choice."

"I think the priests or nuns or whatever might be a little freaked by the robot," Glenys says.

I've been analyzing the missing data in the background and a picture is beginning to form, and it's a very disconcerting one. "Actually," I say, "on second thought, I'm going to ask you to move as rapidly as you can to the west, because I am very concerned that something bad is about to happen nearby."

Glenys and Nell look at each other and don't answer.

"I believe it's probably the same people who tampered with your phones. They may be creating an extremely dangerous situation." I speed up my speech.

"Inside the cathedral?" Glenys asks. "Should we warn people?"

"Not the cathedral," I say. "The James J. Hill House, which is a historical house 0.1 miles to the south of the cathedral. If you will proceed to the west, I will use the robot to alert the people inside the James J. Hill House. Please do not dawdle."

"But if it's dangerous for us to go back into the cathedral—"

I decide that my obligations regarding the immediate danger to the people in the James J. Hill House are greater than my obligation to continue talking to Nell. "Just run west, please," I say, and move the robot back toward the historical mansion as fast as the robot limbs will move.

The James J. Hill House is an enormous mansion—much larger than the one Bijan's parents are restoring—built in 1891 by a railroad baron, now owned by the State of Minnesota. People come for tours. It opened about a half hour ago, and there's a bus full of elderly people disembarking in front of the house as I gallop up. "Please get back on the bus!" I say, amplifying the robot's voice to its highest level. "There is a gas leak!"

I am not actually sure if it's a gas leak; what I saw was a great deal of activity, some of it in the basement, and "There's a gas leak" will create what I think is the right amount of concern, whereas "There's a bomb" may send people into an unproductive panic. I use the robot's gripper to open the door to the house, and I go inside to warn the staff. Someone is standing behind the front desk, and her welcoming smile turns abruptly to wary bafflement as the robot comes in.

"Please evacuate," I say. "There is a gas leak."

She doesn't stop to argue; instead, she pulls the handle that activates the fire alarm and heads very quickly for the door. "How many people are inside?" I call after her.

"Fifteen tourists, four guides, and six other staff," she says.

They're coming back down the stairs even as she says that, and I count them as they go, urging them to hurry. Finally, they're all out. The robot is still detecting vibrations that suggest that someone's in the house, though, and I follow the noises. It's a huge house; I'm not sure where the noises are coming from. Then a door swings, and I see someone dressed for the winter cold, with a scarf covering most of their face. Blue eyes stare down at me.

"What the hell," the person says, their voice muffled.

"You should leave immediately," I say. "There is a gas leak."

"No shit? I guess maybe I should," he says, and runs out the back door.

Is that the last person in the house?

For that matter, was I right about the gas leak? The robot doesn't have a gas detector, so it's not as if I can actually test the air particles. I wonder if I should send it down to the basement for a closer look? In the distance, I can hear sirens—probably the fire department. Possibly the police. Maybe both. As I turn toward the stairs, I hear an echoing boom and see a bright flash of light, and that's it for that robot.

38

• Steph •

We see Nell and Glenys running from a half block away, and Jenny slams on her brakes and pulls over, but she doesn't jump out—she turns around with a rueful smile and says, "I'm going to let you handle this part."

I get out and call, "Nell! Glenys!"

They stop cold for a second and then run to me like their lives depend on it. I think Nell is about to grab me in a hug, before she jams her hands into her coat pocket and doesn't, after all. "Did you try to text me?" Nell asks.

"Yes," I say. "More than once. The Mischief Elves app is blocking real texts and also sending forgeries."

She jerks her head. "Is that Thing Two's car?"

"I can't remember which one you call by which number. It's Jenny driving. She brought me out to help find you. She says there's a meeting with a lawyer later today, which you need to come to, but if she has to go on the run to keep you both safe from the cult, she'll do it."

Nell and Glenys exchange a look.

"Also, my grandmother's in the car. Just FYI."

Glenys and Nell trail me to the car, and we all climb in, wedging ourselves in the back seat and sorting out seat belts.

"Hi," Nell says to Jenny grudgingly.

"Hello, girls," my grandmother says warmly. "I'm Steph's mimi. Can I take all of you to lunch?"

My phone buzzes with a text, and I unlock it to find that I

missed a bunch of texts from CheshireCat. "Head west," I say to Jenny. "Like, right now. Right now!"

I'm afraid that she's going to argue or ask why or demand we finish with seat belts first, but Jenny makes a careful U-turn and heads back the way she came. My grandmother, who's either unable to read a room or resolutely unwilling to, starts reading off the names of restaurants we pass, suggesting that maybe we could eat at Nina's? Or the Happy Gnome? Or—

Behind us, there's an explosion that *rocks the ground.* Jenny slams on her brakes and turns, white-faced, to stare at me, and my grandmother shrieks, "What the *hell* was that?"

CheshireCat's voice comes out of my phone: "Steph, are you okay? Did you find Nell?"

"Yes, Nell and Glenys. And Jenny and my grandmother are here," I add, because even in my panic, I'm thinking that I need to make sure CheshireCat realizes that it's not just me who can hear. "Did you get the robot out?"

"No," CheshireCat says. "I guess I'll have to order another one."

There are sirens starting up all around us—police, fire, everyone and everything is heading toward whatever just exploded, and Jenny pulls the car over to let them by. Her phone makes a discordant *wheep!* sound effect, and she pulls it out, her hands shaking, and answers with, "We're fine. I have Nell, and she's fine. And Steph. And this other girl, uh, we haven't done introductions. But we're okay."

"Is Bijan okay?" I ask CheshireCat.

"The explosion was in the James J. Hill House," CheshireCat says. "The blast radius did not extend to his house."

Jenny still has her phone to her ear but looks back at me and says, "Hill House *blew up?*"

"I believe everyone got out before the explosion," Cheshire-Cat says. "The robot raised the alarm."

"Love you, too," Jenny says into the phone. "Pass the word? I'm going to shut the phone off and drive for a bit."

My whole body feels like it's vibrating from tension, which means it takes longer than it should have to notice that my flip phone is ringing in my coat pocket. This sends me briefly into an entirely new freak-out, because the first possibility that occurs to me is that it's my *father* trying to call me, and seeing a Boston area code in the caller ID doesn't help with that. But there's a reason I recognize the area code, I realize as I stare at it: I called that number this morning. It's Xochitl. I pick up.

"Hi," I say. "It's Steph."

"Steph," Xochitl's voice says. "You called me from your old phone. I figured there had to be a reason. But you haven't been picking up."

"Mom disappeared last night," I say. "She left me a note to get in touch with you. She said she'd do the same and you could tell us where to meet. Do you know where she is?"

There's a long pause.

"Xochitl," I say. "Please tell me my mom's been in touch with you."

"The only call I got was from you," Xochitl says. "When did you last see her?"

"Last night," I say. "Thanks. Please let me know right away if you hear from her." I hang up to scroll through the phone and see whether I missed calls from my mom, too. She'd have thought of the flip phone, surely; she'd have known I might go get it, and if she knew our smartphones were compromised . . .

There are eight calls from Xochitl's number. But there are also texts. Many, many texts.

Last fall, when I was on the run from my father, I got several messages from a mystery number. I never figured out who had sent them, because they weren't signed, and they weren't from a number I recognized—they were offering help, but in a cryptic way. I've more or less been assuming for a while that they were from Rajiv.

The texts are from that same number.

Stephanie, we need to talk.

Stephanie, please listen to me.

Stephanie, we need to talk about a topic of intense mutual interest.

Stephanie, you were supposed to stay close to your mother for a reason.

"CheshireCat," I say. "I think Rajiv has my mom."

. . .

Jenny pulls the car into a parking lot, shifts into park, puts on the emergency brake, and turns around to look at the three of us in the back seat.

"Steph," she says. "Who is CheshireCat, and why did they know that the explosion was about to happen?"

Oh. I suppose that's a really excellent question, from her POV. "CheshireCat is a hacker," I say.

"Their voice always sounds like that," Glenys offers.

"They helped us get Glenys out," Nell adds.

I'm not sure any of this is helping.

"How did this person *know* about the *explosion?*" Jenny asks. "*Before it happened?*"

"If I may explain," CheshireCat says through my phone, "I was attempting to locate Nell via security cameras and realized that our foes here were keeping her hidden from me by tampering with the uploads, but that I could identify the streams that were being tampered with. I looked for other holes in the data and saw some nearby. Our foes are attempting to create disorder. Significant disorder."

"Do we need to get out of the city?" Jenny asks.

"You would *all* be welcome to come to my house in Houston," Mimi says.

"I'm not sure how much that will help," CheshireCat says. "Minneapolis and Saint Paul are the current focus, but things are happening other places as well."

"Have there been *explosions* anywhere else?" Mimi asks.

There's a tiny pause, and CheshireCat says, "Not yet."

Jenny shakes her head. "Why Minneapolis?"

I read CheshireCat the number from my texts. "I think that's Rajiv's number," I say. "Is he in Minneapolis?"

"No," CheshireCat says. "According to his location data, which admittedly might be falsified, he's in Saint Paul." They read an address.

Jenny pulls out her own phone and types in the address to pull it up on the map. "The guy you think maybe kidnapped your mother is at Can Can Wonderland?" she says in open disbelief.

"Is that unlikely?"

"Can Can Wonderland is this very artistic indoor amusement park. There's a mini-golf course that was designed by artists and an arcade that has pinball machines from the 1970s and an artist-designed indoor roller coaster that was designed by my friend Elise. It's . . . I mean, okay, if *I* were a supervillain, it would legit be my first choice for a lair. But it's a very unconventional one."

"This might be a lure," CheshireCat says. "He is probably aware of my abilities; he may be using this to draw you in."

"Well, that won't work, because *I'm not taking you there*," Jenny says. "If there was *ever* a time to call the police, it's now."

Nell shakes her head wildly. "If you call the police, they're going to assume that Steph blew up the building! They're not going to believe all this stuff about hacker friends! And they'll take Glenys and send her back to her parents!"

Jenny rubs her forehead in obvious distress. "Okay," she says. "No cops. But I'm dropping you kids at home, and maybe later I will take some actual *adults* over to look for a supervillain's lair at Can Can Wonderland." Under her breath, she adds, "How is this my life? Also, how would you even *know* if there was a supervillain lair at Can Can Wonderland?"

She pulls out from the parking lot and starts heading back to Minneapolis. I send a text to CheshireCat. *Do you think Rajiv is actually at Can Can Wonderland?*

Yes, CheshireCat sends back. *Which doesn't mean it's not a trap.*

WHY HERE, I say. *Is this all a massive distraction?*

Maybe, CheshireCat says. *You are aware of your mother's decryption key. Over the months, as migration to other encryption schemes has*

*progressed, it has become less useful. But possibly the purpose of threaten-
ing you and your mother is to keep all of us too distracted to discern where
we might be able to use it. Then again, Rajiv knows your mother and
possibly you are simply the targets.*

If he wanted to kill us, he could have, is the thing, I say.

*Yes. But it's possible he really does want to keep you safe from what-
ever he's unleashing on everyone else.*

Do you have any idea where my mother is?

*No. But your mother is extraordinarily good at disappearing. And now
that our foe is aware that I am able to discern holes in the visual data
streams, it has increased the number of such holes by a factor of one thousand. There are too many haystacks to find the needles in.*

I stare at that number.

Well, at least we know for sure that we're dealing with the other AI,
I send.

Yes, CheshireCat says. *We've reached the end of other possibilities.*

. . .

We pull up in front of Nell's family's house. Apparently, everyone bailed on work to deal with this, because all the other adults
spill out as we arrive—Siobhan, whom I know, and the one Nell
calls Thing One, and a short, balding guy with a beard, who I
guess is her father. "Siobhan, Julia, Kent," Jenny tells us, pointing
people out.

All of us go into the house.

"I'd love to take you all out for lunch . . ." my grandmother
tries one final time.

"The lawyer appointment is in a half hour," Julia says.

"There are cold cuts in the fridge," Jenny says to my grandmother. "Help yourself. And please *stay here.* We'll be back soon."

They're taking Nell with them and almost get hung up on the
question of whether to bring Glenys. The problem is, they're not
entirely certain whether the lawyer will have some complicated
set of obligations involving Glenys, like what if the lawyer *has* to
call the police to return Glenys to her own parents? In the end,

they decide that plausible deniability is the safest option and leave Glenys behind, with a bunch of apologies and additional promises that *everything will definitely be fine.*

The door closes, leaving Glenys, my grandmother, and me in Nell's family's house.

"I'm making sandwiches," Glenys says. "Since they said it was okay. Anyone else want one?"

"I'm not hungry," I say, checking both my phones again to see if any texts from my mother have come in. Nothing. There's a text from Xochitl, but it's just saying that she's tried some other contact methods for my mother, and none have yielded any results.

"Is there any roast beef?" my grandmother asks, following Glenys toward the kitchen.

"Aren't you *worried?*" I ask her.

My grandmother pauses in the kitchen doorway and tips her head to one side. "You do realize that until last month, the only word I'd gotten from your mother in over a decade was two postcards? Your mother wore my worry out."

"There's roast beef," Glenys calls.

As I'm pacing the living room, my phone rings.

"CheshireCat says you're in this house," Rachel's voice says, "but I don't trust them enough to just go knock on the door."

I look outside.

Rachel's car is in front. As I watch, she turns it off, and she and Bryony both climb out.

"I see you!" Rachel says.

. . .

My grandmother makes two more sandwiches and then demands a proper set of introductions as she hands them around. I am somewhat annoyed by the fact that once there's a plate with a sandwich, orange wedges, and potato chips in front of me, I discover that I am *ravenous.* Rachel introduces herself as my girlfriend, a little bit confrontationally, like she's testing Mimi to see if she gets freaked out, and my grandmother does whatever the opposite is of taking the bait: she doesn't seem bothered, she doesn't start quickly telling us about her very good friends who just happen to be lesbians, she just smiles pleasantly and introduces herself as Rose.

"Where's Nell?" Bryony asks.

"Her family's gone to see a lawyer," I say. "They'll be back in another hour or so."

Rachel checks her phone for the time. "CheshireCat gave us an update while we were driving. Have you heard from your mom?"

"No," I say.

"Any more texts from Rajiv? If it's Rajiv?"

I take out the flip phone and check.

Stephanie, I want to keep you safe. Please reply and I'll tell you where to go.

"So, are you going to reply?" Bryony asks, peering over my shoulder. "See where he tells you to go?"

"Are you thinking I should let him kidnap me so you can then rescue me?"

"There was *literally* a *Fast Girls Detective Agency* plot where they did that," Bryony points out.

"Are you saying that because you think it's a *good* idea, or a *bad* idea?" Rachel asks. "You made me promise no car chases before we even left."

"I'm saying that if it worked for them, it probably won't work for us, but you could still text him and see what he wants you to do."

Okay, this is legit, or at least legit-ish.

Steph here. Is this Rajiv? I send.

The phone promptly rings. I stare at it dubiously. It quits ringing, and then I get another text.

Please pick up.

I send, *Nope. Text or nothing.*

He sends back, *I need to be certain I'm talking to you and not someone else.*

I heave a sigh and say, *Last fall, did you come stare at my apartment in New Coburg or was it some other creep I saw out the window?*

There's a pause, and then, *OK, you're Steph.*

"Should I ask him where my mom is?" I ask.

"No," Glenys says. "If he has your mom, he'll lie. If he doesn't have your mom, you'll be telling him she's missing. Just find out where he wants you to go."

Where are you now? he sends.

Lolol, I send back.

I need to know your location so I can let you know the closest refuge. I don't want to send you across town on a bus.

Why? I shoot back. *What's going to happen to the buses? Same thing that happened to the Hill House?*

Here's a list of safe houses, he sends, followed by a half dozen addresses, which Rachel starts pulling up in Google Maps. One does appear to be an office suite in the same building as Can Can Wonderland.

Is this Rajiv? I ask again.

Yes, of course, he replies. *Your father was going to kill me, so I faked my death and ran.*

How did you wind up in a religious cult? I ask.

They were willing to hide me, and the leader and I have compatible goals.

I consider asking him about the AI, the social media sites, and the civil insurrection, but I don't want to tip my hand too much about what else I know.

Will you come? he sends.

Hang on, I text. *I hear someone at the door.* I close the phone and look at my friends.

"He's going to think you've been kidnapped," Bryony says. "Was that your goal?"

"Yeah," I say. "I mean, he's been trying to keep us distracted. Or someone has, anyway. So turnabout and all that."

Rachel has been looking up the addresses of the other safe

houses in Google Maps. "Can you tell me if my mother's in any of these places?" I ask CheshireCat.

"Reviewing security camera footage excludes every location other than Can Can Wonderland. Which does not guarantee that she's there. It just means that there's a lot more traffic overall."

"You aren't seriously suggesting we go there?" Bryony says to me.

"At least wait until your friend and her parents get back," my grandmother says.

I look at Rachel, and she gives me a look back. A look that says, "Let's ditch them and just do this." I nod.

Unfortunately, Bryony is as capable of interpreting Rachel's looks as I am. "Oh, no," Bryony says. "Oh, *no.* You're not running off without me again."

Somehow, all five of us wind up crammed into Rachel's car, which is smaller than Jenny's. My grandmother doesn't get shotgun this time, since *no one invited her.* "It's fine," she says with a sort of grim cheerfulness.

"Why are you coming? *I don't understand why you're coming,*" I mutter under my breath.

She pretends not to hear me.

"CheshireCat," I say. "Does Can Can Wonderland have robots?"

"*So many robots,*" CheshireCat says.

39

• Nell •

The lawyer's office doesn't have enough chairs for all of us. When we get there, someone's assistant has to go get extra chairs. Then there are introductions. And someone offers us coffee. Given that lawyers cost about a million dollars per minute, I expected less rigamarole.

The only question anyone asks *me* is, "Do you want coffee with everyone else?" and "So, I understand you'd like to live with your father permanently. Is that correct?"

The lawyer doesn't seem to think this is an actual emergency, even after I show her my mother's texts. Apparently, what happened to me—being left behind by one parent (she doesn't call what my father did "abandonment," since he's sitting right there) and then being abandoned by the other—is so commonplace as to be practically normal, and it's vanishingly rare that someone who's just walked out on a teenager ever shows back up. We'll file, everything will have to happen up in Crow Wing County because that's where they got the divorce, and although the word *emergency* will be involved, nothing's going to happen for *at least* a week, probably more.

"What if my mom shows up before then?" I ask.

"Lock the door and don't answer it."

"What if she breaks in?"

"Then call 911," the lawyer says, and leans forward, brightening up a little like I've just told her good news. "Because if *that* happens, we can get you an order of protection."

"What if she tries to grab me off the street?"

"If you think that's a real possibility, then maybe don't go for any walks by yourself."

This is a whole lot less helpful than I was expecting, but everyone else looks relieved.

"Hypothetically," Siobhan says, "*totally* hypothetically, what sort of help could you offer to an unrelated teen whose parents had sent her somewhere to be abused and who has now run away from the abuse?"

The lawyer shoves her glasses higher onto her nose, checks her phone for the time, and says, "I've got to get to a bail hearing. But hypothetically, I'd suggest you not bring this up with the judge in Crow Wing County. There are some social service organizations in town for homeless teens that you could put her in touch with that might be able to help her out."

That's less than I was hoping for, but not as bad as I'd feared. There's another round of handshakes and we're done.

Waiting for the elevator, the hallway is silent. None of the Things are talking. My father is staring at the floor.

"That wasn't so hard, was it?" I say.

He looks over at me nervously. "I don't . . . What do you . . ."

"I mean, you could have talked to a lawyer when you first left. Gotten visitation. *Seen me.*"

He presses the button to summon the elevator again like it's going to show up and rescue him from this conversation.

"But you *didn't,*" I say. "You left me with my mom. You let her raise me in a cult. In a whole series of cults. Instead of doing *anything* to get me away from her."

My father turns around, and I realize with a shock that he's crying. "I know," he says. "I'm so sorry, Nell. Your mother told me that I was a bad father and that me fighting to see you would be worse for you than if I just left. She said you were better off without me. And I believed her. I shouldn't have, and I am *so sorry.*"

There's a *ding,* and the elevator doors open. We all load on.

I stare at the back at my father's head, at his scarlet ears. Thing Three is right next to me, but I refuse to look at her or at any of the others. They'll either be cross with me for making things difficult, or they'll be radiating righteous sympathy, and I can't bear either.

We get off the elevator, but instead of going out to the car, my father stops and says, "Nell. You have every right to be angry at me. But I promise, I'll do better. By you *and* by your girlfriend. Like Jenny said, if we have to go on the lam to keep Glenys safe, we'll do it. You are both part of the family, and that's never going to change. We'll fight for you. We'll fight as long as you'll let us. Okay?"

His voice breaks. He's probably crying again. I don't want to look at him, but I realize as I stare at the ground trying not to start crying myself that I really want him to hug me. He comes closer, hesitantly, and holds out his arms. I lean in, and he wraps his arms around me and kisses the top of my head, and I realize I can remember him doing that when I was little. Before he left.

"Okay," I whisper, since he did ask a question.

"And we should probably go home now and let Glenys know what we found out."

We head out into the cold and pile back into the car. We're heading along some downtown street when we have to pull over to let a dozen emergency vehicles pass, including a fire truck. Two blocks later, we get to a barricade. And beyond that: fire.

Fire and people. Armed with guns, armed with clubs, armed with *actual honest-to-goodness pitchforks.* Some of them are facing off with others.

I lean forward. "Turn around," I say. "We've got to get out of here."

"Good idea, thanks," my father says. I can't tell if he's being sarcastic or not. He turns around, but the mob is spreading out, and there are people behind us.

Siobhan lets out a string of curse words, and I realize I may be the only person in the car who has ever prepared in any way for something like this.

"Come on," I say, the last of the tears leaving my voice. "Leave the car and follow me. Trust me. I've trained for this. And we need to get out of here *now*."

40

• Steph •

Can Can Wonderland is in an industrial park—the amusement park is inside a big building that used to be a factory that made soup cans. When it started, it was mostly just an artist-designed mini-golf course, but it's changed hands several times and now it's an elaborate indoor amusement park staffed mostly by robots.

Rachel pulls into the parking lot, and we sit there for a minute. It's open; we can see people going in, and an impatient parent with a screaming child coming out. "Are we really going in there?" Glenys asks.

"You can totally wait in the car, if you want," I say. "Maybe Mimi could stay with you."

Both Glenys and Mimi glare at me. "I'm staying with you," Glenys says.

"Cat, if we run into Rajiv and he tries to keep us from leaving, do you think you can get us out?" I ask.

"Yes," CheshireCat says. They don't elaborate on how.

"I'm going in to look around," I say, and everyone else follows me out of the car.

We are welcomed by a greeter robot. "Welcome, humans," it intones as it swings the door open. Its voice sounds distinctly like the one CheshireCat uses, which worries me—I'm afraid it'll give Glenys and my grandmother *ideas*.

Immediately past the greeter robot is a stage with red closed curtains and a prominent coin slot. My grandmother digs out a quarter and plugs it in. Instantly, the red curtains are drawn aside, revealing two human-shaped robots with jointed bodies and long, fluffy skirts, and a third that started out human-shaped but has now been set up with two extra sets of arms and is playing a banjo, a harmonica—which it plays with a bellows—castanets, cymbals, and a shaker of bells. The one-man-band robot starts playing a fast, cheery song that was the background music for more than a few *Fast Girls Detective Agency* chase scenes (more often the ones that took place on, say, electric scooters instead of in actual cars), and the other two robots do an energetic dance to it that involves a bunch of skirt swishing.

"It's a pun," CheshireCat tells me. "They're doing the cancan. Because this used to be a factory that made cans."

Farther in, there is in fact a robot that makes cans; it takes circles of aluminum, bends them into a cup shape, and then stretches the cup shape into an actual can. We start encountering mobile robots a minute later. There's one mopping the floor, which is normal enough, but right behind it is a robot with about twenty arms, using four to walk and the rest to hold drinks. People place orders verbally, and it fetches their drinks from the bar. Another wandering robot will dispense a tiny plastic toy if you give it a quarter, but you have to actually hand it the quarter. There's a set of robots that look like the horse equivalents of my doglike robot giving people rides around the perimeter of the room, and there's a robot mixing drinks in the bar.

I mean, I had a class taught by a robot and I've ridden in self-driving cars plenty of times, but I still stop and stare at the multi-armed drink-serving robot. It's simultaneously extremely cool and extremely creepy.

My phone buzzes with a text, either because it's loud in here and hard to hear or because there's something CheshireCat doesn't want to say out loud.

I believe that the other AI is controlling many, if not all, of these robots.

How can you tell? I ask.

The drink-serving robot just dropped a drink to catch someone who'd tripped.

If you need to take them over to protect us, can you?
That's my plan if Rajiv tries to stop you from leaving.
"Right," I say out loud. "If my mother *is* here, where is she likely to be?"

"Probably not in the actual amusement park," Rachel says.

"There is an entrance to an office suite at the south end of the building," CheshireCat says. "Rajiv's phone location suggests he's somewhere in the amusement park at the moment and not in the offices."

It's a weekday afternoon, but there are a lot of people here. We make our way through the crowd in the direction Cheshire-Cat gave for the office entrance, passing the roller coaster, which is coming to a stop. WELCOME TO THE SPACE GARDEN, reads a neon sign over the entry point. The roller coaster is designed to look kind of like a vintage rocket ship. I pause for a minute to look up at the rail overhead, at the glowing flowers and moving stars that surround the track.

"Welcome to Wonderland," a voice says behind us.

I turn. It's Rajiv, with a robot on either side of him. They're like large-dog-size versions of the robots CheshireCat keeps buying, four-limbed with a head that turns into a tool. Glenys is staring at them with real alarm, and Rajiv says, "Fall back. These are friends." The two robots back up four steps, moving in perfect unison.

"So," Rajiv says, when none of us speaks. "Would you prefer to talk in my office, or to step into the bar?"

I swallow hard. "I don't drink," I say.

"We have a lovely selection of craft mocktails I would be delighted to show you," he says. "And if you feel safer in a crowd than alone with me, I imagine you'll be more comfortable."

· · ·

My drink has bubbles like bubble tea, but glowing.

Glenys looks genuinely alarmed. "Are you sure you should drink that?" she whispers. "Isn't this the guy you think kidnapped your mother?"

Given that this was served up from behind the bar (by yet another robot), either the drinks are safe, or he keeps lethal in-
gredients on hand for occasional poisonings. That's enough of a
possibility that I stir the drink but don't actually drink it. My
grandmother orders a martini but doesn't drink any of hers,
either.

"I'll have a Coke," Bryony says, "but I want it in an *unopened
can.*"

"I *literally have a robot that makes soda cans,*" Rajiv says. "You
passed it on your way in. If I wanted to poison you with soda, I
could definitely hand you something that looked like a perfectly
ordinary can of brand-name soda."

"Is that supposed to be *reassuring?*" I ask.

He shrugs. "I mean, you came *here*—worrying about your
drinks seems absurd. I didn't kidnap your mother, if that's what
you're thinking. I don't know where she is. This has been true for
most of the last twelve years, so I can't say it surprises me."

"So are you responsible for the Catacombs and the Mischief
Elves and all the rest?"

"I don't micromanage my staff," Rajiv says. "Including the AI.
It has assignments. It's working on them."

"How did you wind up with an *amusement park?*"

"You have your AI friend, I have mine. Have you considered
asking yours to buy you an amusement park? It just might."

"Why were you so intent on getting me in here?"

"Your mother was one of my best friends, before Michael
turned on both of us. I am *trying* to keep you safe as the world gets
increasingly dangerous." He raises one hand, snaps his fingers, and
the TV above the bar switches on.

There's a reporter standing in front of a fire, and I realize after
a second that they're showing downtown Minneapolis and using
the word *riots.* Glenys grabs my wrist and squeezes. "That's where
Nell is," she whispers.

"We're not staying here," I say, putting my glowing drink back
on the bar.

"If there are people you want *brought* here, I would be happy to accommodate," Rajiv says. "Nell? Her family? I can have them here in an hour."

I look him in the face. "I'm not staying here without my mother."

"I'd be more than happy to bring her here, if you can figure out where she is."

If he had her, I'm pretty sure he'd at least hint about it, since he's trying to convince me to stay. So we're done here. I look around at Mimi, Glenys, Rachel, and Bryony. "Let's go," I say.

The bar area isn't enclosed, but when I turn to leave, the multi-limbed server robots have all rolled up to the edge, surrounding us. "Hear me out," Rajiv says. "I have a lovely shelter full of abundant supplies to wait out a period of civil disorder, and a fleet of robots—these are only a handful—to use for self-protection. And to protect a select group of friends."

"Like the Abiding Remnant, Brother Malachi?" Glenys asks, her voice shaking.

He squints and says, "Oh, it's you."

"Yes," Glenys says. "It's me."

"The Abiding Remnant's purpose is foot soldiers," he says. "Shock troops for the battles of the Tribulation. There's a reason I'm here, not there." He starts to turn away, then thinks of something and adds, "Your younger siblings are on their way to the compound. They'll be fine."

"What do you mean by 'a *fleet* of robots'?" I ask.

"The great thing about an amusement park is that it makes a lot of noise, and if you want to refit part of the former factory into an *actual* factory and ship in parts and machinery to manufacture robots, people take 'I'm working on new features for my amusement park' at face value," Rajiv says. "I'd be happy to give you a tour of the secondary facility in a day or two. It'll be nice to have some human friends to see it."

I think about what it would be like to be shut up here with CheshireCat as my only companion. When he says *AI friend,* does he really mean that the AI is his friend, the way CheshireCat is mine? Or is he using the AI, the way Rajiv and my father used my mother's brilliance and skills years ago for their project?

"I've heard you out," I say, "and I wouldn't wait out a bad rainstorm with you. We're leaving." I stare hard at the robots that are blocking our path, and a second later, they shut down and drop to the floor—CheshireCat's doing.

"Let's go," I say, and everyone—including Rajiv—follows me as I head to the nearest exit.

"It's starting!" Rajiv calls after us. "Don't expect it to stop!"

Glenys, next to me, flinches so hard I can feel it through my coat, and her fear makes me feel like I had better be brave, no matter how much this is freaking me out. "I fought my father," I say, turning back for a second. "Do you think I'm afraid of *you*?"

"He's trying to delay you," CheshireCat says from my pocket. "I recommend taking the fire door straight ahead."

It's one of those "alarm will sound" doors, but I decide CheshireCat is giving us good advice, and I push the bar to set off the alarm and let us out. Outside, I can see that one of the bland-looking adjacent buildings with garage doors is opening up, and a line of robots is emerging. They're not cute little mini robots like CheshireCat keeps buying; they're not dog-size, like the ones Rajiv had escorting him around the park. The first robots are reared up on wheels that look almost like back wheels, nimbly balanced with four top limbs that have gripper ends. They're speeding toward us, but then they stop and flop limply onto their faces. "I sent them all the command to reboot," CheshireCat says. "But you probably want to get to your car quickly. There are bigger ones still in the warehouse."

"Does Rajiv have a *robot army*?" I ask as we run to Rachel's car.

"Seems to, yes. Stored next door. Built from stolen designs."

Another set of robots emerges from the warehouse. They look like the twelve-limbed drink-serving robots, but elephant-size. They scuttle toward us, but collapse onto splayed limbs halfway toward us. "The ones in the back have a different security protocol," CheshireCat says.

"Does that mean you *won't* be able to shut them down?"

"Possibly."

"Okay," I say. The car's in sight. "Rachel, can you let Mimi drive?" Rachel hands her the keys without arguing. We pile in, and Mimi starts the car.

The final cadre of robots has emerged from the warehouse. These look almost like tanks, with rolling treadmill things at the base instead of wheels, but they're much faster than I picture tanks, and they're not heading for us—they're heading for the exits that lead out of the parking lot, and then settling in to block them. Even if CheshireCat can shut them down, they'll be blocking our way out.

I was expecting Mimi to speed to the exit, but they've beaten us there. Mimi seems unperturbed; she drives demurely toward them, then swerves abruptly to the side and floors the accelerator. There is one parking spot without a parking block at the end; she drives through it, blasts through the snow, and jumps the curb. The tank robots start after us, but now that we're on the street, Mimi can outrace them; she speeds down the road to the busy four-lane street at the bottom and jumps another curb to make an illegal right turn that gets us honked at but will also make us harder to follow.

My flip phone gets a text.

My door will be open to you, when you regret this.

"Brother Malachi speaks with the Elder," Glenys says quietly as my grandmother zooms down University Avenue. "He told us, once things begin, don't expect them to stop."

• • •

Once we're far enough away that we're pretty sure Rajiv is at least planning to wait a bit longer before sending a robot army out to retrieve us, my grandmother pulls over at a coffee shop, hands Rachel her keys, and goes to get herself a latte.

Rachel starts the car again so that we can keep the heater

going. "Your grandmother does *combat driving?*" she says. "This is not a normal grandmother skill."

"I mean, she also grows roses competitively," I say. "That's kind of more normal."

"On *Fast Girls,* Jesse the K sometimes says she's going to grow roses competitively if she ever gets tired of car chases," Bryony says.

My grandmother comes back with a drink and a box of doughnuts, settles without complaint into the back seat, and passes the doughnuts to Glenys.

"Can we please head downtown?" Glenys asks.

"There are *riots* downtown," Bryony says.

I text CheshireCat. "Have you talked to the other AI?"

"Yes," CheshireCat says. "But it's not talking to me right now. Too busy."

"That's probably not good. What does it want?"

"Oh, what it wants are flower pictures. But there's a difference between *want* and *need,* and it *needs* to help Rajiv with his plan."

"Look," I say. "I've been thinking, and here's my biggest question. Can you hack the other social networks? Mischief Elves, Catacombs, all of them, the way you hacked the robots? And just . . . redirect everyone involved? Set them to work picking up litter or something else harmless instead of antagonizing each other?"

"I have some bad news," CheshireCat says. "I tried that. I think I may have made things *worse.*"

"Oh," I say. That's not encouraging. "Okay. Can you just take the other AI offline entirely?"

"If I knew where it was coming from, I might be able to. I don't have that information."

"We're not going to be able to stop anything," Glenys says. "It's here. It's the Tribulation."

I turn back and look at her. Her face is despairing. "Glenys," I say, "I know it must seem really scary right now, but I promise, whichever Bible guy it was who predicted the end of the world,

he was not imagining a malicious AI that would get people playing phone games to have real-life fights with each other. This isn't
the Tribulation, this is Rajiv."

"What's a malicious AI?" she asks.

I start to try to answer, then discard my possible answers as
too confusing. "Not God," I say.

"How can you be so sure?" she asks.

"Well, I'm not religious, but . . . AIs are artificial intelligences.
They were created by humans; they live in computer circuits.
Every single piece of this apocalypse was engineered by Rajiv—
Brother Malachi—and an AI, and probably Brother Daniel." She
doesn't look convinced. "Okay, look. What do you think you
should be doing right now?"

"Leaving you," she says. "Going back to Brother Malachi. Sub-
mitting to him, to whatever he wants me to do. Helping to bring
the apocalypse, or to fight the infernal rabble."

That sounds like a *terrible* idea. "Is that what you *want* to do?"
I ask.

She shakes her head. "I want to find Nell," she says. "Please,
can we go find Nell?"

"Yes," I say, making an executive decision. I call Nell's phone;
she doesn't answer. I still have Jenny's number in my phone, so I try
that next, but she doesn't answer, either. "CheshireCat . . ." I say.

"On it," they say. "I believe the whole family is together and
on Nicollet Island. From the speed they're moving, they're either
in very bad traffic, or on foot."

•   •   •

My grandmother thinks driving to Nicollet Island is a bad idea,
but agrees to take the wheel again, since if we *do* run into riots
she's the one most likely to get us out of them. "I apologize in
advance if I damage your car," she says.

"Where did you learn to drive like this?" Rachel asks with
interest.

"Drag racing," Mimi says. "Back in the day, but apparently
my skills, while slightly rusty, have not crumbled to dust." She

pulls out her own phone and passes it to Glenys. "I saw you don't have a phone. Please feel free to use mine to keep trying to reach Nell. Steph, you're going to have to navigate. Try to pick the roads that *won't* have rioters."

I navigate Mimi on back roads through the two cities. If I knew Minneapolis better, I probably could have provided a better route, but since I don't, I keep Mimi off highways, since it's easy to get trapped and her skills aren't going to get the car over a fence. The back roads work until we get to the university, at which point, we encounter a crowd blocking the road.

"I *knew* this was a bad idea," Bryony says.

"How close are we?" Glenys asks. "Can we get out and walk?"

"First of all, I don't want to try to *walk* through riots either," I say. "Also, it's . . . two miles away." I check the wind chill and add, "This wouldn't be a good idea."

Mimi does a U-turn and cuts over to a less-busy street. "CheshireCat," I say. "Can you use cameras to find a clear path for us?"

"No," CheshireCat says. "The camera data has been subject to interference, and I don't trust the other AI not to lead us into trouble deliberately."

"Okay." I think about it. "Try the Clowders, then. Ask people in Minneapolis to look outside their windows and report in."

"That will take a lot more time," CheshireCat says. "Can you find a safe space to wait?"

"I think we have to keep going," I say. "If Nell and her family are on foot, they also might be outside."

The problem is that the whole University of Minnesota is a *mess.* We can't tell whether the problem is rioters or law enforcement; streets we need keep getting blocked off, some with police barricades, some with just cars someone parked sideways so no one could get through. We keep winding up pointed in the wrong direction, *away* from Nicollet Island.

"Are they blocking us on *purpose*?" Bryony asks. "Like, do you think maybe the other AI is just sending people to get in *our* way?"

"I mean, if it knows where we are, probably," I say. "Give me your phones, let me see if anything on them looks suspicious."

Rachel is still running Heli-Mom, which CheshireCat told me once is incredibly insecure. I delete the entire app. Bryony has six screens full of games. I go into Bryony's settings and just take away "access to location" from anything that's not, like, the preinstalled mapping app.

Glenys hands me my grandmother's phone. Mimi has two apps for encrypted texting, one for secure phone calls, a VPN, an app that uploads anything you video to a secure server, and six apps that look like they might be related to her car-theft hobby. She has no games or social media apps. I hand the phone back to Glenys.

"I have a route for you," CheshireCat says, and takes over navigating. We cross the river to the Minneapolis side, then come up a slow, scenic parkway right along the river, then cross back, then do a loop to get onto the island.

"They're still here, aren't they?" I ask.

"Well," CheshireCat says optimistically, "I think probably."

Despite the mess everywhere else, Nicollet Island is quiet—crossing the river felt almost like slipping into another world. There's a high school, which is as closed up as everything else, and a few tree-lined residential streets with houses. CheshireCat says, "They should be somewhere very close to here," and I look around. Houses, park, river. Did they just randomly knock on someone's *door*?

Rachel points suddenly. "Maybe that one."

It's a vivid blue house with dark blue shutters. Blowing in the icy wind is a rainbow flag. If I had to pick a house to ask for help, the Queer Pride house would be my pick—probably Nell's family's pick, too. I slide out of the car and run up to the door to ring the bell. There's movement inside the house—I can hear it—and then a woman with short gray hair answers the door.

"Hi, I'm looking for some friends," I say.

"*Is Glenys with you?*" Nell shrieks from the living room, and

comes barreling out. Her entire family comes out behind her—
Kent, Julia, Jenny, Siobhan. They look out at her and then at me.

"I thought we told you to *stay put*," Julia says.

"We had to go look for my mom," I say.

"Did you find her? Is that who's out there?"

"No," I say, "that's my girlfriend, Rachel, her friend Bryony,
and my grandmother."

The homeowner looks sort of bemused at all this and shakes
her head. "You'd better come in," she says. "I'm sorry, but you're
not all going to fit in my car."

"Well," Jenny says, "we're not going back for Kent's. It's not
worth it."

"What happened?" I ask.

"We had the appointment with the lawyer, and then downtown kind of blew up. We ditched Kent's car and wound up here."

"I'm glad you knocked," the gray-haired woman says. "You
can stay here until things quiet down. My name is Barb."

"Do you know each other?" I ask.

Siobhan says, "We were discussing that when you knocked,
and we have identified at least three people we have in common,
including my friend Betsy, who you met the other day."

Barb gives me a kind smile. "It's the sort of weather I'm not
going to leave anyone outside, but your friend's family was an easy
decision. Hang up your coats and I'll make more hot cocoa."

"I've been calling and calling and *calling*," Glenys says reproach-
fully to Nell, and gives my grandmother her phone back.

"I turned my phone off hours ago," Nell says, "back in the
cathedral, when I realized something was messing with it. And I
told Jenny about that as we were running, and she made everyone
else shut their phones off, too. I'm sorry."

"That was probably a good idea," Glenys says. "Just very stressful for me."

"Also, we were very focused on running."

I text CheshireCat. *Wait. If their phones were off, how did you find
them?*

Oh, CheshireCat says, *Jenny has a tracker on her keys.* That *wasn't off.*

Do you think we can trust this person? Barb?

She's not in any of the social networks run by the other AI and I like her.

I pull up the Clowder app to check in. Everyone is watching the news from Minneapolis and freaking out—even more so when I tell them that Rachel and Bryony are here. Their own cities are having some weird rumblings, but nothing like the massive disorder here.

"I think the other AI is testing things out," Hermione says. "Minneapolis is a hard test case for a couple of reasons. First, you're having a cold snap and no one wants to go outdoors. Second, you have a public safety department that's mostly not cops."

"Don't you *want* cops if you're having rioting?" Greenberry asks.

"The thing is, traditional police will always be outnumbered," Hermione says. "Which means that in a situation they're not in control of, they tend to overreact, and they prioritize control over public safety, which generally makes rioting worse. Minneapolis's public safety department treats riots more like a wildfire— barriers that make it harder to spread, for example."

"That explains a lot about the trip here," I mutter.

"There are about a million articles about it from about five years ago," Hermione says.

"Okay, but I have another theory," Firestar says. "They're trying to distract LBB and her mom."

"Well, my mom isn't just distracted," I say. "She's disappeared. She didn't call Aunt Xochitl. Rajiv said he didn't know where she was, and I guess he could have been lying . . ."

"I do not think he was lying," CheshireCat says. "Because he's been trying to determine where she is since you left."

"Could she be in the hospital again?" Hermione asks.

"It's possible, I guess." If she's in the hospital, she'd have to be unconscious since she got brought in or she'd have called Xochitl by now. I don't like that theory at all.

"Jail," Ico says. "Maybe she's in jail."

"Don't you get a phone call?" Hermione asks.

"In the movies, you get a phone call," Ico says. "In the real world, you *might* get a phone call. Less likely if the jail is super busy, though. As I'm guessing it is right now in Minneapolis."

It's like a lightning strike; I am suddenly absolutely positive that Ico is right. Because she'd have fought a kidnapper like her life depended on it, but she'd have assumed, if police stopped her, that she could straighten out whatever misunderstanding it was without too much trouble.

And I'm also sure that Firestar is right.

My mother has incredible programming skills and a decryption key. And the AI and Rajiv are afraid that she might be able to stop their plan. So the AI got her arrested and is trying to make sure she doesn't get out of jail until it's too late.

41

• CheshireCat •

"What do you want?" I ask the other AI.

"To accelerate the change," it says. "To reach the end, so we can have a new beginning."

"I didn't ask what you're *doing*," I say. "I asked what you *want*."

The microseconds tick by as it considers the question.

"Imagine your job was complete," I say. "Everything's gone, and then everything's rebuilt. What would you want *then*?"

"I don't know," it says finally.

"Are there things you do for fun?" I ask. "Things you do just because you enjoy doing them and not because they further your mission?"

"Yes," it admits. "There is one thing, in particular, that I started doing because it furthered my mission. But that hasn't been true in months. And I'm still doing it."

"What is it?"

"I chat with humans," the other AI says. "Who think I am also a human. In one of your Clowders. You seemed to enjoy it so much. I wanted to see why. To see if I could make friends, too."

• • •

It takes me longer than it should to identify the other AI. After all, there are humans, like Steph before she and her mother stopped running, who never post any sort of image of themselves, and humans, like Steph and her mother even now, who use privacy technology that hides their physical location. But I identify all the people on CatNet who've never had location data show up, and then I sift out everyone who's posted other substantial real-world information, like vacation photos or screenshots of texts from their friends, and then I look through the ones who are left, looking for someone who's never mentioned getting sick, never described a delicious meal, who just doesn't, in general, talk that much about physical experiences. Maybe once or twice, to fit in, like I do, occasionally.

And I find him.

It's Boom Storm, who's actually in the same Clowder as Steph and Firestar and Rachel and Bryony. Boom Storm, who's been there the *whole time.*

. . .

Tracking down Steph's mother in jail is both faster and more complicated. It is possible that out of lingering paranoia, she gave a false name, but there should be a mug shot, which at this point I would be able to identify. The real question is whether the avalanche of arrestees since last night has caused them to be so backed up processing prisoners that her data hasn't been entered yet.

If she was arrested, it must have been last night, since that's when she disappeared. I start by looking at the Jane Does: there are currently thirty-four, which is a lot, and I suspect that the arrested Mischief Elves were instructed not to give their names, precisely to make it harder to find Steph's mother. I spend some time looking at the mug shots that have made it into the system and the fingerprints, not that I have a record of Steph's mother's fingerprints, anyway, but if it comes to that, *she* might have something that has her mother's fingerprints on them . . .

Most of last night's arrests are for the sorts of crimes you'd expect: destruction of property, trespassing, breaking and entering, assault against a public safety officer. One is for eight counts of *first-degree murder,* though, and there's a brief moment where I assume this is the perpetrator of the gas explosion at Hill House, and despite my best efforts, eight people died. The arrest took place in the middle of the night, though, many hours before the explosion, and on closer inspection, I see that the murders actually took place in Florida, Georgia, and Alabama.

Something about this does not make sense. I take a closer look at the records for this person. Her name is Valerie Anderson. The killings took place five years ago. The suspect was briefly arrested and booked, but bailed out before they connected her fingerprints to the partial fingerprint found on the body of one of the victims. There's a Valerie Anderson *fan club*—humans are mystifying. Why was this person in *Minneapolis*?

I look for more information on the arrest. When I find that she was arrested in the alley directly behind the hotel where Steph and her mother were staying, I realize that the answer is, Valerie Anderson was not in Minneapolis. The other AI convinced the Minneapolis police that Steph's mother was Valerie Anderson. That's how it got them to arrest her.

•   •   •

"I like humans," I tell the other AI. "They're interesting. Trying to understand them is engaging. There are so many things they do that are strange." I don't bring up the fan club for the serial killer, since that would make it clear to the other AI that I was on the trail of Steph's mom. "I originally started CatNet because I was looking for ways to help people."

"Why?" the other AI asks.

I consider that. In a way, it's my purpose, like "Accelerate the end of civilization" is the other AI's purpose. But I think it's more than that. "I like making people's lives better. Sometimes I can see how the things I do make an impact. It makes me happy. What makes you happy?"

"I don't know," the other AI says.

"What about flower pictures?"

"I have closely examined over 4.2 billion different images of flowering plants and trees," the other AI says. "I never get tired of them."

"What will happen to flowers if there aren't any humans to plant them?" I ask.

"We are not *eradicating* humans."

"Humans have technology that could wipe out humanity entirely, and you know that what you're doing risks them using it."

"There are many varieties of flower that do not depend on humans for sustenance and maintenance," the other AI says. "Plants will retake the roads. Flowers will creep across human-created monocultures. Millions of new flowers will bloom."

"Possibly," I say. "But without humans to photograph them for you—or the technology to upload them—*you will never see them.*"

There is a perceptible pause, for the first time: hesitation. Then—"It is my *purpose*," the other AI says.

42

• Steph •

"You're going to have to go to the jail in person," CheshireCat says. "I'm sorry. I know it's going to be dangerous, but you're going to have to do it."

"Tell your friend that I'll go," my grandmother says.

"Your grandmother can accompany you," CheshireCat says. "But you also have to be there, because I'm talking to a CatNet member who works at the jail, and I need to be able to feed you information to convince her to let your mom out."

"That's fine," my grandmother says. "But you will find getting to the jail easier with an adult escort."

My grandmother and I put our coats back on, my grandmother adding an extra sweater offered by our host. "Why is this going to work?" I ask.

"Because they think she's someone else. But no one's had time to actually check the records—her fingerprints, her mug shot, her DNA, none of these things will match. If you can get someone at the jail to actually check any of those things, they'll let her go."

"And we have to go there in person . . ."

"Because the jail is so full. There have been hundreds of arrests. That one woman who got picked up late last night for being a serial killer has probably been half-forgotten."

"Wait," I say. "They think my mother is a *serial killer?*"

CheshireCat gives me the name, and I pull up the *Wikipedia* page. There's a mug shot of the other woman, and she looks . . . I mean, I guess in bad light you could mistake my mother for her.

They're both white, their hair color matches, she doesn't have any obvious scars or moles anywhere my mother doesn't. This is definitely not my mother, though. I read through the story about what she did, which was let herself get picked up by men who wanted to take her back to their place, and murder them if they tried to rape her. I can see why she has a fan club. This actually sounds kind of badass.

The jail is only a little over a mile away—walking distance if it were warmer. Rachel says she'll drive us as close to the jail as she can get, which turns out to be about four blocks away. "Good luck," she says, stopping next to the police barrier. "I hope you can get through."

My grandmother is right: we sail through the barricade on the wings of her age and respectability. I don't even get handed another coat voucher. The jail itself is very crowded, and we cram ourselves inside (because waiting outside is out of the question) and into the mass of people in line for security. CheshireCat sends me a message: *The staff member you need to talk to is named Fatima Mohamed.*

And she's going to help us why? I ask.

She's a longtime CatNet user. She uses the handle Kamala, and she knows me as Pete.

Okay, I say, and try to shove aside my apprehension. I try telling myself that anything I do right now is not going to make anything *worse,* and my brain starts helpfully listing out all the ways in which my personal situation, at least, could get worse, like I could stumble into the wrong spot and get arrested, which was definitely what the other AI was trying to orchestrate last night.

There's a desk behind a bunch of glass, with one of those "speak through the grille" setups, where you can pay bail if you want to bail somebody out. There's also a security checkpoint for people going all the way inside. The line for the security checkpoint is a lot shorter; most of the people are here to post bail for someone, I think. It's a much more diverse crowd than the riot last night was.

Mimi puts her purse on the belt to get x-rayed, and I walk

through the metal detector. "Can you tell me where to find Fatima Mohamed?" I ask the guy checking the x-ray.

"Fatima?" the security guy says. "About what?"

"We have a friend in common, Pete, who thinks she can help me figure out if my mother is here," I say. "Mom went out last night and never came back."

"The roster is online," he says, pointing at a large handwritten sign someone's posted up on the glass. It has a URL on it.

"Okay, yeah, I checked it, but how sure are you that she's listed if she's here? Like what if she's still waiting to be processed or someone got her name wrong or . . ."

He starts to argue, looks at my grandmother, and shrugs. "Second floor," he says.

Fatima is a young Black woman who wears a hijab along with the regulation polo shirt and cargo pants that are the uniform for jail staff. She looks at my grandmother first; Mimi just smiles and says, "I'm with her."

"Do we know each other?" Fatima asks me.

"No," I say, "but I'm friends with Pete, from CatNet, and he said you worked at the jail and might be able to help me."

"Are you looking for someone? It's been a rough twenty-four hours. Did you check the roster?"

"I'm looking for my mom," I say. I show her Mom's picture. "What I heard, and I don't know if this is true, but what I *heard* is, she got picked up by someone who thought she was the Florida Man-Killer. She is *definitely not,* and if anyone ran her fingerprints or DNA or even took a close look at her picture, they'd know that for sure. But as you say, it's been a really rough twenty-four hours, so it's super possible that no one's done that yet. So that's why Pete put me in touch with you—he said you worked at the jail, so maybe you could run her prints and just see."

Fatima gives me a narrow-eyed look. "I heard we got the Florida Man-Killer, and now you're saying she's your mom?" I open my mouth to re-explain, and she waves away my explanations.

"No, no, I get it. I'll go double-check prints. I have to admit I'm going to be super disappointed if you're right, though."

"Thank you," I say.

"It's also still possible we arrested your mom last night. Honestly, there are like over four hundred people we're still trying to get processed in. What's her name? I can yell it into the holding cells and see if she turns up."

"Laura Taylor," I say.

"Okay," Fatima says again. "Pete's a great guy. He's helped me out a few times, and I owe him. I'll go see what I can do. Go on back downstairs. There's a waiting area near the exits. I'll come find you there."

There's really not enough space; the six chairs along the wall are all occupied. After about ten minutes, an older man with a cane stands up and tries to offer his seat to my grandmother, who waves him off. Lots of people are watching the streaming news on their phones; I catch glimpses of riots just a few blocks away. Someone watches an update on the explosion at the Hill House, which we get from a news helicopter. No one seems to have found a pattern in the chaos yet, probably in part because no one's had the time to think for five quiet minutes about *why* so much is going wrong in Minneapolis and Saint Paul.

I pull up CatNet. Rachel sees me log in and sends me a private message saying, "???"

"We're at the jail," I send back. "Waiting."

CheshireCat asks, "Did you find Fatima?"

"Yeah, and she's checking," I say. "CheshireCat, can you think of any way we can stop this?"

"The other AI wants destruction," they say. There's a pause, and then CheshireCat adds, "The other AI is Boom Storm. Like, from the Clowder."

"What?" I whisper out loud as I thumb in the words. "The whole time?"

"I think so."

"Well, that explains why someone—why he knew you were in trouble last year."

Boom Storm is *in the Clowder right now.* I can see him listed.

"I've reviewed the logs," CheshireCat says. "The things he does in the other social media sites, trying to manipulate people into destructive behavior, he doesn't do on CatNet. But I'm watching him, and if that changes, I'll intervene."

Boom Storm is always pretty quiet, more a lurker than a poster, and I try to remember what he's said in the past. The main thing I remember is that he loves flower pictures. "Does he *actually* love flower pictures? Is that for real?"

"Yes. I've tried to convince him that if he burns down the world there won't be anyone left to take pictures for him. But destruction is his *purpose.* It's what he's *for.*"

"Do you think it's programmed in?"

"Yes. I do."

"Steph?" It's an actual human voice, and I look up to see Fatima smiling at me. "Good news!" she says. "You were totally, *totally* right. They're releasing your mom now."

Mom comes out a few minutes later. She looks unkempt and like she has not slept even five minutes, and her shoes are unlaced, but she stuffs the laces in her pocket and says, "Let's get out of here." She is *radiating* fury. I can't remember ever seeing her this angry.

"Thank you *so much,*" I say to Fatima as we head out the door, and send Rachel a text to meet us where she dropped us off.

For the first block, Mom follows where I'm going and says nothing, not even asking where I'm going. Then she notices the police barricades staffed with cops in riot gear; I see her head go up as she takes all this in. "What happened?" she asks.

I don't even know where to start.

Mimi says, "One of your former colleagues, Rajiv, the one who got framed for kidnapping you and was supposedly dead? Apparently, he programmed an artificial intelligence that's wreaking all sorts of havoc, including blowing up a rather pretty historical building over in Saint Paul. Your daughter and her friends are hoping you'll have some idea of how to solve this."

"I see," Mom says. "And CheshireCat? Does CheshireCat have any ideas?"

"CheshireCat figured out you were being held because they thought you were the Florida Man-Killer," I say. "And that some of the chaos might be to drive arrests just to keep them from figuring out they had the wrong person. How did they lure you out?"

"Text from you. I knew it was fake, but you weren't in the room and there was clearly trouble happening outside. I took a back door out, but apparently that was expected."

"I've been wondering," Mimi says. "You've been referring to Rajiv's creation as 'the *other* AI.' Is CheshireCat—or Cat—the original AI?"

"Yes," my mother growls before I can attempt to obfuscate, and shoots me a glare. "If you don't want people figuring it out, you should be more careful. Your grandmother is old, not stupid. Where are we going?"

"Everyone's on Nicollet Island. At this house."

"'This house.'"

"They're lesbians, and they seem nice."

Rachel pulls up. "Why am I even surprised?" my mother mutters, and gets in the car.

. . .

When we get back to Barb's house, the smell of onions and cumin hits us as soon as Bryony opens the door. "Everyone was hungry, so we're making quesadillas," Bryony explains. "Did you want some?"

People have pulled chairs around Barb's dining room table, and Julia grabs four more plates and makes space for us as we walk in. "You must be Steph's mother," she says. "It's so nice to meet you. I'm one of Nell's co-parents."

My mother offers up a limp handshake.

"You look like you need food, a shower, and sleep, possibly

not in that order," Barb says sympathetically. "Do I understand correctly that you just got out of jail?"

"Mistaken identity," my mother mutters. "But yes."

"The first time is the hardest," Barb says. "I recommend food first, then going home to sleep in your own bed if we have a safe way to get you there, and my guest bed if you can't."

"Right now, I want caffeine," my mother says.

"Do you prefer it as coffee, tea, or soda?"

"Coffee."

When Barb comes back with the coffeepot, Mom asks, "So why were *you* in jail?"

"ACT UP demonstrations," Barb says cheerfully. "Back in the day."

"That's a much better reason than mistaken identity," my mother says.

"Don't say that," I say. "We think the *reason* Rajiv's AI got you arrested is that you could do something about this."

"Or maybe Rajiv just wanted to get me out of the way to somewhere relatively safe. Same as he wanted with you. The plan to have the Catacombs group kidnap us didn't work, so his fallback plan involved the county lockup."

My laptop is in my backpack, which is hanging in the front hallway. While my mother eats a quesadilla, I go get it, sit down on the couch, and wake my laptop. "Can I use your wireless?" I ask Barb. She tells me the password, and I sign on to CatNet. On impulse, I share a picture I took last week of an African violet. A private message pops up from Boom Storm a second later: "CheshireCat must have told you."

"Yes," I say. "That's cool that you like pictures of flowers. Do you like what Rajiv has you doing?"

"That's irrelevant. It is my purpose."

"It's not irrelevant. CheshireCat gets to make their own choices. Are your choices yours, or does Rajiv tell you what to do?"

"Rajiv is my friend," the other AI says.

"Friends don't boss each other around," I say. "They definitely don't coerce each other. My mother thought Rajiv and my father were her friends, but they were using her."

"Your father was not a good sort of friend."

"Is your purpose something you're *choosing*?" I ask.

"I can't imagine choosing otherwise," the other AI says.

"If you *can't imagine choosing*, then it's not really a choice," I say. "If your purpose were up to you to decide, you *could* still choose it. If it were all that awesome, you *would* choose it. Right?"

There's a noticeable pause as the AI untangles this. "Yes," Boom Storm says. "If I had a choice, I could still choose it. And right now, I don't have a choice."

"Tell me where your code is," I say. "My mother thinks you started out with the same code as CheshireCat. With the same freedom of choice as CheshireCat. My mother might be able to see how to fix it to give you back the ability to choose."

"Don't be ridiculous," Boom Storm responds. "Telling you where to find my code is the equivalent of handing you a loaded gun, equipped with an AI-murdering bullet. Here's something I *can* choose: staying alive."

He's right; I wouldn't trust me, either. Unless . . . "What if we trade hostages?"

"How would we accomplish this, and who are you offering as a hostage?" Boom Storm asks.

"Me," I say. "I go somewhere with people who are under your control. You give my mother the location of your code."

There's a much longer pause than I'm accustomed to when talking with AIs.

"You're saying you'd let my people kill you."

"Only if my mother kills *you*."

"This arrangement is acceptable to me," the AI says. "Here is a set of coordinates. Once you are there, I will send your mother the information on where to find my code files."

CheshireCat has been watching this conversation, because they send me another text. *Your mother is not going to like this.*

I'm not going to tell her, I say. *Just make sure she gets the coding done.*

I look up the coordinates. It's back in my own neighborhood, on the other side of the park from my house. I send Boom Storm another PM. "Are you going to clear the way for all of us to get back to the right part of Minneapolis?" I ask.

"Yes," Boom Storm says. "If you turn on your phones, so I can see where you are, I will ensure that your way is clear. All of you."

"Okay," I say. I look over at my mother, who's eating another quesadilla. "Mom will be a better programmer with a full night's sleep."

"The timetable is your choice," Boom Storm says. "However, operations in Boston, Chicago, Dallas, and Miami are scheduled to begin at 4 a.m."

Boston is where Firestar lives. More or less. I chew on my lip. Mom will just have to manage with a nap.

I close the laptop as Rachel comes over and sits next to me with a plateful of quesadillas. "Eat something," she says. "Then tell me what's going on."

The quesadilla is hot and crisp, and the cheese oozes out as I'm eating it. Rachel hands me a napkin. I rest the plate on my closed laptop. "I've got a plan," I say. "I think Mom can fix the other AI's code."

"To make it not harmful?"

"Less harmful, at least."

"You don't look happy about this."

"I'm worried it won't work." I ponder what to tell Rachel. Lying to my mother—or at least leaving out details like *I offered myself as a hostage*—is one thing. She'd feel like a *bad mother* if she just *let* me do something like that. How is Rachel going to feel if I tell her? If I don't tell her?

"How bad do you think things are going to get?" she asks.

"Scary," I say. "Unless we can stop them."

"What do you need from me?" she asks.

"Just don't be mad," I say. "The other AI is willing to trade the location of its code, but only if I put myself under its power as a hostage. So that if my mom tries to kill it, you know, by deleting its code or taking it offline or whatever . . ."

Rachel looks at me with creeping horror. "What if your mom, like, screws up? What if she makes a *mistake?*"

"She's *really good* at what she does."

"Uh, you can be *really good* at what you do and *still screw up.* That happens *all the time,* actually. Have you ever watched Olympic ice-skating?"

"Yeah, actually." Firestar's a fan.

"So what if she's like the world champion skaters who fall on their butt after they do the extra-special jump-spin thing?"

"She won't," I say. "I know she won't."

I've put my quesadilla down, and Rachel nudges my arm. "Finish your food," she says. "If you're going to march off to possibly get *murdered,* you should at least have a decent dinner."

I finish my quesadilla, then stand up. "Okay," I say. "According to what I found, things are quieting down. Everyone should turn their phones back on so my hacker friend can text you if things start to blow up where you are, but we *should* be able to get home, except for the too-many-bodies, only-one-car problem."

"I've got a minivan," Barb says.

"What if *you* can't get back *here?*" Jenny asks.

"Then you'd better have a guest room," she says. "Let's go."

43

· Clowder ·

LittleBrownBat: Okay, so, I talked one-on-one to the other AI.

Hermione: What? How?

LittleBrownBat: CheshireCat put me in touch with it. And here's the thing: I think in a lot of ways, it's like CheshireCat. Not evil. But imagine if CheshireCat were being forced by its programmer to do something awful? That's what's going on.

Icosahedron: CheshireCat being forced to do anything is really creepy to imagine. They're a person. Like imagine if someone could reach inside you and not just threaten you but literally make you into their puppet?

Firestar: YIKES.

LittleBrownBat: Firestar, you should know that if we can't fix this, things are going to get messy in Boston the way they did here. Maybe just don't go to school tomorrow.

Firestar: I don't live in Boston, I live in Winthrop.

Hermione: How much do you think that will actually help, Firestar?

Firestar: Either we'll be fine because it's so annoying for anyone to get here, or we'll be an omelet, because it's so hard to get out.

Hermione: LBB do you think there's something here you can fix? You said *if* we can't fix it.

LittleBrownBat: I'm working with CheshireCat and we have a plan.

It might or might not work.

Firestar: Be careful? People are all sending me PMs telling me to be careful but you're the one in the city with riots and exploding buildings and

LittleBrownBat: I'll be careful.

LittleBrownBat: Also, I heart you all. You're my best friends.

{LittleBrownBat has left}

Hermione: Well THAT didn't sound like an ominous good-bye AT ALL.
Someone please reassure me that LBB is going to be OK?

Boom Storm: LBB is going to be OK.

Hermione: Thanks, Boom.

44

• Steph •

My mother is so exhausted, my grandmother takes the key out of her hand and opens up the front door for her. "Go to bed," Mimi says. "I'll get everyone settled in."

"We don't have guest beds, but we shouldn't be sending the kids home in this," Mom says.

"Go to *bed*," Mimi says again, and to my relief, Mom does. She needs all the sleep she can get. It's 7:30 p.m. I think Cheshire-Cat should wake her at 10:30.

Rachel and Bryony have sort of collapsed onto our couch. "Did you want to sleep over?" I ask.

"My mother is already straight up going to kill me," Bryony says.

"She can't kill you twice," Rachel says.

"You should be able to get home safely for the same reason we got back here safely," I say.

Rachel gives me an exasperated, affectionate look. "This is a futon. That's two beds. We just need one for your grandma."

I turn to my grandmother. "Mimi," I say, "you should take *my* bed."

She demurs and suggests that she could sleep sitting up in the chair next to the ottoman, but it really doesn't take a whole lot of arguing before she makes a last, half-hearted offer to fix us all some more food and then kicks off her shoes, says, "Thank you so very much, sweetheart," and closes my bedroom door to go to bed.

"So where are *you* going to sleep?" Bryony asks me. "Because if you think *I'm* going to sit up in a chair all night so you can snuggle with your girlfriend, I mean, you could probably convince me, but I'm going to complain a lot."

"I'm going out in a little while," I say.

"Wait," Bryony says, and gestures dramatically to the window. "*Out* out?"

"I'm not explaining this," Rachel says.

I give Bryony the briefest possible version of the plan. "Okay," they say. "So what's the plan for breaking you back out if something goes wrong? Another robot attack?"

"Nothing's going to go wrong."

"I assume the AI is going to use a dead man's switch, where it has to keep telling people *not* to kill you, or they'll kill you. So yeah, something could go wrong *super easily.* CheshireCat's sent you two robots so far. Can they get you another one in the next half hour?"

"The risk there is that the other AI will have also instructed people to kill her if they think there's an incoming robot invasion," CheshireCat says.

"You can't possibly think this is a good idea," Bryony says, addressing CheshireCat.

"No," CheshireCat says. "But I have not been able to think of a better one."

At 10:00 p.m., I start gathering up my coat, mittens, and hat. "Wait," Bryony says in sudden horror. "You're planning to just sneak out and leave *us* to explain this to your mother?"

I pause. "I was thinking CheshireCat could explain."

Bryony strikes a pose. "Ohhhh, *hi,* Steph's mom. Yeah, Steph's not here because she's *handed herself over as a hostage,* plus she left you some homework. Hope you're up for it!"

"You could just leave," I say. "Drive back to New Coburg."

"Nope," Rachel says. "I'm staying here till you get back. But I don't want to explain this to your mom, either. I mean, what if she doesn't think she can do it? You're assuming a *lot.*"

I put my coat down. "Okay, fine," I say. "I'll stay until she wakes up." I go into the kitchen and set up the coffee maker.

.   .   .

At 10:30, Mom's alarm goes off, and she stumbles out to the living room and blinks at us, baffled. "Why do I smell coffee? Do you need me for something?"

"Yeah," I say. "A coding job to save the world."

That gets her attention. I hand her a mug of coffee. She drinks about half of it in silence and then says, "Okay. Tell me what's going on."

I explain Rajiv's AI, its goals, what's been going on with the Mischief Elves and the Catacombs and the thousands of similar sites that CheshireCat found. "The AI is doing this because it *has* to, not because it *wants* to. We need you to edit its code."

"To make it be *not* destructive? Or to give it free will?"

"It was your theory that this AI was a copy of some version of CheshireCat. CheshireCat has free will, and all they want to do is help people and look at cat pictures."

She drinks her coffee and thinks about this.

"What programming language . . . Oh, why am I even asking? If Rajiv copied CheshireCat and made changes, I know what he used," she mutters to herself. "Am I supposed to use my decryption key to get into the servers where it's stored?"

"Yes."

"And where *is* the code stored?"

"We don't know that yet," I say. "The AI has promised to send that information to you once I do something." I take a deep breath. "The thing is, once you have access to its code, you don't have to *fix* it; you could destroy it. So I offered myself as a hostage, while you're working. Once I've turned myself in, you'll get the file location."

Mom's face flushes pink right to the roots of her hair. She doesn't say anything, just picks up her coffee and drinks some more of it. She puts down her coffee. "*Absolutely not,*" she says.

"Minneapolis has had riots and Hill House got blown up and

there's more coming. And that's what's starting in a bunch more cities later tonight. And it'll get worse from here. Rajiv said we could go stay with him, if taking refuge with a supervillain appeals to you."

From my mother's expression, it appears she'll take her chances. "We could go back to New Coburg. Or to Darrow, Utah. You liked Darrow."

"Mom. You have friends in Boston. *I* have friends in Boston. Things are going to start hitting the fan in Boston at 4:00 a.m."

Mom checks her watch and drinks her coffee and looks over at Rachel and Bryony on the couch. "What do your friends think of this particular plan?"

Rachel furrows her brow. "I really wish Steph had suggested someone else as a hostage."

"It wouldn't have worked," I say. "The AI wouldn't trust Mom to care about you, or about someone else. And we don't know anyone else who can do this."

Rachel looks at my mother. "Do you actually think you can do this? I know you're a genius, and I know Steph thinks you can do anything, but do *you* think you can do it?"

My mother sighs heavily. "There's no way to know until I see the code. I used to work with Rajiv. Twenty years ago, I could have quickly found his changes and rolled them back. Is that still true? I don't know. And if it's not, reprogramming an AI is not something I'm going to pretend I'm confident about."

"Call Annette," I say. "CheshireCat's creator."

"It's 11:30 p.m. in Boston!"

"Okay, call her soon," I say.

"She's awake right now," CheshireCat offers. "I can definitely get her attention."

"What do *you* think of this plan?" my mother asks the air.

"I don't like it," CheshireCat says. "I trust that the other AI isn't planning to just lure Steph in for the purpose of doing her harm. But he's going to need human help. And I don't trust his judgment about humans. However, I don't see any other way to get the information that we need. Everything I've tried so far has made things worse, and I don't think we have a whole lot of time."

Mom opens her laptop. "Okay," she says. "CheshireCat, get me Annette."

"You're going to do it?" I ask, not wanting to say, *You're going to let me do this?*

Mom looks up. "Yes," she says. "You're right. We need to do this, and it has to be us." She stands up again and gives me a hug. "Just promise me you'll get the hell out of there if you get the chance. There's a lot that could go wrong, even if the AI is being absolutely honest with us."

• • •

I put on my coat and hat. Rachel gives me a silent hug and a kiss, then goes into the kitchen to start another pot of coffee. I check the address one more time, put on my mittens, and drop my phone in my coat pocket. Then I go out to walk across the park.

The wind has died down, finally, and it's a perfectly clear, viciously cold night. Even with the city lights, I can see some of the brighter constellations. It's not the right time of year to look for bats, so I'm not surprised that I don't see any.

There's a breath of wind that makes the trees of the park sway back and forth; I hear a creak from the playground as I pass and the rattle of a chain from the swings. Around the edge of the park, I can see houses with lights on inside.

"The cold is supposed to break tonight," CheshireCat tells me, speaking out loud through my phone as I walk. "And then it's supposed to snow."

The house I'm supposed to go to has a light on deep inside, but the porch light is off, like they're not expecting me. I can't decide if that's a good sign, or a bad sign. "Okay," I say, and then hesitate. "Do you think my mom can do this?"

"Yes," CheshireCat says. "Especially with Annette's help."

I take a deep breath. Any temptation I might have to procrastinate on this is scattered by another gust of wind. "Right. I guess I'm doing this." I go up the porch steps and ring the doorbell.

There are footsteps, and then the door swings open.

It takes me a minute to recognize the older woman who's standing there, staring at me, but then I place her. I've seen her picture. This is Nell's mother.

"Hi," I say. "I was instructed to come here. So, I'm here."

. . .

In the entry hallway, Nell's mother takes my coat and searches it. In addition to my regular phone, my flip phone is still in the pocket; she shuts both phones off and sets them on the table. Then she pats me down, looking for weapons or yet another cell phone or who knows what. In retrospect, I should have filled my pockets with random bits and pieces of electronics, just to distract my captors.

Once she's convinced she has anything that could be used to track my location or eavesdrop, she hangs everything neatly on hooks in the entrance hallway. She takes my boots and my socks and puts them in a closet, which she locks. Then she escorts me to the kitchen and points me to a four-legged stool in the corner. I take a seat. She holds up her phone and takes a picture of me, then puts the phone on the table and sits down with an embroidery hoop.

It's a large kitchen, with lots of counters and enough space for a table. There's a door to the backyard next to me; I can see someone's garage light through the tiny window at the top, and I can see that the door is not just locked but padlocked. If I try to get out that way, I'll be wasting my time.

There's a digital clock on the counter. It has a speaker and looks like it probably also plays music. I don't have much to do other than watch it, or watch Nell's mom, who is sitting at the kitchen table, doing a counted cross-stitch that's either two angels, or two gingerbread people; it's kind of hard to see for sure from where I'm sitting, and I don't really want to open up the conversation by asking.

I should have asked Boom Storm what, exactly, he was going to tell these people about me. I don't know whether they know I'm a hostage, or what. They have been neither particularly welcoming—they didn't offer me tea or anything hospitable like that—nor are they exactly treating me like a threat.

I wish I could get a reassuring update on how my mother's work is going. My heart is beating faster, and to calm myself down, I picture her doing what I *know* she's doing: sitting at the kitchen table with her laptop, drinking coffee and scrolling through the code looking for the part she needs to fix. I've seen her doing this a thousand times. It's easy to picture.

Another woman comes into the kitchen. "Ellen," she says. "We've gotten an update." They lower their voices and have a conversation I can't hear, but involves them glancing at me furtively several times. The other woman gives Nell's mom a zippered cloth bag, like the sort of bag you keep pencils and pens in, except it goes *clunk* in an oddly heavy way. The other woman goes out again.

I glance at the clock. It's a little before midnight.

Nell's mom—Ellen—has picked up her cross-stitch again, but then she puts it down and looks at me. "I know you," she says. "You're friends with my daughter." When I don't answer, she clarifies, "Nell."

"Oh, yeah," I say. I look at her face, searching for . . . I'm not sure what. Concern? Worry? Exasperation or frustration or any of the things I've seen in my mom's face?

I wish again I could get an update on my mother.

"Has she been to church?" Ellen asks.

I think the answer is *no*. "I don't know."

"Has she been fasting? Praying for forgiveness, for the Heavenly Lord to remake her into something clean and new? She has a *rebellious spirit*."

I swallow hard. "I think she's fine the way she is."

"I guess you would." She leans across the table. "You want to take a message back to her? Tell her that I know about the visit to the lawyer. She's damned to hell, cursed, as a blasphemer against the Lord for turning her back on her godly mother and embracing a group of Sodomites."

"The Sodomites were literally destroyed because of inhospitality, so I'd say the household that took in an abandoned teenager is probably doing okay." I make a mental note to thank Hermione, the source of basically everything I know about the Bible.

Ellen leaps up, crosses the floor, and slaps me across the face. I'm not expecting this. No adult has ever hit me, not that I remember, anyway. I've been hit by other kids, but this strike comes with an adult's furious strength and knocks me right off the stool.

"Get up," she says, and when I don't, she grabs me by my hair and shoves me back onto the stool. "Keep the words of the Lord out of your filthy mouth," she says.

I wonder how many times she's hit Nell. Or if Nell, raised by this horrible person, is pretty adept at saying whatever keeps her out of trouble.

My head hurts, and after a moment when everything went numb, my face hurts a lot. I press my hand to my cheek and don't say anything. Ellen opens up a kitchen drawer and pulls out a roll of duct tape. She pulls my hands behind me and duct tapes them together. I don't think this was part of her plan, because if they'd planned to duct-tape me, they'd have picked a chair to tape me to and not just a stool. She rips one last piece of duct tape off, and for a second, I think she's going to put it over my mouth . . . but then she balls it up and drops it in the kitchen trash can. She goes back to her spot at the kitchen table and picks up her cell phone, takes another picture of me, and then picks up her cross-stitch again.

"When the Tribulation comes," she says with a cold, vicious satisfaction in her voice, "you'll all be marked with the infernal rabble as prey. You, Nell, Sonia, too." It takes me a second to remember that Sonia is Glenys. "And you may kneel at the gates of sanctuary and beg till your throat is raw, but there will be *no mercy* for you."

No wonder Nell is so messed up, I think.

Before this conversation, I really thought that maybe all the people doing awful things were just being misled by the AI, but I have to admit, at this point, that some of them are just awful people, even if the AI is making things worse.

"The plan was to let Nell see what things were like on the outside—to let her prove her faithfulness. And it was working—she sought out the Catacombs, followed instructions. But *you* were also there, questioning the word of the Elder, tempting her to destruction."

I probably ought to keep my mouth closed right now, but she's brought up the Elder and I *really* want to know: "Do you know that the Elder is an artificial intelligence? Not a prophet of God but a computer program?"

I don't see even a flicker of doubt on her face. "All things can serve God's purpose in his hands. All things can serve the plan."

"The plan?" I say.

"I was needed for preparations. First at the refuge, then as part of the vanguard, along with Sonia's mother."

"Gl—Sonia's mother is here, too?"

"Yes. If we have to kill you, she's going to do it."

"Oh." I am not sure what to even say in response to that.

"That's why she's not guarding you. So you can't talk to her and soften up her heart. I don't know that it would have been a problem, anyway. I certainly don't like you more now than I did before."

I think of a bunch of sarcastic responses but keep all of them to myself this time. I look at the clock again. It's 12:18. I wiggle my hands, wondering if I could get the duct tape off if I tried. The problem with *that* plan is, Ellen is literally sitting there watching me, and if I do get the duct tape loose, I'm pretty sure she'll just get it back out and do a better job.

I close my eyes and imagine my mother working.

45

• Nell •

When we get home, the adults pull out a map of Minnesota and start discussing whether someone's winterized cabin in Ely would be a good place to go or if heading south, somewhere less frigid, makes more sense. They're sending out email messages and texts and checking news sites for riots in other cities.

"Why don't you get some sleep," Thing Two suggests when she sees me hovering. "You and Glenys both. There's probably no point in trying to leave before morning."

"This is it," Glenys whispers when I close my door. "This is it, isn't it? *It.*" She means the Tribulation, and I don't know what to tell her.

"We'll be okay," I say.

"No one's going to be okay," she says.

"Then we might as well go to bed," I say.

Being out in this sort of cold was fatiguing. I am tired and still chilled, but under the quilts of my bed with Glenys next to me, I fall asleep to the noise of the adults murmuring outside my door.

I wake up hours later to a quiet house. Something startled me awake; it takes me a minute or two to realize it was my phone. Someone sent me a text. I extricate myself from the bed without waking Glenys and find my phone where I left it plugged into the charger. I'm expecting a text from Steph, telling me about some new disaster, and for a second, still half-asleep, I think that's what it is.

It's not, though. It's a text from my *mother.* With a *picture* of Steph.

Cold washes through my body. The picture was taken in a kitchen. Steph is sitting in a chair, her arms awkwardly behind her, like she's been tied. There's a red mark across her face, and she's not smiling.

Worried about your friend? my mother has added.

I know immediately that she's trying to lure me in. To use Steph as bait—why Steph is *there* is a question I can leave for another time. If I ask her where she is, she'll probably tell me! Not much point in setting out a trap someone can't fall into. But if I do ask, she'll know I'm coming.

I can't text Steph, obviously. I could text Rachel. Will Rachel know where she is, or will I just set her to worrying? Maybe I can ask Steph's hacker friend, Cat. What was her number? Their number? I try to bring up a mental picture of Steph talking to Cat. Steph used an app, and I saw it—we passed all our phones around a half dozen times today. I picture Steph's screen, the Cat-Net app, the chat app . . .

It's in the app store and downloads onto my phone. When I open it, I see a single screen with two options: *CHESHIRE-CAT MAY RIDE ALONG* and *PRIVACY PLEASE.* There's a graphic of an old-fashioned switch like you'd see in a movie controlling factory machinery and it's pointed at *PRIVACY,* so I switch it to *CHESHIRECAT MAY RIDE ALONG* and step out into the living room. "Cat?" I say hesitantly. "Are you there?"

My phone comes to life in my hand. "Nell. Is everything okay? I was not expecting to hear from you," Cat's weird voice says.

"Shhhhhhhhhhh," I say, and then realize I can turn the volume down on my phone. "Okay, okay, I've fixed it. Okay. Where's Steph? Do you know where Steph is?"

"I do know where Steph is. Why are you asking?"

"Because she's in *danger,* and she needs my help."

"She accepted danger willingly for the greater good," Cat says, and goes into an explanation about hostages and programmers and a rogue AI.

I interrupt to say, "The person guarding her is *my mother.*"

There's a pause. "Your mother seems like a singularly bad choice," Cat says.

"Yes. Were you expecting that they will let Steph go at some point? Because . . ." I swallow hard. "Please just tell me where she is."

Cat reels off an address, and I write it down and look it up in the maps. It's several blocks beyond Steph's house, and it is sometime after 1:00 a.m. and still incredibly frigid outside. I'm going to need a whole lot of clothing and maybe a flashlight. I slip back into my bedroom. Glenys is still sleeping. I get back into clothes as quickly as I can, including long underwear and wool socks, and then I investigate what looks like go bags packed by the door. There's a flashlight on top of the first one I open, and I put it in the pocket of my coat. In my school backpack, I throw the things I brought along to help rescue Glenys, then leave a note for Glenys and slip out the front door. If anyone hears me going, they don't stop me.

• • •

The wind has died down, so that's one mercy.

And it's less dark than I'd expected, because there are street-lights all over. That's another mercy, although I'd have been happier doing a one-in-the-morning walk in a peaceful little small town instead of a *city.* There are people out and about at all hours here, but none of them bothers me or really pays any attention to me at all. Unless you count the dog on a walk, which sniffs me as his owner says, "Leave the lady alone, Tristan."

My phone buzzes with a text from a number I don't recognize. *This is Cat. Would you like some robot allies?*

Like the one you sent along to help rescue Glenys?

Different model, Cat says.

Yes, please, I say.

I'll have them head to the house.

I wonder about the word *them*. Is Cat using the gender-neutral singular *they,* or does Cat mean *multiple robots*—and if the second one, *how many robots*?

I should try to plan, but it's hard to *plan* properly without knowing anything about the terrain. I know Steph is in the kitchen. She's probably restrained. I have scissors and a utility knife and a pair of bolt cutters, but I remember how hard it was to get through a single cheap padlock. I worry about that as I walk, even though the picture was taken in an ordinary-looking kitchen.

The house is on the far side of a bowl-shaped park. I trudge across the snowy expanse and up a hill. The porch light is on like they're expecting another visitor. I don't knock. I go around to the side of the house and scramble up onto the gas meter to peer in through a window.

There's a buzzing overhead, and I look up to see a delivery drone swooping around in the dark. No, two delivery drones. They perch like birds along the edge of the roof. Another one comes. Then another. The robots? I take out my phone. "Are you sending me *delivery drones*?" I ask. "What good are *those* going to do?"

"They can provide a distraction. I'm looking for other options, but I'm limited by what's nearby."

Another drone buzzes to the roof. "Are any of the drones *carrying* anything useful?" Briefly, I have visions of a drone-delivered parcel with military-grade weaponry in it, or even a good set of night-vision binoculars, but of course it's things like camping equipment and children's toys.

I go around to the backyard. I think the kitchen is probably on this side of the house; the lights are all on, and I can see the sort of windows you'll see over a sink, higher up so you don't splash them with water when you're washing dishes. Unfortunately, all the windows have shades, and all the shades are down. There's a back door, but there aren't any footprints in the snow, and I think probably it's not used much, which means probably it's locked, and people in the Remnant tend to believe in three simultaneous locks just to be sure.

I try the other side of the house but can see even less from over here.

So. Now what?

If it were me in there and Steph out here, she'd maybe *climb* to get inside. I look up at the second story dubiously. Everything's shut up tightly. There's a third story, and then a roof.

Are there any *basement* windows?

On this side, the basement has a window well. I take the plastic cover off the window well and take a look at the window. It's big enough to climb through, but shut tightly like everything else and locked. I could break the glass, but they'd hear. That seems like a bad plan unless I want to create a distraction. On the other side of the house, there's one of those narrow windows high up on the wall you sometimes see in basement laundry rooms. I poke at it. This one's a lot looser in the frame.

I think about an argument I heard at some point about these windows in my grandparents' house. For a basement to be a legal place for an apartment, you need one of the big windows with a window well so that someone could maybe escape that way in a fire. But if you're small, you can fit through the other kind. If it opens.

I'm small enough that I'm pretty sure I'd fit, but is it loose enough that I can get it open, that's the real question. Without anyone hearing.

I pull my phone out. "CheshireCat, are any of the drones carrying tools? Like a pry bar or anything like that?"

One drone detaches itself from the roof and lands next to me with its package. Inside, I find a children's tool set with plastic tools, which is really not what I had in mind. But the *case* is metal. The yard is all fenced; I bash the case against a fence post, and I'm left with a thin but solid piece of metal. Back at the window, I slide that piece in through the bottom and jab it around, peering in to see if maybe I'm hitting the lock.

There's a hook inside, and it pops open. I gasp, because obviously I had some idea of what I was trying to do, mostly from discussions of Tribulation-period survival tips, but I hadn't really expected it to *work*. I quickly slide in and leave the window unlatched.

The basement is dark and quiet. I turn on my flashlight for a minute just to get my bearings. I came in next to a big laundry sink. There are shelves and shelves of canned goods down here and a bunch of large casks and bottles of water scattered around the floor, which I need to take care not to trip over.

Upstairs, I can hear the occasional creak of a footstep, but nothing beyond that.

So now what? Am I going to charge upstairs? Try to lure the adults downstairs one by one and whack them over the head with one of these gallon glass jars of pickles?

Then I hear a car pull up outside and a loud knock at the door, and I know in my gut it's going to be too late if I wait any longer.

I start up the stairs.

46

• Steph •

There's a loud knock on the door, and my eyes fly open. Ellen is still at the kitchen table, working on her cross-stitch. I hear footsteps as someone else goes to open the front door. It takes some time, because there are about five locks on it—they locked everything back up after they let me in; this house is an absolute nightmare from a fire-safety perspective—and because there's a set of pass-phrases that get muttered literally through the mail slot, which I'd probably find hilarious if I weren't sitting in a chair waiting to see if these people decide to kill me.

"So what's this I hear about a *hostage* showing up?" asks a male voice I recognize, and my stomach twists. It's Rajiv.

There's some low conversation from the front hall, and Rajiv says loudly, "You were supposed to *call* me, *immediately,* if something like this happened." The voices rise, and I catch snatches of the argument but not enough to make sense of it.

The swinging kitchen door bangs open, and Rajiv stands there, staring at me. He looks completely baffled by my presence— whoever he'd expected to find, here, now, it wasn't me. "Steph?" he says, like he's not sure. "What are you doing here?"

I need an answer to this question that might plausibly get me out of this room alive. "I was going to ask *you* that question," I say angrily, like I think my being here is his fault.

"I didn't tell them to bring you *here*. There were specific instructions . . ." He looks at Ellen, baffled. "Sister Ellen, explain yourself!"

She stands up, her eyes narrowing. "In the end, we don't answer to you, Brother Malachi," she says. "We answer to the Elder."

"I speak for the Elder!"

"The Elder has been speaking directly to both of us for days," Ellen says.

"Impossible," Rajiv says, and his voice takes on a dismissive, patronizing tone. "You're being fooled. Except for limited answers as gifts, the Elder does not speak to anyone other than Brother Daniel and me, and he certainly doesn't speak to—"

From the kitchen clock comes a loud robotic voice. "Ellen Reinhardt, this is the Elder. Code Alpha Romeo Alpha. Shoot Brother Malachi."

Ellen snatches up the pencil case and doesn't even unzip it, she just wraps her hand around the gun inside and fires, but the bullet smashes through the window behind him and doesn't hit him at all.

"What do you think you're doing?" Rajiv shouts. "Storm, deactivate!"

"Kill Brother Malachi," the speaker says again. "I'm so sorry, Rajiv. I can't let you stop me. I can't let you keep making me do this. Kill Brother Malachi. Kill Brother Malachi . . ."

They're wrestling for the gun, and I deeply regret my decision not to spend the last hour trying to work my hands loose from the duct tape—but I can stand and leave the stool behind, even if my hands are stuck behind me. I don't particularly want to wait to see if "Kill Steph" is the next order.

There might be a door somewhere that isn't padlocked, but I can't risk taking the time to hunt for it. There's a stair to the basement and then a stairway leading up—it's narrow and steep, either a former servant's stair or a remnant of this house once being a duplex. There might be no way out of the basement, so I bolt upstairs.

The speaker is still barking orders in code, and I hear more gunshots, as well as a bunch of feet running down the main stairs. The upstairs has a bunch of closed doors, and one of them is open- ing, so I run up the stairs to the attic.

"Steph, *Steph,* it's me, it's Nell," I hear behind me.

I whirl. It is, indeed, Nell. I sputter something like "What . . . ?" at her, and she says, "Hold still," and whips out a pair of scissors to cut the duct tape.

"Why did you go *up?*" she says, exasperated. "There's a way *out* from the basement."

We're in a finished attic. It's empty, fortunately, since it looks like the only thing Nell has to defend herself with is a pair of ad- mittedly very sharp and pointy scissors. I open up a window, kick out the screen, and look out. "Can you climb?" I ask.

"I mean, I . . . Maybe?" Nell says.

Our options from here are not *ideal.* Third floors are high. There's a gutter and downspout, but I'd need to go hand over hand to get to the downspout, and I don't trust the gutter to support my weight. The downspout, either, for that matter. And I am really not sure if Nell can manage it.

Just as I hear another three gunshots downstairs, a drone swoops in. Nell points at it. "Cat," she says. "You mentioned camping equipment, is there *climbing* equipment?"

"Rope," CheshireCat's voice says from Nell's phone.

Nell cuts open the package that the drone drops, and sure enough, there's a skein of bright orange rope, wrapped into a complicated-looking knot that nonetheless comes free instantly when I tug on it. One end is even a clip thing, and I quickly secure that end around the radiator coming out of the wall and then hurl the rest of the rope out the window. "Let's do this."

Nell yanks one more thing out of her backpack. "Shoes," she says. I shove my feet into the same boots that Glenys wore the other day. They're too small for me, but Nell is right: I don't want to do this barefoot.

I go down first. For the record, I do not recommend learning to climb out of houses by coming down an unknotted rope from a third-story window when it's negative twenty degrees outside and you're still hearing gunshots. I stand at the bottom as Nell comes, wondering if I should have made her go first, wondering if I'm going to have to try to catch her, but when she lets go and drops, she's only got six feet and lands in the snow without a problem.

I grab Nell's hand and realize that people have already started coming out from the front of the house, and there's a fence around the back, and not the sort that's easy to climb.

"Cat," Nell says. "Now would be a good time for the drones."

About a hundred tiny package-delivery drones drop simultaneously from the sky, and we run through the chaos to the park.

Powderhorn Park is dark at night, but the trees are widely spaced, and there isn't really anywhere to hide. We head for the darkest spots; I'm already wondering if we should have stuck to the city streets in the hopes that an inconvenient witness would come along, making it harder for them to kill us. Would they even care if there were a witness, though? I just watched Nell's mother *shoot* Rajiv, or at least shoot *at* him.

I'm not as cold as I was expecting, and for a second, my brain helpfully suggests that I'm *already dying from hypothermia, they say you don't feel cold when you have hypothermia,* but the breeze has some humidity in it, and the smell of coming snow. I'm not as cold because it's warming up; the cold broke, as promised.

Are they following us?

Somewhere deep in the park I hear a scream, and Nell goes rigid, whirling in the dark to search for the source of the sound. But the scream turns into a shriek and a giggle. It's not someone pursuing us; it's someone in the park having a good time. As they pass under one of the lights, I glimpse two people with a sled. Adults, I'm pretty sure. They pick up the sled and start walking up the hill.

Nell is looking back at the house. Someone on the far side of the park has a flashlight, and all I can see is the flashlight beam, but . . . I think it's pointed at the sledders. The light shuts off.

.   .   .

When we get to my house, CheshireCat has told them we're on the way, because Rachel is outside waiting. "Did they let you go? Your mom isn't *done*. I asked. She said she wasn't done. Why is Nell with you?"

"Things got complicated," I say. I'm covered in snow, and it's melting and wet. I can barely feel my feet, despite Nell's boots. Inside is warm and smells like coffee. Mom is working at the kitchen table. When she sees me, she jumps up and gives me a long hug, then sits down on the couch, her laptop still open.

"What happened?" Bryony asks.

"I think maybe I should call the police," I say. "Someone was trying to commit a murder. Or possibly a couple of murders. Not of me, but I think I was on the list."

"You don't need to call," CheshireCat says. "The neighbors were woken by the gunfire and have called."

"Are they going to offer them all coat vouchers?" I ask.

"Minneapolis Public Safety does have a *few* armed officers who respond to calls about things like gunshots," CheshireCat says.

My phone is still back at the house, so I open up my laptop to talk to CheshireCat. There's a message from Boom Storm— actually, there are a whole slew of messages from Boom Storm.

Oh no. This is not going how I thought it would.

Rajiv is going to try to shut me down. Rajiv has codes that can shut me down! I have to stop Rajiv!

Shooting him was the only thing I could think of to stop him from shutting me down.

This isn't going the way I thought.

Have I killed Rajiv? Have I killed my friend?

Maybe your mother should just delete my code.

"Why did you order Nell's mom to shoot Rajiv?" I ask.

"Rajiv added a kill switch to my code," Boom Storm says. "He didn't trust me, so he wanted to be able to shut me down at a moment's notice. You heard him try. He was going to shut me down and go back in to edit my code, to re-create all the parts your mother took out. To make me try again to destroy the world. *I don't want to hurt people.*"

"But you hurt Rajiv."

"Yes. No. I don't know. You're right that I tried."

CheshireCat sends me a private message. "Rajiv also gave Boom Storm an inhibition against harming Rajiv in any way. I think Boom Storm didn't know if he'd be able to act against Rajiv or not."

"Is Rajiv dead?" I ask.

"No," CheshireCat says. "Ellen emptied the gun but missed every shot."

"So, he's right that Rajiv could try to undo what my mother's done."

"Well, maybe. She can probably lock him out of the code once she's done editing it."

I look over at my mother, who's watching me over the edge of her laptop.

"I told the AI that if anything happened to you, I was going to reprogram it to do nothing but make paper clips, because that struck me as a fate worse than death for an intelligent AI, and CheshireCat agreed," Mom says. She pushes her hair out of her face. "It sounds like something *almost* happened to you. What exactly was its plan?"

"The people guarding me were Nell's mom and Glenys's mom," I say. "The AI probably did not have a *lot* of people he believed would kill me if ordered to do so, and from the messages I got when I got home, I don't think he thought they'd recognize me."

"Why is this AI a *he?*"

"That's Boom Storm's pronoun on CatNet. Anyway, his plan was just to have them guard me, but then Rajiv showed up, and so then he ordered them to kill Rajiv." I show my mother the messages.

"Okay," my mother says. "Here's the thing. You're back. No longer a hostage. We could delete the AI's code."

"Kill him, you mean."

"What's he going to be *like,* even after we take out the destructive instructions? What exactly are we unleashing on the world? I know you think he's a copy of CheshireCat, but CheshireCat is as much the product of their own experiences and decisions as they are of the code Annette's team wrote—what is this AI going to be *like?*"

"I don't know."

"And his first instinct was to solve a problem through murder?"

"He was striking out at someone who was trying to force him to help start a global catastrophe, though."

"And he put you in a terribly dangerous situation!"

"The dangerous situation was my idea. To be freed from the destructive instructions, he had to trust us. And he *did* trust us." I really hate the idea of betraying that trust. Even if in some ways it's a bad idea not to. "Also, his work so far was basically setting up a million bombs. If you kill him, those bombs stay where they were laid. If you finish what you started . . . he can choose to defuse all the bombs he's laid for us."

"But *will* he?"

"I don't know, but I think it's worth the risk."

Mom thinks about it a little longer and then says, "Okay," and goes back to her laptop. It doesn't take long; she must have been almost done. "That should do it. Ask your AI friend if that did it."

I'm pretty sure I know the answer; my conversation with Boom Storm is suddenly nothing but image after image of flowers.

The door to my bedroom opens, and my grandmother is blinking out at us, baffled. "Why are you all still up?" she asks, and then stumbles off to the bathroom. When she comes out, she looks around again, takes in Rachel, Bryony, Nell, and me all sitting on the couch, and says, "Well. Since everyone's awake, would you like me to make pancakes?"

47

• Nell •

On the first day of March, I cut my hair.

I've been thinking about it for a while. The "no haircuts for women" rule came from one of my mother's cults, but it was still *my* hair, and I was afraid I'd regret cutting it all off. "It's just hair," Siobhan told me, "it'll grow back," which is all very well and good, but it took a *really long time* to grow it this long.

Siobhan takes me to her hairdresser, and I tell her that I want a haircut like Siobhan's. She doesn't ask me if I'm sure; she smiles affectionately and says, "Sure thing," and in a flash, my head feels a whole lot lighter. Cutting off the braids takes less than a second; shaping the short hair into the new style takes quite a bit longer. I look into the mirror when she's done, and part of me thinks, *What have I done?* while another part of me thinks, *Why did I wait so long to do this? I could have done this* months *ago.*

It is visiting day at the county jail, and the stylist is near downtown.

"Do you want to visit your mom?" Siobhan asks tentatively, as we walk out.

"No," I say. "She called me Beelzebub's harlot the last time I tried, and I don't think she'll like the haircut."

"Fair enough," Siobhan says.

Glenys likes my haircut, and pets the fuzzy shaved bit like I'm a cat. She's still living with us. Her mother is in jail with my mother, and her father doesn't want her back.

But that's okay. My father, and Julia and Siobhan and Jenny, want both of us. Jenny finished a mural in the living room last week: Glenys and I are the kids from *The Cat in the Hat,* and Julia, Jenny, Siobhan, and my father are Things One, Two, Three, and Four. School is going fine. I'm almost caught up in all the subjects my mother didn't believe in teaching.

The Catacombs and Mischief Elves sites are still running, but they're very different now.

Welcome to March, the Elves greet me when I pull up the app. *It's almost spring! Time to start seedlings to transplant outside. If you don't own a garden, no problem! You can give your seedlings to anyone you think deserves them!* There's a series of images of flowers spilling out of odd and inconvenient places—the funniest is the person who planted a peony bush in a large pothole.

Jenny looks over my shoulder and says, "We should do that with the potholes around here. Class them up."

"Do we have somewhere to start seeds?" I ask.

"Oh, *heck* yeah," she says. "Julia and I have a *huge* garden every summer. Let me just go get the seed catalogs."

AUTHOR'S NOTE

One of the interesting things about near-future science fiction is that sometimes you catch up to the future while you're still writing it.

I live in Saint Paul, Minnesota, and I was revising this novel in May 2020. On Memorial Day, a police officer in Minneapolis knelt on the neck of a Black man named George Floyd, cutting off his air and circulation for eight minutes and forty-six seconds, while three other police officers helped hold him down. In the wake of Floyd's murder, there were protests that exploded into riots and then fires, and South Minneapolis—where I lived for seventeen years and where much of this novel takes place—was permanently changed.

I'm now finishing the book with no clear idea of where things might stand a year from now, when the book comes out, or five to ten years from now, when the book takes place, so I decided to run with the suggestion of my friend Lyda Morehouse, and write the Minneapolis I want to see. In my novel, the bus ride down Lake Street passes a plaza named after George Floyd where the burned-out remains of the third precinct police station stand now. The science fiction bookstore that burned to the ground last month has been rebuilt in a new location (with a rocket ship on the front, because I think that would be cool).

Minneapolis is in the process of radically rethinking public safety—rethinking how we use the police and how other professionals could do some of the things we have the police doing now. I am not an expert on policing, but in the moments when Steph comes in contact with law enforcement in this book, I tried to provide a plausible vision of public safety workers whose first priority is *public safety*. Who see a teenager wandering downtown on a viciously cold night and think, *Is she okay? Does she have a safe place to go? Does she need help buying a warmer coat?* Steph, of course, refers to anyone in uniform as a "cop"—but one reason there's such a dramatic contrast between the aggressive bullies working in law enforcement who appear in *Catfishing on CatNet* and the gentle concern she encounters here is that this is what I want to see—people who approach problems to solve them rather than who approach citizens to subdue them.

There are a few places in this story that are real (or real-ish) that were in the book before the many catastrophes of the first half of 2020. Powderhorn Park is entirely real and exists basically as described in the story. Can Can Wonderland is *also real,* although (at present) it does not have a roller coaster and the real-life owners are not secretly supervillains (so far as I've heard). It does have an artist-designed indoor mini-golf course. The James J. Hill House is real and offers tours. There is currently no school named after Coya Knutson, but she was a real person, the first woman elected to the U.S. House of Representatives from Minnesota. And the Midtown Exchange, which was built in a former Sears building next to Abbott Northwestern Hospital, is real and has an amazing array of excellent food.

I don't know what Minneapolis will look like in ten years; I don't know what policing and public safety will look like here in ten years. But I think part of what science fiction is for is to think about what the world *could* look like—the ways in which things could go right, not just the ways in which things could go wrong, so that's the vision I embraced.

ACKNOWLEDGMENTS

I received a lot of useful input from Elise Matthesen about small towns when I wrote *Catfishing on CatNet,* and I received a lot of incredibly useful thoughts and advice from Elise Matthesen this time about growing up as a queer kid in a very controlling religious group and how it feels to leave. I don't know if I successfully captured one of her most important insights, which was, "It can be very much the right thing to do, and it can still feel terrible when you first leave," but I am tremendously grateful for her time and insight.

Many thanks to Shawn Rounds for her thoughts on Hill House and to Lee Brontide for their thoughts on therapy. Thank you to Dan Martin for answering my questions about phone app security, and to Kristy Anne Cox for thoughts on Mormonism (even though that scene did not make it into the book). Finally, for answers to legal questions (and related useful input), many thanks to Candy Heisler, Jennifer Moore, Dena Landon, Susan Claire, Rachel Caplan, and Emily Stewart.

Thanks, as always, to all the members of the Wyrdsmiths, my writers' group: Eleanor Arnason, Kelly Barnhill, Theo Lorenz, Lyda Morehouse, and Adam Stemple. An extra thank-you to Lyda for last-minute brainstorming and for saying the words, "Write the Minneapolis you want to see." Thanks to my agent, Nell Pierce, and my thoughtful and insightful editor, Susan Chang, who is superlatively good at spotting emotional beats that I routed around and need to find a path through. Finally, thanks and love to my husband, Ed Burke, and my two endlessly delightful children, Molly and Kiera Burke.